Se

She peered at her face in the mirror. The swelling and bruising would take some days to go down, and she would have to wait for that. You couldn't start a new life looking battered and bruised – what would people think? When it had gone down enough not to be noticeable, she would pack a few things and with the little money she had saved from the housekeeping, take the train to London. She had never been there, but a big city would soon absorb her and the children. No one would ever find her. She would walk to the station in the early hours and put a note in Dora's door, hoping no one would see her. If she waited and posted a letter to her, Dora would see the postmark and that would never do.

For she wanted to sever all ties. No one would know that little Vida's father was a drunkard, and no one would ever suspect who was the father of little Freddie. She could work to earn money to keep them all, she was sure of that. She had never been afraid of hard work.

It was a case of waiting for the right moment, after she had found out the times of the trains, written the note to Dora, packed a few things. The fewer the better.

Mixed in with the feeling of trepidation was the faintest glimmer of excitement. She would manage. Wasn't she a Yorkshire Lass?

Rose Boucheron is the author of six novels: *The End of a Long Summer, Pollen, The Massinghams, September Fair, Promise of Summer* and *The Patchwork Quilt*. She lives in Gerrards Cross, Buckinghamshire.

September Fair

Rose Boucheron

Woman's Weekly Fiction

A Woman's Weekly Paperback
SEPTEMBER FAIR

First published in Great Britain 1992
by Judy Piatkus (Publishers) Ltd
This edition published 1995
by Woman's Weekly
in association with Mandarin Paperbacks
an imprint of Reed International Books Ltd
Michelin House, 81 Fulham Road, London SW3 6RB
and Auckland, Melbourne, Singapore and Toronto

Copyright © 1992 by Rose Boucheron
The author has asserted her moral rights

A CIP catalogue record for this title
is available from the British Library
ISBN 0 86056 016 4

Printed and bound in Great Britain by
BPC Paperbacks Ltd
A member of
The British Printing Company Ltd

Chapter One

Riding in her pony and trap through the park-like grounds of Aldebourne Grange, Mrs Gerald Ogilby caught a glimpse of a white pinafore darting through the trees. She smiled indulgently. Wherever little Hetty was you could be certain that David was somewhere nearby. Hetty, the groom's daughter, was her son's constant companion. They had played together since they were small children. Mrs Ogilby was only too thankful that he had a companion, for an only child could get lonely sometimes, and David was not the strongest of children, a serious attack of pneumonia when he was six years old having left him prone to coughs and colds.

Hetty, bless her heart, more than made up for any weakness David might have. She was strong and healthy and full of energy, as pretty as a picture. At fifteen, two years younger than David. Ah, there they both were, making for the paddock. Mrs Ogilby supposed they would both go riding. Jessops would look after them – see they were both safely mounted. She gave a light tap to the pony who trotted obediently, his mistress holding the reins to curb his youthful exuberance.

Hetty, one arm around David's shoulders, approached her father who was tending a bay mare.

"Father, may we go for a ride?"

He looked up, always pleased to see this youngest child of his, so dear to his heart. Within reason there was nothing he could have refused her. The sheer vitality in that pretty face, the shining eyes, the eagerness. Beside her, the boy stood tall, like a young colt, his pale fairness a perfect foil for the girl's dark beauty.

1

"Aye, tak' Moonshine and Blaze – and coom back when y' set – I'll check on y' then."

They rode out of the muddy courtyard and across the dry field, presently breaking into a canter. Hetty knew David did not like to go fast, for her sake as much as his. Although she was stronger and more daring, he treated her with respect and deference, never seeing her as the tomboy that everyone else thought she was.

They came to a halt beneath the large oak tree, the tree that had been theirs for as long as they could remember. Dismounting, they tethered the horses and lay down on the dry grass gazing up at the sky. They often stayed like this for a long time, words being unnecessary such was the long forged bond between them.

"It's six days now before you go back to school," said Hetty.

"I know. I shall miss you."

"I should hate to go to boarding school. I would miss my family, and the horses, and the dogs – and you."

"I do," he said. "But it's not so bad, really. There are some good chaps there."

"Come on." And she stood up. "I'll show you where I found the bird's nest."

He followed her to the small copse where stood a ramshackle hut. She pushed through the brambles and nettles to expose a beautifully made nest of bits of twig, moss and feathers. David peered inside at the blue speckled eggs.

"Blackbird's eggs," he said. "The mother must have deserted them. Come on, race you to the pond."

Their summer days were spent like this, rambling over the moors, searching the ponds for frogs and newts, helping with the harvest.

"Will I see you before you go back?" she asked.

"Of course you will – I'll meet you at the gate. We're going into the village, aren't we?"

"Yes – what's the time?"

"Almost four."

"Golly, I must fly. I've forgotten to collect the eggs."

David made his way slowly back towards the house. His music lesson was at four-thirty, and he never looked forward to that.

2

Hetty lived on a tied cottage on the estate. There were six of these in a row, and the Jessops lived in the end one which had the largest garden. At the end of the narrow garden was a chicken shed where the hens roosted for the night. Otherwise they roamed on the grass, sometimes when broody "laying away" as her mother called it. Hetty went straight to the wire netting enclosure and, ducking her head, crept through to the corner, where sure enough she found eight large eggs, and joy of joys, one beautiful brown one. The brown eggs were laid by Nellie, Hetty's favourite hen. The eggs safely tucked in her pinafore she made her way to the kitchen. Her mother was baking, her sleeves rolled up, her round rosy face shiny with heat from the kichen range.

"Eight eggs, Ma. One brown."

Mrs Jessops nodded, busy beating, her strong freckled arms moving like lightning above the great yellow mixing bowl. When she stopped, she put her hands on her hips, her eyes resting warmly on Hetty.

"Did y'see the lad, then?"

Very occasionally she worried about the friendship between the lad and Hetty, but generally she thought that things have a way of working out, and what was to be would be. They were only children, the pair of them. But Hetty being a girl was more forward than the lad, and she prayed with all her heart that this youngest child of hers would not be hurt. There had never been time to dwell on the other children. They had grown up and married and made their way in the natural order of things, but she had had Hetty late in life, at a time when she thought she would have no more children, which accounted for the way she and Jessops tended to spoil her.

Well, the lass was but fifteen yet, and due to leave school, and things would change quite a bit after that.

"We went riding on Moonshine and Blaze. David goes back to school next week."

"Aye, time'll come when you'll not think that important, luv." And she resumed her beating. "Taties are ready for scrapin' and there are peas to pod."

"Yes, Ma." Hetty pushed her hand into the sack which stood in the corner. "How many?"

3

"Dora's coming to supper with little Tommy, so do a few more."

"Oh, good." And she began to hum a little tune. She always liked it when one of the family came round. There was not much life to be seen around the Grange, for three of the tied cottages were empty because the men had gone to war, and Colonel Ogilby had not replaced them.

Hetty had never known anything else but life at the Grange. Both her parents came from hard-working farming people, athough her father had made a natural progression to horses, and now looked after the stables for the Ogilbys, who were very good employers. A man knew he would be looked after if he went to work for them, for they were kind and looked after all the families on the estate.

Colonel Ogilby, David's father, worked in an advisory capacity at the War Office in London, while Mrs Ogilby spent almost all her time doing charity work, visiting the sick and helping the poor. She was most highly thought of in Yorkshire, and more's the pity, people said, that she'd only one bairn to follow on, and he a weak and sickly lad. They'd not much time in Yorkshire for weak and sickly men, but it wasn't her fault, poor lady, nor his, come to that. When he was older a spell in the army would sort him out, there was nothing like the army for turning a boy into a man.

In the meantime, it was as much as the Jessops could do to keep body and soul together, for all the generosity of the Ogilbys. Life had never been easy for them, life on the land never is, but Colonel Ogilby was determined to hold on to his horses come what may and so far had managed to do so. Things had become very difficult after the war, and there was no knowing what might happen in the future. The prospect could be bleak for Jessops who was no longer young.

Still, Mrs Jessop consoled herself, all the children but one were off her hands and safely married, while Hetty, once she had left school and found herself a job, would meet a nice local boy, they would start walking out, and in no time it would be wedding bells. She herself had married at sixteen and never regretted it. Hetty would probably do the same.

Sometimes Hetty thought about her future but not often. It was already ordained. Like her mother and her sisters before

4

her she wanted to marry as soon as she could. Going into service did not appeal to her although she hadn't much choice. Her secret wish was that she could work up at the Grange for Mrs Ogilby, although she was not sure what a lady's maid did, nor if Mrs Ogilby had one, and she thought not. She was not the sort of girl to spend much time day dreaming, for she was a worker and liked to be busy. Lately, though, she had thought some very odd things, thoughts connected with David which made her blush, things more to do with his touching her. Knowing about horses and animals as she did she guessed that this was to do with growing up. Sometimes David seemed so young compared to her, although he was two years older.

The day before he went back to school they went for a last ride. When it was over they walked towards the cottage. Other years he had dashed off with a "Cheerio, Hetty," and she had run indoors. This time she stood before him uncertainly, feeling that something was missing.

"Goodbye, David," she said, holding out her hand to him. Somewhat surprised, he took it. To hide his embarrassment, he laughed. "I'm not going away forever, Hetty". And she fled, her face crimson, into the house and up the narrow stairs to her tiny bedroom where she flung herself down on the narrow bed and lay with her eyes tightly shut.

Later that year, tragedy overtook the Jessops family when Hetty's father died as the result of an accident with a piece of farm machinery.

This meant a great deal more to Mrs Jessops than the loss of her husband, for as a result she had to leave the tied cottage. The Ogilbys were kindness itself to her, and found her a tiny cottage in the village. Hetty was in two minds about leaving the Grange. It pleased her that she would see a bit more of life, but coupled with that was the fear that she might lose touch with David.

Events moved swiftly once they had established themselves in the tiny two up and two down house. At Easter, Hetty left school, and with many other girls in the same situation tried to find a job, but times were hard. Going into service was the only option open to her, much as she disliked the prospect, but what was a girl like her to do? She had not been educated for anything else and had no particular talent except a capacity for hard work.

Her new job was as nursemaid to Mr and Mrs Brotherton who lived a mile outside the village. Her charges were two little girls, three and five years old. She would have to live in, and had her own tiny room at the top of the house next to the nursery. Mrs Jessops was very pleased, it was such a step up from housework. She looked forward to Hetty's half days off when she came home and told her about life at the Brothertons and stories of the two little girls.

There was no one more surprised than Hetty one day in the summer to find David standing at the front door of the cottage. In response to his knock, she had hurried to the door and opened it, and it was with a sense of shock that she recognised him.

"David!" She blushed to the roots of her hair.

He grinned back at her, while her heart raced. In the time that had passed since she had seen him, he had grown taller, filled out more, was quite the young man. She closed the door carefully behind her and came out to stand beside him on the step. "How did you know I was here?"

"Your mother told me. I met her in the village, and she told me you had two days' holiday. I couldn't pass up the chance of seeing you. How are you? You look wonderful."

"So do you." She smiled, and remembered her manners. "How is your mother?"

"She's well, busy as usual. What are you doing with yourself these days?"

"I am working at Rokeby Hall for Mrs Brotherton as a nursemaid," she said proudly. His blue eyes twinkled at her.

"Good for you," he said. "Look, why don't your come up to the Grange tomorrow – it would be like old times. I've missed you."

Hetty was shocked.

"Oh, I couldn't! It wouldn't be right! Whatever would your mother say?"

"What do you mean? What could she say? My mother was always very fond of you, Hetty."

She was pleased. Nevertheless, she felt years older than

him in experience. He had always been so sheltered while she had been brought up with the knowledge that everyone had his place, and mixing with the gentry was not hers.

Her soft brown eyes looked up into his. "It's really nice of you, David, to call. But I've had one day off already. I go back to work tomorrow."

He looked disappointed.

"Oh."

"How are you getting on at school?"

He made a face. "It's awful – nothing but exams. Mother wants me to go to Oxford, but I'm not sure I shall make it."

"Of course you will," she said staunchly. "I think you are jolly clever."

"Dear Hetty," he said, and this time it was he who took her hand, while his blue eyes looked down into hers. "Take care," he said.

She watched him go, a tall slip figure striding down the narrow path. Going indoors she closed the door behind her, putting the hand he had held to her lips.

Dear David. She would love him for ever and ever.

Chapter Two

"We are going to have a special tea party for Hetty's birthday," Daisy Brotherton announced solemnly when Hetty took the little girls into the drawing room for inspection before going to bed.

Mrs Brotherton smiled at her two pretty little daughters.

"I see. And when is that to be?"

"Tomorrow," Laura said. "May we, please, Mother?"

"I think so," Mrs Brotherton said. "I shall have a word with Cook and see if she can make a special cake, shall I?"

"Oooh!" The small girls cooed delightedly. They adored Hetty as Mrs Brotherton knew, and she never ceased to thank the fates for sending the nursemaid to her. After two disastrous predecessors Hetty had proved a Godsend. Her employer hoped and prayed that the girl would not go and get married now that she was sixteen, so often they did.

"Say thank you and goodnight to Mother." Hetty said, and in turn each little girl went forward to kiss her mother, delighting in the scenty smell of her, the softness of her cheek.

"Goodnight, Laura. Goodnight, Daisy. God bless."

Holding each child by the hand, Hetty mounted the steep climb to the fourth floor, where beneath the eaves the three of them slept, on summer nights to the sound of the owls' too-whit too-who, a distant fox barking, and sometimes the bleat of a stray lamb, the scent of the heather-stewn hills coming in the open window. In the winter it was a different story, the windows shut tightly against the howling bitter winds and the snow which often kept them housebound for days on end.

After listening to the children saying their prayers, she

tucked them up for the night and went to her own little room, where she curled up by the open window looking out at the magnificent view, the fields and meadows, the bracken and heather, the distant spire of St Luke's church, the tiny village nestling in the valley. Her mother was down there some-where, knitting perhaps, or talking to a neighbour, or giving one of her high teas or suppers to one of the family.

Now Hetty had an extra worry, for Mrs Jessop's rheu-matism was getting worse. Knitting, which was her favourite pastime, was becoming more difficult because of her poor hands which were bent and the knuckles swollen, the joints so large that she could hardly hold the needles. She also had difficulty walking and getting out of her chair. Altogether Hetty was concerned for her mother. She wished sometimes she could stay at home and look after her, but that was out of the question. She knew that once she herself was married, her mam would go and live with Tom and Dora, although they hardly had the space. But they would manage some-how. She sighed. Marriage was a long way off. There were few chances of meeting boys when you were in service, only the occasional village dance or local fair. Sometimes, like now, on this lovely summer's evening, she thought of David, and wondered what he was doing. They had spent such won-derful summer evenings together when they were young, and she smiled at the thought. When they were children, she amended, for they were grown up now. David would be at Oxford, living the life of a rich young man, his days filled with study, and who knew how he spent the rest of the time. Down there and over the hill, just out of sight, was Alderbourne Grange. Sometimes she thought her past life there was like a dream.

Hetty was not a girl to mope. She got up and brought out her sewing, there was always plenty of mending to do for the two small girls.

Fate took a hand in things a few weeks later, when Rokeby Hall saw the arrival of strangers who looked everything over with great attention to detail. That week when Hetty went home, her mother, who knew all the local gossip as did everyone in the village, told her that the Hall was up for sale. The Brothertons were unexpectedly going abroad.

9

"They haven't said a word!" Hetty gasped. "I had no idea."

"Well, you wouldn't, luv," said Mrs Jessops. "Us'd be the last folks they'd tell."

"That means I shall have to find another place," Hetty said, her eyes lighting up. Truth to tell she was a little bored up at Rokeby Hall. The job was easy enough, but she welcomed the idea of a change.

"Aye." Mrs Jessop wrestled with her knitting pins. "They'll tell you when they're reet good and ready. In the meantime, you could look around. They need a girl in the baker's shop, Goodbody's."

Hetty frowned, "Oh, not the baker's shop, Mam."

"And why not?" Mrs Jessops' face was stern. She would brook no nonsense, although she herself was not keen on the idea. "The pay's better, but then it's not all found. I couldn't afford to keep you at home."

"Course not, Mam," Hetty said. "Well, I'll have to wait until they give me notice, won't I? After all, it may not come off. Their going abroad, I mean."

"Oh, they're going all right," Mrs Jessop said, as though she knew something that Hetty didn't, and wasn't going to say.

A month later, as Mrs Jessops had predicted, Hetty left Rokeby Hall for the last time, having taken leave of two tearful small girls.

"You will come and visit us in India, won't you?" they both cried.

"Of course I will," Hetty promised, and kissed them both. India indeed! Fat chance of that, she thought, although having no particular wish to travel and see the world she could wish them well and goodbye without a pang of envy. Nice little things, she thought fondly, feeling suddenly quite grown up.

Now what? she wondered, as she made her way down to the village.

On Saturday, they were holding the September Fair and local Agricultural show. There would be sideshows and coconut shies, Punch and Judy, swings and roundabouts, horticultural exhibits and vegetable competitions. It was the biggest day of the year in Barnsdale, and everyone, simply everyone, went.

She was going with Eleanor Norcutt who had been in her class at school. They had not been particularly friendly then, but now that they were older, seemed to have something in common. For one thing, Eleanor also had an older mother, most of their classmates having mothers in their twenties when they started school while Hetty's mother and Mrs Norcutt had been at least forty years old.

Eleanor's father worked at the pithead, while Eleanor herself had got a job working in an office close to the mine. She had been the cleverest girl in the class, and was known as the brainbox, but now Hetty quite liked her and was glad she had someone to go with on the day of the agricultural fair.

The day dawned, and much to everyone's relief was warm and sunny. The music shrilled out from the hurdy gurdy, the roundabouts swung out and round accompanied by their passengers' delighted screams. Indian toffee was on sale everywhere while at the back of the field was the real reason for the show, the pens containing the animals where the farmers gathered together on this one day in the year to compare stock and prices.

Most of the stalls charged a penny a go, and with only sixpence to spend you had to think out very carefully what you wanted to do most. The hoop-la stall was a must and Eleanor won a china dog which pleased her no end. Then there was the ride on the roundabout, when Hetty sat astride a horse and Eleanor an enormous colourful chicken, both girls laughing and almost falling off in their excitement. After that, a toffee apple at a halfpenny a time kept them busy for quite some time. Hetty eventually wiped her hands on her clean handkerchief, and the two girls made their way towards the fortune-teller's booth.

There was always a fascination about Madame Salome who came to the show every year, and weird and wonderful were some of the things she forecast. Neither girl was prepared to go in, on Hetty's side because she knew her mother would highly disapprove, but when Eleanor's cousin Myrtle came along and dragged Eleanor inside with her, Hetty began to mooch around on her own. Several boys who had been at

11

school with her whistled admiringly after her, for she made a pretty picture with her blue flowered dress and shady hat around which she had tied a silk scarf and a bunch of daisies. A little smile on her face and her head held high she found herself at the coconut shy and it was as she was watching a very clever young man knock one down after the other that she felt a hand on her shoulder.

She turned, and her heart missed a beat as she found herself facing David Ogilby.

"David!" she cried, delighted to see him. How tall he had grown, handsome and fair, those blue eyes regarding her now with fond affection. He took her hand.

"Hetty." He smiled. "I'm so glad I have found you – I have been looking everywhere for you – I guessed you'd be here."

But she was already having misgivings. She had called him "David", and a tell-tale blush stained her cheeks.

"You look wonderful," he said. "Quite grown up, and very pretty, if I may say so."

Her brown eyes sparkled up at him.

"Shall we walk?" he said, and Hetty, feeling like a duchess, matched her stride to his.

"Well, and what have you been doing with yourself, young lady?"

Somehow he seemed to find an easy path through the crowds as Hetty tried to keep up with him.

"Working. What about you?"

"Same as you – working, but I expect your work is much harder than mine." They had reached the fringe of the crowd now, and she walked beside him until he stopped and turned to face her. "Look, there is a seat over there – shall we sit down?"

Hetty, who was in a seventh heaven of delight, agreed. It was an old seat, carved out of a log, and she leaned back surveying the scene in front of her. She was so happy she wanted to stay here forever.

"Do you sometimes wish we were young again – without a care in the world?" David asked.

"We're still young," she laughed, "but I know what you mean. You never appreciate childhood until it has gone."

"We were lucky, weren't we?" David said. "Not a care in the world."

12

"You make it sound as though life is full of troubles," Hetty said. "Aren't you enjoying Oxford?"

"Yes, of course – up to a point. But you know I'm not the academic type, Hetty. I'd like to be back here with the dogs and horses, going around the farm."

"I know what you mean. I never see a horse to ride nowadays, since Father died."

"Yes, that was awful. How is your mother?"

"Not too bad, I suppose. Her rheumatism is playing her up, and she is getting on, you know, but she is happy enough and never complains."

"But what about you, Hetty. Are you still a nursemaid?"

"No, actually I have just left. The Brothertons are going to India, so that's that. I have to find something else to do – but I don't know what."

"Do you have to go into service, Hetty? It must be jolly boring, and such hard work – always being at everyone else's beck and call."

She could have hugged him. He was so nice, such a gentleman, there was nothing he didn't understand.

And now they could hear the sound of applause coming from the marquee, where apparently the judges of the fruit and vegetables and the home made cakes and jams had made their final decision.

"Mother is presenting the prize for the best cake," David said, and Hetty came down to earth with a thump.

Mrs Ogilby here! Well of course, she would be – but what would her reaction be if she knew that David and Hetty Jessops were sitting here together? It was just not done. If David had no idea of the order of things, Hetty certainly had. She got to her feet and smoothed down her skirt.

"David, I must go. I came with a friend."

He was apologetic. "I am so sorry. I didn't realise."

"It's all right, really. She went into the fortune teller's."

"And you didn't want to find out what the future held in store for you?"

She picked up her small purse. "No. I don't believe in that sort of thing. Well".

They faced each other, and for some reason Hetty found it difficult to look into his eyes, perhaps knowing what she

13

would find there. But slowly she did so, and what she saw caused her blood to go rushing through her veins, and sent a thrill through her body. Her face flamed. He went to take her hand, but she moved back.

"No, David. I must go. It was nice to see you. Goodbye." And holding her hat, she almost ran back to the fortune teller's booth where she found Eleanor waiting for her, and in none too good a temper.

Where've you been?" she demanded crossly. I've been looking everywhere for you!"

"Sorry," Hetty said, still trying to compose herself. "I got lost."

"Hmmm", Eleanor said. But she could be as cross as she liked, Hetty decided. She had just seen David again.

"Come on," she said. I've still got twopence left. "What shall we do now?"

It was not until much later that evening, when the washing up had been done and she had helped her mother climb the stairs to bed, that she sat downstairs in the little front room by the window with the Nottingham lace curtains, the oil lamp alight by her side. She rocked to and fro in her father's old rocking chair, thinking.

Hetty Jessops, she told herself, you must be mad. You want your head examining. Just who do you thing you are? David Ogilby is not for the likes of you. Here you are, a Yorkshire lass, your head filled with daydreams. It's time you went out and got yourself another job and found a nice young man to marry.

She turned off the oil lamp and made her way in the dark across the room to the kitchen, where she drew herself a glass of cold water. Then bending down she picked up the family pet, a large black cat who nestled into her.

She cuddled him closely to her for a minute, before putting him down and opening the back door.

"Out you go, Blackie," she said, and closed the door after him.

14

Chapter Three

Fate stepped in when Mrs Jessops fell in the back yard and sprained her ankle. She was a large woman and had grown stouter with the years, so it was important that she kept the weight off her damaged ankle. Hetty knew now where her duty lay. She must get a local job and stay home and look after her mam, at least until her leg was healed.

With this prospect in mind she applied for the job in the baker's shop, and was quite pleased when she got it. She started at eight in the morning and worked until five-thirty in the evening, with half an hour break at midday – ample time for her to call home and see to her mam.

It was surprising, she though, how a bit of trouble brought them all running home. She saw sisters and brothers she only met at Christmas time, for apart from Dora and Tom who lived in the next street, they all lived quite a distance away. There was Polly who was married to Arthur and who lived close to the border, Ida and her husband Ned, who lived in Grimsby, and Eva, nice gentle Eva, who was married to Ted. Eva was Hetty's favourite sister, a pretty shy young woman with dark brown eyes like Hetty's, and a cloud of dark hair. She had such a hard life on a farm, what with the work in all seasons and a brood of five, yet she managed to find time to come by train to see her mam.

When they had all made their felicitations and departed again, Hetty settled down to her new job. She found it quite pleasant. The time passed quickly for she seemed to be serving non-stop and soon got used to the names of the various home-made cakes and buns and the different shapes of bread.

Sometimes, at the end of the day, Mrs Goodbody presented her with a bag of cakes, which delighted Mrs Jessops who had a very sweet tooth. Neighbours, too, called in to see her, giving her all the gossip, while Dora called in every day to see how she was. With five daughters and two sons, there was always something going on, although her youngest son, Gervase, had emigrated to Australia soon after the war with his wife Florence.

Hetty had been in the shop for two weeks when the dark haired young man with dark eyebrows came into the shop for tea cakes. He looked a little familiar to her, but she couldn't place him as a local man. When she gave him his change his hand lingered a little over hers. Looking up, she met a pair of dark, almost black, flashing eyes which almost took her breath away – they were impudent, laughing eyes. She immediately took on a haughty demeanour.

"Next, please," she said imperiously, and the young man left the shop.

That evening her mother regaled her with bits of local gossip.

"There's new people in the corn chandler's" she said. "Scotch people, by all accounts. Fancy Enticknaps giving it up – they've been there for donkey's years, even before your father's time. 'Course, Silas Enticknap were getting on a bit and she warn't too well. Any road, Mrs Appleton said the new people are in. Seems it's an elderly couple, and a young man works in the shop. 'Course, I dunno if 'e's the son . . . grandson more like." She wrestled with her knitting needles. "'andsome young fella, Mrs Appleton said, more like a gypsy." And Hetty stopped peeling the potato, the knife held up in the air. Was that the young man who had come into the shop today? And she suddenly remembered where she had seen him before. He was the young man she had seen knocking coconuts down one after another – a right proper show off, she thought.

"Well, supper's on," she said, "It'll be about half an hour, so I'd best get on with the ironing."

"Ye're a good lass, Hetty," Mrs Jessops said.

Several times after that the young man came into the shop for bread, and since not many men shopped for food, Hetty

16

suspected that he came in to see her, for he always made a point of touching her hand and smiling at her.

"Ye've a new admirer, then," Mrs Goodbody said one day when he had gone. "Young Maclaren from the corn chandler's."

"Oh, is that who he is?" Hetty said idly. "I thought he was new round here."

"Yes, his grandparents have taken the shop over. Seems his father was killed in the war and his mother died when he was born, and they've brung him up. They've done a good job. He's a fine upstanding young man – and good prospects, what's more. You could do worse, young Hetty."

She blushed to the roots of her chestnut curls, while her dark eyes looked ominously angry. She hated the way everyone talked about good prospects and the importance they attached to money matters. She had said as much to her mam one day and she had rounded on her fairly and squarely.

"There's nowt wrong with valuing brass, lass. When everything else goes, it's brass as matters. Ye'll not get far in this world wi'out it, that's for sure. Ye can take mam's word for that."

One day when she came out of the shop the young man was waiting for her outside. She looked at him, her brown eyes meeting his, and felt a strange excitement.

"Will ye let me walk home with ye?" he said, his black eyes warm with admiration.

"If you like," Hetty said. He didn't sound very Scottish, she thought, more like a Geordie.

They fell into step. Hetty trying to keep pace with his stride, for she was a small, slight girl, and he was tall with broad shoulders, and, she thought, stealing a sidelong glance at him, very handsome.

"You could tell me who you are," she said lightly.

"Oh." He stopped short. "I'm John Maclaren – but my friends call me Jack." He smiled at her disarmingly.

"And what shall I call you?"

"Jack – if ye like," he said. "My grandfather has just taken over the corn chandler's. That's where I work."

Hetty nodded. "I thought you were new around here. I'm Hetty – "

" – Jessops," he finished for her, and she laughed. "Oh, you know that, do you?"

"I made it my business to find out," he said, and she felt a sudden shiver go through her, whether from excitement or apprehension she didn't know.

As they passed the corn chandler's, with its jute sacks full of maize and bran, garden forks and spades all stacked neatly outside, she glanced across.

"That's it," he said proudly.

It certainly was, Hetty thought, one of the busiest shops in the village.

"I've seen you pass on you way to and from work in the last couple of weeks."

"Yes, I've only been there that long. Before that I was a nursemaid up at Rokeby Hall, but the people went to India."

"But ye'd not be sorry about that," he said. "I canna imagine anything more dull than looking after other folk's bairns. Ye're much too pretty to be doing that."

Hetty blushed. No one had ever said anything like that to her before. They came to a stop outside the cottage. "Here's where I live," she said.

"I was wonderin' if ye'd come out with me tomorrow afternoon? It's my half day. Yours too?"

"Well . . ." Hetty said. Oh, if she only could. But what about Mam? It was the one time she could do all the housework and washing. There was never time to do it all on Sunday, what with church and all, and besides you couldn't put washing out on a Sunday.

"I'm sorry," she said. "I would have liked that – but my Mam has hurt her leg and until it's better I have to look after her."

To her surprise, Hetty saw his eyes darken and his brows draw together.

"Don't you have any time off?" he asked. "What about this evening?"

"Yes," she said, anxious to please. "I could manage that."

He smiled, a brilliant smile that showed excellent teeth and quite took Hetty's breath away.

"Seven o'clock then," he said. "See you then."

"I think," Hetty said, explaining to her mother, "that he is a young man who likes his own way."

18

"They all do, luv," Mrs Jessops said, "and it takes a long time to mould 'em – you'll learn."

At seven o'clock, Hetty in her second best dress of blue cotton opened the front door and emerged just as soon as she saw Jack waiting outside. He had put on a suit and a collar and tie and looked very smart. Handsome, she decided, he certainly was. But handsome is as handsome does. She would see.

They walked along the river bank, exchanging confidences. She learned that he came from a Scottish family, but that he had lived in Newcastle all his life. He was twenty-two years old and had done his National Service.

"What about you?" he asked her. "Come from a big family, do ye?"

And Hetty told him all about her sisters and brothers, and Mam and her broken leg, and her father being a groom up at Aldebourne Grange. But she didn't mention David Ogilby.

"I've right taken a fancy to you, Hetty Jessops," he said.

"Oh, have you now?" she bantered.

"Ye're not going steady, are ye?" he asked. "There's not another chap?"

"No," she said truthfully.

"Well, then," he said, taking her hand, and they walked like that all the way home until they came to the village street when he let it go.

Outside her front door, they paused for a moment.

"All right for Saturday at the same time?" he asked, his splendid dark eyes looking down into hers. Hetty was quite overcome.

"Well, I – "

"See you then," he said with his dashing smile, and Hetty let herself in. She had heard of people being swept off their feet and wondered if it was happening to her.

It was a whirlwind courtship, and sometimes Hetty was left quite breathless. Mrs Jessops was as pleased as punch.

"Well, young Hetty," she would say when her daughter came in after yet another evening out with Jack Maclaren. "Someone up there is certainly looking after you. I don't know when I saw a more handsome chap, and he thinks the world of you. And like to come into the business," she

19

stressed. "You play your cards right, my lass, and you'll be wed in no time."

But Hetty didn't like that kind of talk.

"That's not what I'd be marrying him for, mam. I like him and, well, I know he likes me – but he's nice, and he makes me laugh." She smiled, but then her eyes darkened. "He's got a temper, though."

Mrs Jessops threw her a suspicious look. "And what would you know about that, my girl?"

"Well, he gets annoyed if I'm a minute or two late, and sometimes on a Saturday at dinner time, when he's been to the Rose and Crown, I can tell he's had – well, a drink too many."

Mrs Jessops was thoughtful, eyes on her knitting. At length she put down her work and looked up. "They're all the same, Scotch men," she said. "They like their drink. Spend most of their evenings drinking, from what I've heard. Still, lass, that would change when you are wed."

"He hasn't asked me yet," Hetty laughed. "Chance would be a fine thing."

But she thought about it more and more. That she was attracted to Jack Maclaren she knew for sure, painfully conscious that he aroused her physically. When he took her in his arms to kiss her goodnight, it was all she could do not to give way to his ardent caresses. He was a masterful lover, and she suspected he had had some experience, but not knowing much about such things herself, she accepted the fact. After all, he was almost five years older than her, and a good-looking man like Jack must have had lots of girls after him. She was at once captivated and aware. When he kissed her, and he knew how to kiss, Hetty felt like melting butter, and when his hands began to roam it was all she could do to struggle faintly, and as time went by, more weakly. Sometimes, when she looked up, it was to find his black eyes, glowing like hot coals, looking down into hers with a kind of mesmeric quality. She wanted to swoon, to allow him to do anything with her that he wanted.

One Sunday afternoon he took her to tea to meet his grandparents, Mr and Mrs Maclaren, who lived over the shop. Hetty, fussed over by Mam, put on her best dress of white cotton with the navy embroidery, and her Sunday hat. She took a small posy of pinks from the garden, and when Jack called for her and stood silently for a moment watching her, Hetty knew in an instant that this was the man she was going to marry.

He held out his arm. "Ready?" he said.

She smiled at him.

"Of course," she said, and stepped out confidently.

She was fascinated by the flat over the shop, never having been in one before. The parlour, which was bright and clean, was directly over the shop, and quite large. Jack's grandmother, an elderly lady with snow white hair, had a lovely kind face, and welcomed Hetty with open arms. Her Scots accent was so strong that Hetty had some difficulty in understanding her.

"So ye're Hetty," she said, looking at her approvingly. "Sit ye down, lass, Mr Maclaren will be here the noo."

Hetty felt at home at once. She knew she was on approbation, as it were, being looked over, and there could only be one reason for that. She was here as Jack's intended bride. She found that the prospect excited her.

She looked across at him, at his wonderfully handsome face and broad shoulders, and she felt a thrill run through her. What more could she ask? To be married to such a man, with all that he had to offer her, and to know that as a Yorkshire lass she was being true to her roots. It was fine to have security, but that was not half as important as having the man you wanted. Her soft eyes met his, and her heart began to beat fast. Then she dragged her gaze away from his to greet old Mr Maclaren who came in apologising for the delay. He had the nicest manners, the courtesy of a gentleman, and she was a little surprised. Had these two gentle people really brought Jack up? He was so strong and so vibrant, you might have thought he was a foundling child, a gypsy, but as the afternoon wore on and they brought out old sepia photographs of Jack's long dead parents, she could see where he got his looks.

For his father had been a big man, with the same black curling hair, and dark eyes, eyes that held a glint in them, even in a faded photograph, while his mother had the sweetest expression. Hetty sighed. She really was a very lucky girl.

Tea followed, a real high tea, with toast and sandwiches and lots of home-made bread and scones and jam. "Tuck in, lass," Mrs Maclaren said, and watched with approval as Hetty waded in to the gargantuan spread. Every now and again she looked across at Jack who, catching her eye, twinkled back at her. "She will do nicely," she seemed to say.

Hetty, conscious of what was going on around her, thoroughly enjoyed herself. What a lot she was going to be able to tell Mam when she got home, and how pleased she would be. For she was going to marry him – when he asked her, she reminded herself, but she had no doubts about that. When he took her home that night he kissed her gently when he left her, surprising her. He really loved her, she thought, it wasn't that he was just after – well, you know. Letting herself in, she tiptoed up to bed, putting her head round Mam's door to see she was all right.

A few nights later, Jack asked her to marry him. They had walked up the lane after a storm, and the road was awash with water, while the overhanging trees dripped, and the grassy meadows sparkled with the sun which suddenly came out, flooding everything with a golden glow.

"Yes, Jack," she said, putting her arms around his neck.

He bent low and kissed her passionately, until she felt delirious with desire for him. "Jack, Jack – "

"You won't be sorry, Hetty." He buried his face in her neck. "I'd do anything for you, anything."

He lifted his face, his eyes like black jet as they met hers. "We'll make a good pair," he said.

She closed her eyes and smiled.

22

Chapter Four

The news Hetty brought home that evening was just what Mrs Jessops needed. Her last and youngest daughter to be married – and such a catch. The most handsome young man in the village, and with such prospects. When his grandparents died he and Hetty would be the owners of a shop, the busiest shop in Barnsdale, except for the grocer's and the public houses, of course. She couldn't wait to tell everyone the news, and the family rallied around with much excitement. Think how impressed the neighbours would be, although they had a good idea by now as to what the outcome of Jack Maclaren's courtship of Hetty Jessops would be.

He bought her a ring, a real diamond ring, a small stone surrounded by seed pearls which she chose herself.

"Pearls!" Mrs Jessops wailed. "Pearls are unlucky."

"Not for me," Hetty laughed. "You're superstitious, Mam."

"Who, me?" Mrs Jessops cried. "Never! – I've no time for that sort of rubbish, but pearls are unlucky – everyone knows that."

Sometimes, at night, Hetty lay awake thinking over the events of the past three months. It has all happened so quickly. Since the night that Jack had escorted her home she had hardly had time to call her own. What with Mam, and Jack's proposal and the wedding plans – and how exciting they were. In the still of the night she sometimes thought of David Ogilby, and wondered what he was doing with himself now. News filtered down to the village sometimes from the Grange. She knew for instance that he had left Oxford and had gone on a Grand Tour of Europe. Perhaps, she thought, he will come back with a foreign bride. The thought made her sigh.

There were times when she compared her love for David with her overriding passion for Jack, and knew that they were two very different things. Her love for David was as for a friend, a close friend; it was warm, affectionate, gentle, something that made you smile to yourself when you thought about it. She would always love David, nothing could change that. It was not as if she could ever have married him, that was out of the question, and a girl had to get on with life, plan for her future as a married woman and the mother of children.

What she felt for Jack was something else. Passionate, with a sense of urgency about it. Physical – yes, that was it, except that they also got on well and understood each other. She knew by now that he liked his own way about most things, but also that he would do anything for her. He was generous to a fault, think of all the lovely presents he had given her, and he had the power with his lovemaking to set her senses on fire, to rouse her to an extent she had never dreamt of. Thinking about marriage to him and sharing the same bed, she was overcome with desire for him. Yes, she was a lucky girl, as Mam said. Mam also said that a wife must be dutiful and not nag, except that if he seemed to like the drink a bit too much, then she must make herself so attractive to him that he had no wish to go out. A couple of babies would soon see to that, Mam said.

One evening he called round to tell her he had found a small cottage farther along the village. It was right on the village street. His grandparents had been told about it when they delivered goods to the house next door. The old man who lived there had just died, and the cottage had become vacent. They knew the landlord and Jack had just been around to see him.

"Come on, Hetty," he said. "I've got the key – we'll go right now."

She took his arm proudly as they walked along the street, aware that behind the lace curtains many a curious eye was watching their progress. When they reached number forty-seven, he inserted the key in the lock.

Once inside the narrow hallway he wrinkled his nose. "Phew! It could do with some fresh air – let's leave the front door ajar."

Hetty bent down and put the doorstop against the small wooden door. "He'd lived here a long time – all his life, I daresay – no wonder it's stuffy."

She thought of her own home which was about the same size, and how it smelled of polish and soap and carbolic. Mam was very fussy about the house. She even kept lavender bags in the cupboards. Her father had always grown lavender bushes and rosemary. She glanced outside at the minute patch of earth. She would do the same. The garden would be filled with flowers, and she would press them in the winter and make pictures."

"Did you know him?" Jack asked, going into the tiny front room.

"Yes, everyone knew old Mr Pickering. He used to garden up at the Grange," she said, but Jack was not listening.

"Of course, this all needs doing up, but I'm not bad at this sort of thing," he said.

There was a small black iron fireplace surrounded by tiles. The room was full of antiquated old and dusty furniture, and the curtains up at the window were in rags.

"Ugh!" Hetty made a face. "Clear this lot out and burn it, and a good scrub through will work wonders. Let's see the kitchen.

The kitchen was even worse than they had imagined, dark and dirty with a yellow porcelain sink, but it did have running water and there was a copper in one corner. Beyond it was a narrow garden, full of overgrown flowers and weeds. Hetty's eyes began to sparkle. If she could just get her teeth into all this, she would have it looking like a new pin in no time. The outside privy hardly bore inspection. Jack closed the door hurriedly. "That's a job for me," he said. "Have no fears about that. I'll not have ye doing the dirty work."

Hetty looked at him suddenly, seeing the big, strong man that Jack Maclaren was. Yes, she need have no fears in that direction.

They climbed the narrow staircase which led straight into a bedroom, and with a hasty glance inside, Hetty withdrew.

25

Poor Mr Pickering had probably died in there. But she put it once and for all at the back of her mind and entered the other bedroom, a much smaller room. Jack was just behind her. Turning to him, she saw the black eyes full of unspoken thoughts, and smiled at him. They were thinking the same thing – a spare room for children. She kissed him lightly, but he dragged her to him and kissed her passionately, almost causing her to lose her balance. "Jack!" she cried. "Mind!" Catching hold of the iron bedstead.

He looked around with distaste. "Ye can thank your lucky stars this room is in a disgusting state – otherwise I might . . ." And he glanced down at the bed then at Hetty with a wicked gleam in his eyes.

She blushed furiously. "Jack Maclaren!" she hurried down the staircase and into the back garden where she stood for a moment or two until he reached her side.

"Well, what do ye think?"

"It could be wonderful, and I'm not afraid of hard work."

"Ye'd not have to be," he grinned. "We'll tak' it, eh?"

She nodded, eyes dancing.

He put an arm round her shoulders and hugged her to him. "We can set the wedding date now, eh?"

"September," Hetty said firmly. "Is that all right with you, Jack?"

"Today would be fine with me," he grinned, "but, yes, love, September will be fine. Of course," he went on, "later when the old folks retire we shall be able to live above the shop. It's not a bad flat, that."

"But it doesn't have a garden, Jack," she said, and he squeezed her hand. "I forgot, love," he said. "We must have a garden, eh?"

So the wedding was fixed for the second Saturday in September and the Jessops family got to work. Dora offered to make the bride's dress if Hetty would help with the bridesmaids'. There would be four of them, all Hetty's nieces. Her dress was to be a traditional gown of white art satin, and the bridesmaids were to be in pink. "No expense spared," Mrs Jessops told them. "Well, within reason. Little Hetty is the last of the brood, and we'll make a reet good day of it. We must show Jack and his family how well we do things in

26

Yorkshire." They were to be married in St Luke's like Mrs Jessops and her other daughters. The church would be decorated with flowers, and Hetty would wear a wreath of orange blossom and carry a spray of pink carnations and roses.

It was a wedding day that was long remembered in Barnsdale, for it was a fine day, and the bride looked simply lovely. All in white, with bridesmaids in pink, and the groom the handsomest man you could ever wish to see. There were crowds outside the little church, for everyone loved a wedding. Afterwards it was almost open house at the Jessops', where the tables groaned with home-made cakes and cold meats, salads and jellies, while to crown it all, the wedding cake sat in the middle of the table, a grand three tier cake, a present to the happy couple from Mrs Goodbody.

Afterwards, dressed for going away, Hetty ran down the confetti-strewn path to the pony and trap which was to take them to the station where they would catch a train to Scarborough. Just for the weekend, for Jack was needed back at the shop. It all seemed like a dream to Hetty, the day had flown by, but here she was, sitting next to her new husband, wearing a new gold ring, no longer Hetty Jessops but Mrs Maclaren.

"Happy?" Jack asked her. "It was a nice wedding, wasn't it? You Mam did us proud."

Hetty nodded. "It was wonderful, Jack."

"And that's not all," he said, his black eyes dancing.

"Oh, Jack!" Hetty said, blushing to the tips of her ears.

"You were the most beautiful bride I have ever seen," he said.

"And you were the best-looking groom," she laughed.

"That makes two satisfied customers."

The guest house, called Shangri-la, was on the Esplanade. They walked up the steps and through the open door into the hall. A Mrs Throckmorton welcomed them and showed them to their room. It didn't overlook the sea, but they didn't mind that much. Jack put the case down and Mrs Throckmorton gave them a look which brooked no nonsense.

"No visitors mind – and dinner's at seven," she said, closing the door behind her.

27

They both burst out laughing from sheer exuberance, and then the laughter turned quickly to desire as Jack devoured her with kisses. He threw her hat on the bed and pulled the pins out of her hair. 'Jack, Jack, it's only six o'clock!" she remonstrated, but not very strongly, as he helped her out of her jacket and began unbuttoning his own.

Hetty, excited, but unsure, glanced towards the window. "The curtains, Jack – pull the curtains."

"Eh? Oh." And he crossed the room and did so, leaving them in darkness, just a filtered light coming through the thin curtains. "I want to see you," he said.

"Time enough, Jack," she said, turning to him. He embraced her and kissed her passionately, her eyes, her lips, arousing her to such an extent that she no longer cared what he did. He pulled her down on the bed and lifted her clothes and she felt her body flush with desire as his hands moved over her, exploring her, caressing her. If the thought crossed her mind that he hadn't wasted much time, she stifled it. She knew Jack was a hot-blooded man and had no wish to be thwarted, and she wanted him desperately. All coherent thought stilled, she surrendered herself to what he was doing, marvelling at the intensity of her own passion, giving herself to him totally. Never had she supposed, for all her girlish dreams, that it would be quite as intense as this, the overpowering sensation of two bodies becoming one. Exhausted and breathless, they lay back. Then Jack looked down her and smiled. In the darkness she could see the gleam of his fine teeth and the brilliance of his dark eyes. He bent over and kissed her again, and then gently began once more to make love to her while she lay responding to his caresses. This time it was slow, he took his time, which made it even more exciting, almost unbearable in its intensity.

It was seven-twenty before they put in an appearance in the dining room where the small servant waited by the door and Mrs Throckmorton eyed them with disapproval.

"You're late," she said with jaundiced eye.

Jack took out his pocket watch and glanced at it.

"We are? Sorry – I thought you said seven-thirty." And he winked at Hetty.

"Dinner is at seven," Mrs Throckmorton said sourly, "and you'd do well to remember it."

28

"Sorry," he said again with all the charm he was capable of. The week end flew by with them spending almost all of the time in bed, although they did go for a walk along the sea front before dinner. Arm in arm they faced the oncoming breeze which whipped up the colour in their cheeks and gave them such a sense of well-being that they were ready for anything.

"I am looking forward to our little house, aren't you, Jack?"

"You bet," he said. "You wait 'till you see it. Sarah's done a good job, and I've done a bit myself."

Sarah was the strong local cleaning woman who never minded how dirty the work was. Jack had engaged her to thoroughly clean the house so that Hetty could go into it at least cleaner than it was. By the time the rag and bone man had taken all the old stuff away, and the worn lionoleum had been taken up and carted off, and the ceilings swept of cobwebs and cupboards cleared out, Hetty wouldn't know it. There would be time enough to paint it and buy more things later. Hetty's Mam had given them a double bed and washstand, and his grandparents had bought them a kitchen table and two chairs, so they had a good start. He couldn't wait to see her face when she opened the door.

Hetty was so excited and thrilled when she saw what had been done that her eyes filled with tears and she threw her arms around Jack. "Oh, you are good to me," she said, laughing through her tears. "It's lovely – just wait until I start on it. You won't recognise it, Jack Maclaren."

As the months went by, the little house improved by leaps and bounds Jack painted the doors and windows and Hetty hung freshly laundered curtains that Mam had given her up at the windows. The floors were scurbbed and stained until such time as they could afford new linoleum. As it was, Hetty spent the winter months making a rag rug, sitting by the fire in the small black grate, her nimble fingers working over it. Jack often went down to the Red Lion in the evenings while Hetty always had plenty to do and sometimes went and sat with her mother or Dora. It had been decided that now Mam was on her own, there was no point in her keeping the home going, she needed someone to look after her all the time. Arthritis had set in both legs, and she had great difficulty getting about.

"She must come and live with us," Dora said. "We'll make room."

Hetty felt guilty. She and Jack also had room, a tiny room it was true, and one which they hoped to use for a baby. But she had no need to worry, Dora quite understood.

"You and Jack are only just starting out in life," she said. "You've to have time to get settled and on your feet. Time enough for you to have her later when my children have grown up and need more room."

Hetty was relieved. She knew Jack would never have agreed to Mam coming to live with them. He would have put his foot down very firmly. She was learning more and more about him as the months went by. He was very different from her father and brothers who had been quiet, easy going men. Jack was not in the least like that. When he was quiet he was very quiet, and when he was angry he was very angry indeed. It didn't take a lot to upset him, it was as if he had himself under control most of the time, but there were others when he went over the top, and more than once he frightened her when he lost his temper over something trivial. But he was always terribly sorry afterwards and tried to make it up to her. She was learning the hard way how to deal with him.

They had been married almost a year when Mrs Jessops became ill following a bout of influenza, pneumonia setting in. For three days she lay at death's door, and when they all thought that the danger period was over and she was going to be all right, quietly passed away.

Tearfully attending the funeral, Hetty felt unwell and put it down to the shock of bereavement. There had not been much time to think about herself in the last few days, but when the funeral was over and she sat back quietly in her own little home to count the days, she realised that she was pregnant.

"Jack!" she cried, before he had closed the frong door that night. "Jack – we're going to have a baby. I'm pregnant!" And with a whoop of joy he lifted her up and swung her round in the small passageway.

"Put me down," she gasped breathlessly. "Jack!" But he was kissing her and hugging her, there was no doubt at all about his delight at her news.

"That calls for a celebration drink," he said. "I'll buy them all a round at the Red Lion tonight." And he didn't see the slight frown that appeared between her eyes. Then she smiled at him.

"Wouldn't Mam have been pleased?" she said.

Chapter Five

One cold March evening, Hetty and her sister Dora sat in Hetty's small front room. She was sewing while Dora was knitting, her needles clicking to the sound of the clock on the mantelpiece. Outside lay a fall of snow for it had been a hard winter, and now in late March it was still bitterly cold. The east wind blew itself against the front door and howled around the chimney stacks. Inside the little room it was cosy with a coal fire burning brightly in the grate. There was never any shortage of coal in Barnsdale.

Hetty's baby was almost due. This morning she had had a few pains, so Dora had kept a watch on her in order that she could be on the spot and call in the midwife should she be wanted. Every now and again she looked up and glanced at her sister, her look one of compassion and concern.

Hetty really was a pretty girl. The prettiest girl in the family, with her lovely brown eyes and that cloud of dark hair. Dora could feel the anger rising slowly inside her, anger which up to now she had managed to conceal. The needles flew along the rows of knitting, until suddenly she glanced up at the clock and put the knitting down, rolling it up and placing it in the knitting bag, the words being forced from her, as though she could no longer hold them back.

"He's not working late, is he?"

Hetty raised startled brown eyes.

"What do you mean?" she whispered.

But Dora was ready to speak. She had bottled it up long enough, and now the die was cast.

"Jack," she said. "He's not working late at the shop, is he?"

She could have wept to see Hetty's face, the misery in her eyes. She had no wish to hurt her, especially now, but it was better out in the open. That way, they all knew where they stood. She saw Hetty's shoulders sag, as though at last the burden of silence was broken. Her hands lay limply in her lap, the sewing forgotten, as she stared bleakly in front of her.

Then she shook her head slowly. "No," she said at length. "He's not working late."

"More likely at the Lamb or the Red Lion," Dora said harshly, "while you . . ." her tone was bitter.

"When did you find that out?" Hetty asked.

"I've known for a long time. Tom told me first – said he had seen him times out of number, and he was always there long after Tom and the others had called in for a pint. Not only that – " she took a deep breath " – I've seen the bruises that you tried to hide."

At that the tears sprang to Hetty's eyes and flowed down her cheeks.

"Oh, luv!" Dora was almost crying too. "I didn't want to upset you, honest, – but I couldn't hold it in. Something came over me." And she looked up at the clock. "Look at the time – it's gone ten, and still he's not in. And I s'pose when he does come, he'll be the worse for drink. Oh, you poor little thing!"

"He's not a bad man," Hetty said, sniffing into her hankie. "He's good and generous and kind, but he just seems to want to drink. I've tried to stop him, honestly Dora, and he means to turn over a new leaf, but then, after a time, he just has to go and get a drink – "

"Trouble is," her sister said, "he doesn't know when to stop."

"It's a kind of illness," Hetty said. "He can't take it, really."

"Then it's a pity he starts at all," Dora said acidly. "What'll you do when the baby comes?"

"I'm hoping it will make all the difference," Hetty said. "When he sees the little bairn he just won't want to go out drinking, and I will have something to take my mind off it."

"Leopards don't easily change their spots," Dora said cryptically. "It's the beating I don't like – I'm just glad that Mam isn't alive to see it."

33

"Oh, Dora – "

"How many times . . . how often . . .?" she began, but Hetty stopped her.

"Only once or twice, when he was in a temper, and that was because he had had too much to drink. It's the drink, Dora, that does it."

"I'm sure it is." She spat out the words. "I'll tell you something, Hetty. If I see your face bruised like it was before, never mind the tale that you walked into a door, I'll send Tom around, honest I will."

"Oh, no, Dora!" Hetty wailed. "Jack'd kill him – you don't know his strength when he's in a temper."

"Bugger that for a tale." Dora was in a fine old temper herself now, but tried to simmer down as she realised that she had not exactly chosen the right moment. She sighed. Well, it was done now. At least it was all out in the open. It was a start in the right direction.

"Look, don't seem as if it's going to be just yet. You get up to bed and get some rest – you're going to need every bit of it as soon as the baby is born. Rest and sleep will be a thing of the past then." She smiled reassuringly at Hetty. "I'll clear away the cups and wait a minute or two until he comes in."

"You won't say anything will you, Dora?" Hetty's eyes were those of a faithful spaniel.

"Course I won't," Dora said, although there was nothing she would have liked more. "Pubs will be closed in a minute or two – he can't be much longer now. Up you go, and sleep tight."

"Goodnight, Dora, and thank you," Hetty said, heaving herself out of the Windsor chair and waddling off towards the stairs. What a size she was, thought Dora. It was to be hoped it wasn't twins. Poor little devil! For two pins she'd kill that swine of a husband.

Six days later, Hetty's daughter was born. A fine healthy girl, weighing seven pounds. The midwife, Martha Alsop, who had delivered most of the babies in Barnsdale, had been called in by Dora at eleven in the evening. She knew exactly the state Hetty was at, and got to work at once. With the sheets tied to the bed rail at the bottom of the bed, she urged Hetty on. "Push, push! Come on, dearie, harder, I can see the head. Push a bit more, a bit more, nearly done now . . ." Hetty pulled on the tied sheets for leverage, tugging away to help her deliver her precious burden.

Martha Alsop was pleased with her. She hadn't expected much trouble from Hetty Jessops, and with Dora Jessops to assist her – she never could remember their married names – and the baby wrapped in a shawl, she turned her attention to the new mother whose dark hair was a mass of damp, dark curls, whose forehead was glistening with sweat, her body limp with relaxation after labour, yet whose face wore that same satisfied expression of wonder and gratitude that most mothers wore after they had given birth.

Vida, Hetty called her, from the moment she first held her in her arms. Vida, and Joan after her mother.

"That's a pretty fancy name," Dora laughed, as she looked down at the sleeping infant. "Where did you get that from?"

"I don't know," Hetty admitted. "It's always been my favourite name. I must have read it somewhere."

Jack Maclaren stared down at the sleeping baby in wonder. He seemed quite overcome at the sight of his tiny daughter, and Hetty remembered that he was an only child and not used to having children around. "She's so wee," he said.

"Here, take her," Hetty said. "You won't drop her." And he did so, nervously at first, then obviously gaining more courage as the moments slipped by. "Aye, but she's bonny," he said with pride. "When can the old folks see her?"

"Whenever you like, Jack," Hetty said. "Grandmother Maclaren might like to come over while I'm still abed, or I can take her over when I am up. I shall be in a few days."

"Nae, lass, ye've to stay there for a week. Dora says ye must – once ye're up, ye'll be hard put to find a minute to spare."

Oh, if only it could always be like this, Hetty thought. Without the drink he was such a kind man, thoughtful and so hard-working. He would do anything in the house that she wanted. He had painted the small room for the baby, although she wouldn't need that for a long time. Hetty couldn't bear the thought of having her sleep in another room. A baby's place was with its mother, tucked up in bed beside her, cosy and warm, where she could feed her when she was hungry. But later on, when they had another baby, then that would become Vida's room. In a cupboard in that room she kept all the tiny garments she had knitted, the presents she had received from well-wishers and the family. Jack's grandmother had given her all sorts of lovely baby clothes, things she said had been in the family for many years. Hetty was grateful for anything.

Within a month, Hetty was "churched", going to church to give thanks for her baby. Next would come the christening. Hetty wished things could always be like this, with Jack so attentive, and hardly going out to the pub at all, and when he did he returned after a beer or two. "I only had two, Hetty," he would say, and her heart went out to him. Perhaps now things would be better. Since Vida was born, he had turned over a new leaf.

The baby grew by leaps and bounds. One moment it seemed she was in a shawl, and the next she was crawling. She was a good baby, and as pretty as a picture, with Jack's dark curling hair and large brown eyes, which laughed at you and twinkled. It was difficult to be firm with her, she was so endearing. But Hetty had a lot of her mother's temperament, and knew a spoiled child was an unhappy child. Where Jack would have spoiled her, Hetty was firm. "We mustn't make a rod for our own backs," she said.

Jack's good behaviour lasted for almost a whole year. Then just before Vida's first birthday, Grandpa Maclaren died. He had been hale and hearty one minute and gone the next, the villagers said, adding that it was the best way to go, except for those left behind. Grandmother Maclaren was a doughty Scotswoman, and it took more than the death of her elderly husband to get her down. She worked harder than any man, and with her strong grandson to help her intended to carry on until such time as the Lord called her too.

It seemed to Hetty that her real troubles began then, for instead of Jack rallying round and taking over the reins as everyone expected him to do, he gradually began to drink again. He stayed out night after night, ostensibly to help his grandmother, but Hetty knew that he wasn't there. And yet, she thought, he knew only too well that it was his own business that was suffering, his livelihood, his future. The final degradation came when two men brought him home one night, paralytically drunk.

"Here y'are, missus."

Hetty, as white as a sheet, stood at the door, with as much dignity as she could muster.

"Could you please help him upstairs?" she asked them. "I don't think I could manage him on my own."

"Of course, missus," they said, and hauled him up the stairs.

That night she slept on the tiny narrow bed in the spare room, and the next day was up early to take Jack a cup of tea.

He looked awful, she thought, unshaven and tired, lines around his mouth, his handsome faced flushed with drink, while the smell in the room was indescribable. She wrinkled her nose. Surely that wasn't the smell of beer? It was more like whisky. Her heart sank. He turned away from her when she woke him, as if even he was ashamed to be found like this.

She made her way downstairs, and sat by the fire with little Vida on her lap, thinking. Why did he drink? Was he unhappy – was he so miserable that he could only face life with a glass in his hand? Whatever would her Mam say if she knew that this was what her daughter's life had become? Or Dora? Her sister must never know, but if things got worse how could she keep it from them? As it was, it would be all over the village by now that Jack Maclaren had to be carried home.

She cooked his breakfast and put it in the oven of the kitchen range to keep warm. When he came downstairs he did not meet her eyes, and she said nothing until she had given him a fresh cup of tea.

"Jack," she began.

He glanced up then, and the look in those handsome black eyes was almost enough to make her weep.

"I'm sorry, Hetty," he said, and she remembered Mam's words. Don't nag, it's the worst thing you can do, but make his home life so comfortable that he won't want to go out and drink. Was it her fault? Was he sorry he had married her?

"Jack," she said, "I've been thinking. Would you like to go right away from here, or do something else for a living, set up home somewhere else? We could take Grandma with us."

"What are you blethering on about, woman?" he asked

37

angrily. "Ye're ashamed, is that it? A chap canna have a wee dram without his wife goes on at him, day in, day out . . ."

"Jack! That's not true. I only want to help."

"Help? What do you mean, help? Anyone would think I was ill or something. Where's my breakfast – and where's the babby?"

"In the garden," Hetty said, going to the oven and getting out his breakfast. He at it in silence, and when he had finished pushed his plate away.

Hetty came in from the garden, Vida in her arms, and Jack held out his arms to her.

"My bonnie wee bairn," he said, kissing her. There was no doubt about his feelings for her. He stood her down. "I'll not be in until late," he said. "I've to go to Skipton for the corn meal."

Of course, it was Thursday half day, Hetty thought. Jack often had to go out on those days to buy or collect. Quite often on a Thursday afternoon she walked the pram over to Grandmother Maclaren who was always glad to see little Vida. Perhaps she would do that this afternoon. "I'll keep your supper in the oven," she said as Jack got up to go. On his way out, it was as if he almost changed his mind and came back to say something, then with a quick kiss and a wave to Vida, he was gone, without so much as a farewell.

Sighing, Hetty collected the dishes and washed them up. She always hated these times when there was silence between them, and she had no idea what to do for the best. How best to solve this terrible problem of Jack's drinking? Apart from that they were happy together, and she knew he was ashamed. Going about the household chores, making the bed, cleaning the kitchen and polishing the brass while Vida had her morning sleep, she wondered if she might broach the subject to Grandma Maclaren. After all, she herself knew little of Jack's past life, his immediate family; it was not as if he was a local lad when his life would have been an open book.

After lunch, she washed Vida and put on a pretty pink dress that she had made. Hetty could turn her hand to almost anything. Vida looked a picture, her large dark eyes surveying everything, and Hetty was delighted that she had a great sense of humour. Without that, she thought, life was nothing, and she must try to look on the bright side about Jack's drinking. There had to be an answer to it somewhere.

"We're going to walk to Granny's today", she told Vida, who liked nothing better than to dispense with the pram. Closing the door behind her – no one ever locked a door in Barnsdale – she walked down the garden path, Vida's podgy little hand in hers.

The shop was closed today, the pavement empty of shop wares and the blinds drawn. Holding the bunch of sweet-smelling pinks she had cut from the garden, Hetty made her way to the back of the building and the yard. They climbed the iron staircase and knocked on the back door.

Granny Maclaren stood there, delighted to see them. In her print blouse and long black skirt, she affected the same style as she had throughout her long life. She beamed when she saw Vida and held out her hand.

"Come in, lass, come in – it's grand to see ye." And taking Vida's hand she led the way into the living room. Spotless as ever, Hetty observed, which took a bit of doing at the old lady's age. "Have you brought me a wee giftie?" She took the flowers from Vida's small hand. "Come on, let's find a little pot." And taking the child by the hand, she led her into the kitchen.

Granny Maclaren found a basket of oddments for Vida to play with while Hetty offered to make the tea. Granny sat with her crochet happily watching the child. After tea, Hetty waited for an opportunity to bring up the subject of Jack's past life, and found the opening when Granny Maclaren produced an old photograph album, containing many sepia photographs, some of them so old as to be barely discernible.

"This is Jack at the age of fifteen – ye can see there how handsome he was, even then," she said proudly. "And this is his mother, poor soul – oh, she was the bonniest lass. And, d'ye ken, I think little Vida is like her."

Hetty peered at the photographs. There was a likeness, she could see. "It must be nice for you to have a grandaughter," she said, "only having had the boy – Jack's father. Is that a photograph of him there?"

"Aye, that's him, he was a grand-looking man." But a look of sadness had come over her face.

"Does Jack take after him?" Hetty asked.

"Aye – in more ways than one," Granny Maclaren said, and Hetty decided to take the opportunity of bringing up the subject of Jack's drinking.

"Did his father drink – like Jack?" she asked.

She saw the sudden shock she had given the old woman, and was a mite sorry, but looking straight into Granny Maclaren's eyes, knew the old lady was far too honest to lie.

"Yes, Hetty, he did. It was the scourge of his life, and I prayed young Jack wouldna tak' after him, but I can see from ye face that ye've had a lot to put up with. You know, lass, it's the pride of every Scotsman's life to be able to hold his liquor – and that's something neither of them could do. With some men it's women. With some it's the drink. His father used to get into brawls – he had a fearsome temper. I think he took after my father. As children we used to go in fear of him, and I dursn't think what my Mam's life was like. Still, apart from one case of drunken behaviour when he was bound over to keep the peace, Jack's always been a good lad." She looked over to where little Vida sat playing happily with the basket, then back again with troubled eyes.

"Ye've not – Jack's never – " And Hetty made haste to reassure her. What was the good of worrying the old lady? There was nothing she could do about it. It was too late, Jack was her responsibility, but now that she knew, it was something of a relief. It was not her fault, not entirely anyway. He had been like it before she married him. She wondered if she would have done so had she known. How different her own family had been. Her brothers and her father had been God-fearing men. They liked a drink but she never recalled seeing any of them the worse for liquor.

She reassured the old woman, and saw the relief in her eyes. "It's nothing I cannot handle," she told her. "Jack's a good man, I know that, and he'll come to his senses one of these days." She looked down at Vida. "Now put all the things back in the basket. We mustn't leave Gran's house untidy."

"Ye're a grand little lass," Gran said. "Twas a lucky day for Jack when he met ye."

40

Hetty smiled and took her leave. Well, she had learned something, but nothing that would help.

Jack came home several times the worse for drink in the months that followed, and Hetty learned to say little, since when she remonstrated with him, he was inclined to get violent. Once he hit her across the face, causing her to fall, and her arm was badly bruised. The next day he was so contrite, so abject in his apologies, that she found herself consoling him. He promised her then that he would try and give it up totally, and she knew he meant it – at the time. By now she had come to the conclusion that it was an illness with him, and that drink was like a poison to him, but there seemed to be nothing she could do.

One evening in the summer Dora came round to fit on a dress she was making for Hetty's birthday. Grandma Maclaren had given her the material and Dora was making it. In the years since the war had ended, fashions had changed more than a little. Gone were the long dresses, the tight waists, the restrictions women had suffered for so long. In their place were shorter frocks, casual dresses, but these fashions had taken a long time to reach North Yorkshire. Women up there had more to think about than dressing up. But Hetty liked nice clothes, and Dora liked making them. She had inherited her mother's old sewing machine with its elaborate treddle, and having no daughters of her own thoroughly enjoyed making feminine clothes.

Jack had gone down to the working men's club to play billiards, and Hetty prayed that he wouldn't drink too much. She and Dora had a wonderful evening, laughing over old times and gossiping. Around ten o'clock she stood up in the new dress, with its mid-calf length showing her pretty legs and its sash around the hips. She looked like a schoolgirl, dressed for a party. Dora stood back, delighted with her efforts. "It's so pretty." she said, then heard a sound outside.

"I must go." She was gathering up her things at the same moment as Jack pushed open the front door and lumbered in. They stood aghast as he faced them – "As drunk as a lord," Dora related afterwards to Tom – leering at them, then noticing through a drinker's haze Hetty standing there in all her glory.

"She lookled a picture, Tom," Dora wept, crying quietly, "and he took one look at her, at the dress, and slapped her face. He called her a – a whore, Tom. You should have seen Hetty's face. She was as white as a sheet. I thought she was going to faint, but she stood there, without a word, then he went through to the privy . . . She just stood there, Tom, and I've never felt so mad in my life. I couldn't find anything to say, but suddenly she said: 'You go, Dora, I'll handle him.' 'Go?' I shouted. 'I'll kill 'im!' But she pushed me towards the front door. 'Don't worry, Dora,' she said. 'It'll be all right, honestly – I'll come round tomorrow.' So I came home. Oh, Tom, I'm so worried. Don't you think you should go round there?" But he shook his head. "Do more harm than good," he said. "I don't believe in interfering between husband and wife, but we must certainly see that she's all right tomorrow."

"It may be too late," Dora wailed.

"She'll know how to handle him," Tom said. "She's used to it by now, I daresay."

"The swine," Dora said bitterly. "Thank God Mam's not alive to see this."

Chapter Six

Things were never the same between Jack and Hetty after that night. The fact that Dora has seen him at his worst didn't help, and from then on the atmosphere between husband and wife was cool to say the least. Hetty had come to the reluctant conclusion that she could do nothing to change him; pleading, or even showing him that she was disgusted enough to leave him, at the end of the day did not achieve anything. She busied herself about the house, the garden particularly bring her a kind of solace, while Vida, who was becoming a little person in her own right was the light of her life.

Hetty cooked Jack's meals, and washed his shirts, and kept the house spotlessly clean. She kept her own counsel in the village, and such was her dignity in view of the talk that must have been going on, that no one who had known her family would ever hear a word said against her. Hetty Maclaren, they said, was a grand little woman, a hard worker if ever there was one.

By the time that Vida's third birthday came round, their marriage had settled into a kind of routine. Jack was at the shop all day, although there was talk now that when Vida started morning school in the village, which she was entitled to do when she was three years old, Hetty would help out in the shop. She quite looked forward to this, to have something to do in the afternoons, and they planned that when the boy who helped out went to do his national service, Hetty would take over. In the meantime, she spent most evenings mending and sewing, or visiting Dora and Granny Maclaren, while Jack spent his time at the social club, or at the Lamb or the

Red Lion. It seemed to be a ritual now that he got drunk every Saturday night, and on those occasions he was far too drunk to want her. At other times when he made love to her, she lay passive in his arms, and after he tried to rouse her into some kind of response, which never came, he would turn away from her in a fury. Sometimes on these occasions she thought he would strike her, but up to now he never had, although she lay in fear and trembling more than once.

Sometimes she fretted, but she was a naturally resilient person, and threw herself into whatever she had to do with gusto. Now it was time for the Agricultural Show once more and this year little Vida would be old enough to enjoy it. Hetty became quite excited at the thought of it, and dressed her small daughter in a pink flowered dress and poke bonnet to match. Jack would be going with them. Today was Thursday, his half day, and he was looking forward to it; he enjoyed a fair as much as any man.

They walked along the village street, each holding Vida's hand, Jack so handsome with his gypsy-like good looks. No one would believe what their lives were really like, Hetty thought, but today was different. Today they were going to enjoy themselves. They so seldom went out as a family. The sound of the organ from the roundabouts reached them long before they arrived at the entrance. There, they found crowds milling around the sideshows and the evocative smells of an outdoor show: kerosene and pink Indian toffee, paraffin and toffee apples, horses and all the fun of the fair. They stood and watched while Jack, who was a past master at knocking down coconuts, knocked down four in a row, much to Vida's delight. Hetty's memory went back to the first time she had seen Jack. He had been shying coconuts then. What a lot of water had passed under the bridge, and she smiled indulgently. Today he was like a small boy who had been let off school.

"Daddy, Daddy – could I go on the roundabouts?" Vida's eyes were sparkling with excitement and anticipation.

Jack looked down at her bright little face. "Which one do you want to go on?"

Vida looked from one to the other of the gaudily painted animals. "The horse," she said without any doubt. "The horse!"

"Right." Jack bent down and picked her up. "Leave her with me for a bit." he said to Hetty. "I'll give her a couple of goes on this – she'll be alright with me. Here."

And he handed Hetty two half-crowns.

She looked down in astonishment. Five shillings! He hadn't given her anything for a long time. "See you back here in about half an hour. Come on, Vida."

And he went to pay the roundabout collector.

Hetty waited until Vida was safely sitting on the horse with Jack behind her holding her tightly. She watched as the music blared out and the carousel went round and thought she wouldn't spoil their fun. Jack so seldom had Vida to himself. She wandered off to the various stalls, rolling several pennies into squares without any luck, then past the fortune teller's booth.

Over in the corner sat the huge marquee, where all sorts of things were going on: competitions for cake making, knitting, crafts and vegetable shows. Then there was the field with the enclosed pens for the animals, sheep, cows and shire horses. Drawn to the horses as she always was, Hetty walked slowly towards them and leaned over the iron railing where two thoroughbreds were standing in the sun, their breeding unmistakable. Her eyes shone with sheer pleasure at the sight.

Then her heart gave a sudden lurch as she saw the once familiar figure walking straight towards her – it couldn't be, surely? But it was unmistakably David Ogilby, and his pleasure at seeing her could not be denies.

"Hetty – Hetty, my dear."

"David."

She would never have believed that the sight of him would leave her so shaken. His blue eyes looking down into hers, the familiar look of him, the way he looked at her, after all this time.

David Ogilby was feeling much the same thing. He saw a small pretty girl with unforgettable brown eyes which looked into his with such candour. She was as familiar to him as the air he breathed. Memories came flooding back, everything at once: Hetty in her white pinafore, their riding together, their hiding places, the fun they had had, the talks – how could he have lived without her all this time?

45

Hetty wanted to say so much, but the words stuck in her throat. She could only stare at him, the past five years as if they had never been.

He took her hand, and she made no effort to draw away. It was as if an electric current flowed between them.

"I'm married." were the words that finally came out.

"I know."

"And you?" She asked. "Are you married?"

He shook his head. "No." He pressed her hand. "Are you happy?"

She nodded, she didn't want to take her eyes off him, then suddenly a horse neighed nearby, and she quickly took her hand away and looked around fearfully. "My husband is here somewhere – with my little girl."

He spoke anxiously. "Hetty, I must see you again. I am going away on Saturday, for a long time."

Her look was one of anguish. "Where are you going?" She couldn't believe what she was saying. What did it have to do with her? "For how long?"

"A year, possibly," he said, and his words were like a knife in her heart.

David felt he wanted to take her in his arms. If anyone had told him this morning that later he would be feeling what he was now, he would not have believed it. "I have to see you before I go," he said. "We can't talk here."

"No" Hetty said through dry lips. "I must go."

"Tomorrow," David said urgently. "Tomorrow afternoon."

"I can't," she said. "I have a little girl – she's home in the afternoons."

"In the morning, then? I can't bear to think of leaving without seeing you again."

The temptation was too great, and Hetty succumbed. It was easier to agree, and quicker – if Jack saw her standing here talking to a man, he would go wild.

"Here," David said. "They'll be clearing everything away. Here at ten o'clock?"

Convinced by now she was dreaming, Hetty nodded. "Yes, ten o'clock. I'll try." And she hurried off just as fast as she could go, her heart racing nineteen to the dozen, back to the roundabout where Jack and Vida were just dismounting.

Hetty was quite breathless, and hoped it didn't show. "Was that nice? How many rides did you have?"

"Four," Vida said proudly, her cheeks pink from the exertion of flying round and round, up and down.

"Come on," Jack said. "Let's see if we can win you something on the hoop-la." And he swung Vida high on his shoulders, where she squealed with delight. Hetty followed closely behind them.

That night, she hardly slept at all, tossing one way and then the other, first of all deciding she couldn't possibly go to meet David . . . but how would she let him know? She couldn't bear to think of him waiting there, and in the next moment decided she had to go, without a shadow of a doubt, she had to see him again. What harm could it possible do, meeting an old friend from her childhood days? But she knew deep down that she was not being strictly honest with herself.

She hardly knew how she got through cooking Jack's breakfast and getting Vida ready for school. At nine o'clock she took her to the school gate, where she kissed here and told her she would be waiting for her at twelve o'clock. Then she hurried home and began to get ready, taking time over her hair, and putting on her best dress of pale blue cotton and a white straw hat. She closed the door carefully behind her – what on earth would the neighbours say, or Jack for that matter, if they saw her walking out at this time of the morning without her apron?

When she arrived at the field, she saw that most of the stands had gone, and they were busy dismantling the large marquee. She saw David in an instant, and her heart leapt at the sight of him. As she drew near him his eyes never left her face. Silently they looked at each other before taking the bridle path which led to the woods, a place which they both knew well.

"David," Hetty began, without knowing what she was going to say.

"Seeing you again, it's as if nothing has changed," he said. "Did you feel that?"

She nodded. "Yes – except it's different for me, because I'm married. I shouldn't have come."

"I'm glad you did," he said. "I suppose it's partly because I am going away, and for a long time, that it seemed so important to see you again, to talk to you."

"Where are you going?" she asked.

"To Malaya. My grandfather has a rubber plantation there, and he has just died and left it to me, so the family want me to go over and sort the thing out. I expect to be away for some months, perhaps a year. But tell me about yourself, Hetty. My mother told me you married a man from the village, is that right? I was abroad in Europe at the time. And you say you have a little girl. How old is she?"

"Almost four," Hetty said. "She is a darling, and so pretty – even if I say it myself."

He was smiling. "I can believe it. Does she have your eyes?"

Hetty blushed. They had never spoken to each other on personal terms. "She has dark eyes – her father has, too." She saw his slight frown.

"Are you happy with him? Is he good to you?" He felt rather than saw her faint hesitation. "Hetty?"

Startled, she looked at him. "Oh, yes, he is . . ."

They walked on in silence, "Who is he?" he asked suddenly, without looking at her.

"Not a local man. His name is Jack Maclaren and his grandmother runs the village corn chandler's. Jack works there." She glanced up at him. "He's a Scotsman."

When he said nothing, she spoke again. "How is your mother?"

"She's well. Steeped in good works as usual." He smiled and looked down at her. "Shall we find our tree?" He said.

Hetty felt the years slip away. "Race you," she laughed, and ran to the covert where the huge old tree stood, its leaves now a spectacle of colour. Every now and again a light breeze brought fresh leaves tumbling down. When she reached the tree a moment before him, breathless from exertion, it was to stop beneath one of the great branches where on the bark the initials HJ and DFO could be seen, faint but still there.

She had once asked him: "What does the 'F' stand for?" and he had replied: "Frederick, it is my father's name."

"Freddie," she had laughed. It seemed only yesterday.

48

Now they looked into each other's eyes, and David took her in his arms. It seemed the most natural thing in the world for Hetty to be there. He kissed her gently, and presently, as if by mutual consent, they lay down. The leaves crackled beneath them as David looked down at her, his blue eyes searching hers. Hetty wanted to stay like this forever.

"Don't you feel we belong together?" he asked. "Isn't it the most natural thing in the world for us to be like this?"

"Yes, but – "

"I know what you are going to say – you are married, and you have a child. I know all that. But you can't love him, Hetty, you belong to me – you always have."

She closed her eyes against the intensity of his gaze.

"David – this is wrong. I do understand what you are saying – I feel the same way – but it's just not possible. For one thing we come from different worlds."

"But what's that got to do with it?"

"Everything," she said. "We have nothing in common, nothing at all, except that we like each other, and used to play together as children, and we feel – something. I don't know what it is or how to explain it."

"Did you love your husband when you married him?"

She thought about it honestly. "Yes, I did," she said. "It didn't last, mainly because – well, I won't go into it now."

"There you are, then," he said triumphantly. "We were meant to be together."

Despite her lack of education and worldliness, Hetty felt herself to be the more sensible of the two. She looked at him fondly.

"I suppose I do love you – in a kind of way," she said. "I always have. I used to dream when I was younger . . . but they were girlish dreams, romantic dreams. Every girl has them,"

She looked into his face. It was a man's face now, and she recalled how youthful he had been – how young they had both been. What of David's life since then?" How had he spent the past five years?

"Have you never thought of getting married?" She asked. "Never met a girl that you felt serious about?"

"No," he said honestly. "Oh, I've known some girls – lots

49

of them – girls my mother wanted me to marry, girls my mother didn't want me to marry!" He laughed. "You know how it is in my world."

"That's what I mean." she said, and sat up. "David, we shouldn't have met like this – I shouldn't have come."

"Hetty, please, couldn't we – couldn't you – please?"

And her face flushed, bringing a rosy glow to her cheeks, while her eyes darkened. She couldn't look at him. He was making it so hard for her. He leaned over her and traced the outline of her lips. She felt a delicious thrill run through her. If only.

"I'm going away tomorrow," he said. "I won't be able to see you for so long," he murmured against her ear – and she lifted her face for his kiss, which when it came left her feeling breathless and with no will to refuse him. He made love to her gently, and with great passion. It was a kind of fulfilment, she thought afterwards. It had been nothing like the honeymoon she had spent with Jack; that too had shaken her to her very depths, but that had been purely physical. This was different – it was as if she had been waiting all her life for this. She could never regret it, whatever happened in the future.

Afterwards, he kissed her tenderly. "I love you, Hetty Jessops," he said. "I always will – whatever you think of me. Remember I told you that. You do believe me, don't you?"

She smiled at him, a smile that he remembered of old. "Yes, David, I do. And I love you, too. I always have, and I suppose I always will." She stood up. "And now I must go – I shall be late at the school."

He stood beside her, his eyes pleading with her. "Hetty, could I write to you, get in touch?"

She was horrified. "Of course not! How could you think of such a thing? No – today will be our special memory, something to remember all our lives. I have my life to live, and you . . . well, someday, a nice girl will come along."

"No," she said.

"It's true." She smiled, and he saw the glint of a tear on her lashes when suddenly she reached up on tiptoe and kissed him gently. "Good luck, David – goodbye." And she had gone, running down the bridle path, her skirt flying in the breeze, leaving him looking after her, his life suddenly empty.

Chapter Seven

After that very special day, Hetty felt she had come to terms with her life. Things would never be the same again, whatever happened. It was as if the whole reason for living has been shown to her; she had a new awareness of things, her life had a meaning. Whether it would have been different had David not been going away she never knew, but she settled down with a quiet new confidence, an acceptance of the fact that she would love him until the day she died, and there was never any chance in this wide world of there being more than that. She counted herself very fortunate in her position, the daughter of a groom, from farming stock, that she had the love of someone like David Ogilby, for that he loved her she was in no doubt at all. When she thought of him she did not see him on a rubber plantation halfway across the world, but as she had known him, their life together as children in years gone by, and the ecstasy they had known beneath the oak tree.

As the weeks passed by and she knew she was pregnant, her heart soared. She prayed, indeed believed, that it was David's child, and gave thanks. This would be the ultimate blessing. She hugged the knowledge to herself for some time before telling Jack.

"Nearly three months?" He said, his black brows drawn together. "Why didn't you tell me before?"

"Because I wasn't sure," she said equably. Nothing these days could ruffle her composure.

"I suppose you won't want to come and work in the shop in the afternoons then?"

51

"Not really, Jack. We'll have to manage without the money. When I get bigger I should feel uncomfortable – besides, I couldn't lift the heavy stuff.

"No, we don't want you straining yourself," he said, looking at her. "You feel all right, do ye?"

She smiled at him reassuringly. "Yes, I'm as strong as a horse, Jack. You should know that by now."

Her announcement seemed suddenly to sink in, and his fine dark eyes lit up. "I say, Het, it might be a lad – wouldn't that be grand?"

"You never know," she said. "It would be nice for Vida to have a brother."

"And for a man to have a son," he said importantly.

"That's true, Jack'" Hetty said mildly, and thought, not for the first time, how strange it was that she felt no sense of guilt but went quietly about her duties as if the interlude with David had never been. Jack wanted for nothing when it came to looking after him. She took a pride in her housework, her linen was spotless, and she was a good cook.

Dora received the news with mixed feelings. Hetty knew that she was filled with revulsion at the idea of her sister bearing Jack's child. Jack Maclaren, the village drunk; a hard-working man, but one who couldn't hold his drink. You couldn't sink much lower than that.

"Oh, Hetty," she sighed. "You could have done without this. It's not as if – "

Hetty raised tranquil eyes from her sewing.

"I want this baby, Dora," she said. "Aside from anything else, Vida needs a brother or sister. It's not good for her to be an only child.

"You're right there," Dora said. In fact she had been surprised that Hetty hadn't followed up the birth of Vida with more babies, but as time wore on had come to the conclusion that perhaps they couldn't have any more children. She had put it down to Jack's drinking.

"How are the boys?" Hetty asked. She was fond of her nephews who were growing up fast. Nice boys, all of them. Charlie, the eldest was about to start work.

"They're fine – looking forward to Christmas. Charlie start's at Withy's Farm on Monday. I can't wait for the others

52

to leave school. That extra bit of money, it all helps. When's the baby due, Hetty?"

"June sometime."

"Summer babies are best," Dora said wistfully. "I wish I'd had a girl. Your Vida's lovely."

"I have to agree." Hetty laughed. "She's so pretty – she doesn't take after me."

"You were the best looking of us four girls, but Vida takes after her dad," Dora said grudgingly. "She's like a little gypsy with that colouring, curly hair and those dark eyes, but she's a proper little lady. Wouldn't Mam have loved her?"

She made them some vegetable soup for the midday break, Jack now usually stopping off at the Lamb, and they ate Hetty's home-made bread and farmhouse cheese. Dora made her sit and rest while she cleared away afterwards.

"I'm not an invalid," Hetty laughed.

"No, but you're still my little sister," said Dora.

Hetty watched her retreating figure as she went into the scullery with the dishes, seeing her wide girth and stocky legs, her plump arms busy at the sink. She reminded Hetty so much of their mother – she was like a rock in time of trouble.

The Christmas festivities that year were at Dora's house, and Grandma Maclaren bought Vida a small doll's pram. Hetty made covers for it, and Dora dressed the doll. Vida played with it all over Christmas and hated to leave it to go back to school.

January brought icy weather, with heavy falls of snow. In February the village was almost marooned when transport could not get over the moors, while Hetty's baby grew inside her and she could no longer do up her dresses. Jack, who had been fairly circumspect at the beginning of her pregnancy, now began to drink more, which worried Hetty, for as Vida became older it was becoming increasingly difficult to hide it from her. Once Hetty found her at the top of the steep staircase, her eyes wide, her hand to her mouth as she heard Jack shouting downstairs, his words slurred, while Hetty tried to help him to bed. She let him fall into a chair and hurried up the stairs.

"Vida love, what are you doing out of bed? You'll catch your death of cold. Come on." And Hetty took her hand.

Vida looked up at her with with wide fearful eyes. "What's the matter with Daddy?"

"He tripped up and hurt his ankle – didn't he make a funny noise? I think he was pretending to cry." She made an attempt at a joke, and by the time she had tucked the small girl back into bed, Vida seemed reassured. "Now you get back to sleep," said Hetty, "while I go down and see to Daddy's leg."

She hurried downstairs in a fury with Jack. How dare he come home drunk and frighten Vida? It was bad enough that she had to put up with it. She stood over him, seeing his closed eyes. He was starting to snore, and she shook him awake. "Jack," she hissed, "wake up. You're to stay down here tonight – and don't come upstairs until you're sober. You frightened Vida." She saw what she hoped was a look of shame in his eyes before his drooping lids closed again and he grunted. She got an overcoat from the peg in the corner and put it over him, then made her way back upstairs. For the first time since she discovered she was pregnant, she had misgivings. What on earth would she do when the baby came? She was past believing now that he would ever change.

As the snows melted and spring came in with wild winds which flattened the daffodils and whistled through every crack under windows and doors, Hetty began to think about the new baby. Although it was not due until the spring, she liked everything to be organised. Vida would go to stay with Dora, and Jack would stay with his grandmother for a few days.

Five years on, and Martha Alsop was still helping with the population increase in Barnsdale. It was a fine night in June when she was sent for to assist at the birth of Hetty's baby.

"Come on, my luv," she encouraged. "It's easier second time round." Easier? thought Hetty through the agony, the perspiration running down her cheeks. She bit her lips until they almost bled, and pulled on the anchored sheet until it almost tore in half.

Her son was born at five o'clock in the morning, a long slim baby with fair skin, weighing almost eight pounds, and Hetty knew without the shadow of a doubt that this was David's son. When Martha Alsop gave him to Hetty to hold, she kissed him through a mist of tears, and hugged him close.

"That's it," Martha Alsop said, going about her business. "Have a good cry – it's often a good thing to do when it's over." But Hetty was crying in gratitude. David's son . . . And she smoothed his small face with a soft finger. Little Freddie, she thought, and wondered what Jack's reaction would be.

He came over before the shop opened, and raced upstairs to see her. "Hetty," he said, and she was surprised to see real concern on his face. She smiled, and looked down at the sleeping infant at her side.

"A boy," he whispered. "A son." He moved the shawl a little. "He's not a bit like Vida, is he?" He spoke softly.

"Well, he's a boy." Hetty smiled.

"No, I mean – dark, like Vida."

"No," she agreed, "he may turn out to be fair – like my mother's family." And for the first and only time asked God to forgive her.

"What shall we call him?" Jack asked.

"Frederick," Hetty said firmly in a voice that brooked no argument. Jack's dark brows drew together.

"Frederick!" he almost shouted.

"Sshh," Hetty said soothingly, looking down at the sleeping infant, and then up at Jack. "Yes, Frederick."

"That's a soft name for a boy." Jack said scathingly, but Hetty took no notice. "I expect we'll call him Freddie," she said, and Jack could see by her expression that there was to be no argument about it.

Life settled down again for the Maclaren family, with Hetty busy as a bee looking after her two children. As the weeks went by, and the baby's hair grew, it was seen to be fair and as light as thistledown, while when he opened his eyes they were of such a blue as to startle the onlooker. For the first month, Jack was as pleased as punch with his son, but as time went on he became increasingly annoyed at the amount of time Hetty spent with the children. If she wasn't feeding the baby, she was seeing to Vida. It seemed to him that a man had to take a back seat, that there was no time for him in his own house. Several times he flung himself out of the house, but Hetty knew it was only an excuse to get on with his drinking.

She was delighted that little Vida showed no more than the normal jealousy for a new baby. She helped her mother bathe and change him, and as he grew loved to play with him. She showed him things and tried to teach him words, held his fat little hands in hers and watched him laugh. By the first week in December, he was the proud possessor of two front teeth, had been christened Frederick John Maclaren at St Luke's church, and had a quiff of blond hair above two bright eyes. He was the image of David Ogilby, but no one would have seen it but Hetty.

"Mam's family were fair like that," Dora observed. "My Charlie was when he was born, but it went dark,"

That week, on the Saturday, Jack was in a particularly bad mood. For one thing business was bad and the money wasn't coming in. Hetty sympathised. There was nothing worse than being short of money, and she knew that he felt his responsibilities keenly. "It'll be all right, Jack," she said. "It'll pick up later."

"Fat lot you know about it," he snarled, and flung out of the house. Hetty's heart sank. In this mood, they could be in for a bad time later. She got the children to bed and closed the door firmly, athough she usually kept it ajar, and sat by the fire to wait. She was knitting a dress for Vida. Knitting was all the rage this year, and she hoped to have it finished by Christmas.

Jack was later than usual on this particular evening, and she kept looking up at the clock. Her eyes felt heavy and kept closing despite desperate efforts to keep awake. Presently, too worried to continue knitting, she stood up to stretch, her muscles beginning to feel cramped, and peered at the clock. It was almost half-past midnight – the latest Jack had ever been. Now she was really worried.

Five minutes later he stumbled through the door, and she knew without seeing him what to expect. He could hardly stand upright, and she recoiled when she saw his face. His mouth was slobbering, his eyes half-closed. It was obvious he couldn't see straight, and she went towards him . . .

The next thing she knew she was on the floor and her jaw felt bruised and sore. Holding it, her eyes wide with surprise, she got to her feet. "Jack?"

"Get outa my way." His words were slurred, and he pushed her roughly against the wall. It was then that she became aware of something else, something new, and it came to her in a flash that it was the smell of cheap scent. Although a warning light flashed in her brain, she couldn't help herself.

"You swine," she said softly, a mental picture of Molly Edwards in front of her. Molly Edwards, barmaid at the Lamb and notorious for comforting many a husband with a roving eye. Everyone knew Molly Edwards, her reputation went before her, yet somehow Hetty had never associated Jack with that sort of thing – drink was his failing, she had never had cause to suspect him of this before.

Under the light, it was obvious he had been with a woman. His tie was loosened and there was lipstick on his face, while the smell of the cheap scent filled the narrow hallway.

She turned in disgust to go into the kitchen and imagined he would follow her. He would have to sleep on a chair downstairs tonight. Then she felt her arm grasped tightly, and his disgusting breath hot on the back of her neck. He turned her round to face him.

"Too good for me, are ye?" he asked her. "Too high and mighty, are ye?"

"Jack!" This time she felt the blow when it landed on her face and knocked her to the floor. There was a silence, during which she hardly dared move. Her right eye was so painful she could barely touch it, but she put up a hand and felt it gingerly, feeling the swelling. A thought flashed through her mind incongruously, that this was her punishment for what she had done. Not daring to get up, she stayed there for a moment or two until she felt him step over her and go out towards the back yard. Swiftly she got to her feet and hurried upstairs and into the bedroom. He wouldn't worry her tonight, she thought, he wouldn't be able to manage the stairs. She could hardly open her right eye which was swelling fast. She bathed it in cold water, and held a cold damp flannel to it. A large bruise was coming up below her chin and the thought crossed her mind as to what she would say to little Vida, who would be horrified. Time to think about that in the morning. She felt herself to be ice cold inside with an anger she had never felt before. She heard the outside privy flush

57

just as she climbed into bed, and before she slept, knew what she was going to do.

Jack was still asleep when she took little Vida to school, her hat pulled down over her eyes, a scarf round her mouth. The baby was tucked up warmly in the pram. Vida held on to the handle, her large dark eyes fearful of something unknown.

"I fell down the stairs," Hetty laughed. "From top to bottom, wasn't I silly?" Vida had regarded her seriously, "Bumb, bump, I went, all the way down – " And her breath caught in her throat.

"Did you break your leg?" Vida asked. A schoolmate had broken her leg falling in the snow, and Vida had been very impressed.

"Not this time." Hetty smiled, and kissed her at the gate, watching her cross the playground.

When she got back to the house, Jack had gone to work. Thank God, she thought, and bathed little Freddie and began to make her plans.

She was going to run away.

She would leave Jack forever; she would take her babies and walk straight out of his life. The only regret she would have would be leaving Dora and Tom and the boys, but Dora would understand, and although she would miss her sister, she would be pleased to see her escape. One day, in the future perhaps, Hetty would let her know where she was.

But not yet. Not for a long time.

She peered at her face in the mirror. The swelling and bruising would take some days to go down, and she would have to wait for that. You couldn't start a new life looking battered and bruised – what would people think? When it had gone down enough not to be noticeable, she would pack a few things and with the little money she had saved from the housekeeping, take the train to London. She had never been there, but a big city would soon absorb her and the children. No one would ever find her. She would walk to the station in the early hours and put a note in Dora's door, hoping no one would see her. If she waited and posted a letter to her, Dora would see the postmark and that would never do.

For she wanted to sever all ties. No one would know that little Vida's father was a drunkard, and no one would ever suspect who was the father of little Freddie. She could work to earn money to keep them all, she was sure of that. She had never been afraid of hard work.

It was a case of waiting for the right moment, after she had found out the times of the trains, written the note to Dora, packed a few things. The fewer the better.

Mixed in with the feeling of trepidation was the faintest glimmer of excitement. She would manage. Wasn't she a Yorkshire lass?

Chapter Eight

She laid her plans carefully. So much was at stake, she couldn't afford to put a step wrong. She stuck to her first decision to go to London, and after a lot of thought decided on Greenwich. Her only reason for this was because her brother, who had fought in the war was for a time in the Seamen's Hospital there, and had sent young Hetty coloured postcards which she had kept until she was quite grown up. There was one of the wounded men lying out in the beautiful hospital grounds, then one of the Greenwich Observatory, the Painted Hall and the River Thames at Greenwich showing a fiery red sun casting a glow over the waters. But best of all was Greenwich's history which they had read about at school, especially the story of Queen Elizabeth stepping ashore from the royal barge, after which it had become the Royal Borough of Greenwich. Surely Greenwich would be a lovely place to live.

She must travel light. Carry the minimum of luggage, for with a long train journey in front of her, and no destination, she could not afford to be over encumbered. She had a baby to carry, and a small girl's hand to hold, a light weight basket to hold the baby's things, and a canvas carrier bag for odds and ends. She would take nothing else with her. Once she found somewhere to live, she would work and earn money to buy them necessary things. She went by bus to the station to find out the cost of the fare, and the times of buses and trains, then waited for two whole weeks before she set forth. She wrote a letter to Dora and one to Grandmother Maclaren, which she posted the night before, and a note for Jack:

"Don't try to find me. This is all for the best. Hetty." At the end of two weeks, during which time he had hardly spoken to her, she closed the door behind her for the last time.

Greenwich was not all as she had imagined it, Hetty decided, as they made their way from the station.

"Where are we going?" Vida enquired, holding tightly on to her mother's skirt.

"To find somewhere to live," she said with much more conviction than she felt.

Only once on the long and tiring journey had Vida mentioned Jack, but Hetty was ready for her.

"He's got a lot to do at the shop – and we're going to have a little holiday."

Now, in mid-December, it was growing dark early. It was only half-past three, but the shops were lit up, displaying wares, and there was a kind of cheeriness about the scene. They passed a large, important-looking hotel. 'The Ship Restaurant and Tearooms' it said on the glass over the door, and Hetty made a mental note that if all else failed perhaps she could get a room there for the night. She walked on, looking in all the windows where some of the shops had boards of advertisements, and then she reached a corner grocer's. It was brightly lit in the murky gloom and looked quite inviting. A grocer's or a newsagent's shop would be the best places to find houses to let advertised, she reasoned. Her spirits rose. This was more like it. Tomorrow everything would look different. She pushed open the door and went inside.

Bill Baldwin looked over the counter at the pretty little woman with the sleeping child, and the beautiful little girl who kept her eyes on him without moving. He was up to his neck with Christmas trade, and the shop overflowed with extra stock for the holiday season – biscuits and bacon, hams and cold meats, boxes of sweets and chocolates – all the things that a working-class neighbourhood was determined to have whatever the cost. Neighbourhood people had paid into Christmas Clubs all the year round, and now would spend it all in one fell swoop.

"I'm sorry to trouble you," Hetty said in her soft Northern voice, "but would you have any idea where I could find accommodation – permanent, if possible? Although I will take anything for the time being."

Busy as he was, Bill Baldwin was moved by the sight of the trio, although he had no idea how he could help. "Have you tried the police station, duck?" he asked. "It's only round the corner."

She shook her head swiftly.

"You're new around here, aren't you?" he asked curiously.

Hetty nodded, and stood her ground.

"I've just come down from up north, and I was hoping to find accommodation, even temporary like, over Christmas."

Bill whistled. "It's a bad time, duck. Where's your luggage?"

"I've not much – at the station."

He pursed his lips and thought hard.

"I'm prepared to work hard for my keep – I don't want any favours, I'm a good worker, I'd be no trouble."

She didn't say that she was dying on her feet, that she was exhausted after the long journey south.

Bill Baldwin looked down at the little girl, and it was her eyes that finally decided him to call his wife. He couldn't see a wee mite like that without a bed to sleep in.

"Betty!"

She came, a handsome little woman, still plump after the birth of her fourth child.

"This lady – what's your name, love?"

And Hetty gave him the first name that came into her head – her mother's maiden name.

"Keane – Mrs Keane." She saw Vida look up at her.

"Mrs Keane wonders if we know of anywhere where she can stay – permanent if possible, otherwise just for the night."

Betty Baldwin clicked her tongue.

"You've chosen a bad time, duck. Let me see . . ." She and her husband looked at each other, then doubtfully she said; "Pop Collins?"

He looked shocked. "Oh, I don't think . . ."

"Well?" Betty raised her eyebrows. "She doesn't have much choice, does she?" And she walked back to the storeroom. The meaning of her look at Hetty was clear. What is a young woman doing looking for somewhere to stay on a dark winter's afternoon, with a babe in arms and a small child in hand?

"I'll take anything," Hetty said. "I don't mind what it is."

"Well, duck, I don't know if he'll take you, but I know he does have the room. It's very poor, mind. Still, it might do for now."

"Anything," she said.

Bill was writing now. "He keeps the old toot shop." He saw Hetty's sudden frown.

"It's a second hand shop, number twenty-one Queen's Row, and he lives over the shop. I know there's a basement. He must keep all sort of things down there. Still, you never know." He handed her a slip of paper. "This is the address, duck. Turn right when you leave here, go to the end of the street, it's a long one, and you'll find twenty-one on the right-hand side. Mr Collins is his name – everyone knows him. And don't let him scare you. He's all right really. 'Course, he don't always open on a Monday – but just knock at the side door."

"Thank you," Hetty said gratefully, and turned to go.

"Just a minute." Bill leaned over and gave Vida a lollipop. Her eyes widened.

"Thank you."

"And the best of luck," he said, watching the little trio. He shook his head. He'd better get on with the orders. Still, what a turn up for the book. Talk about no room at the inn.

The shop was in darkness when Hetty finally reached it, so she walked round to the side door. When she knocked with the blackened brass door knocker, clutching the little girl's hand and the baby to her bosom, there was no one more surprised to see her than old Pop Collins.

Her heart sinking, she saw an old man with white hair, stooped, for he had been tall, with rheumy blue eyes and a scowling face.

"Whatdjerwant?"

He regarded her with suspicion, the blue eyes below the thatch of white hair narrowing as she explained that she must find a home.

"'Oo sencha?" he kept asking, and over and over again she told him the man at the corner grocer's shop, and then, because she was not without pride and was afraid of no one, drew the children closer to her.

"Whatsyername?" he asked.

"Mrs Keane," she said with dignity, "and if you can't take me, say so. I'm not asking for charity – not from anyone. I'll pay my way. If you can take me at least until after Christmas, I'll see you don't want for a bit of cleaning and cooking. I'm a good cook," she added.

It might have been the cooking that did it, for he turned his head sideways, still regarding her, and seemed to waver. Finally, as she waited, he said: "Come in, you'll catch yer death."

And the old door was closed behind her.

Chapter Nine

It was late when Jack Maclaren arrived home. After the shop closed he made his way to the Rose and Crown where he stayed until eight-thirty, so by the time he reached his home it was almost nine. Somewhat befuddled, and his vision not too clear, he pushed open the front door. The first thing that struck him was how dark it was. It dawned on him that there was no light on in the passage, and he slammed the door behind him. "Hetty!"

But there was no reply. He took out a box of matches and struck one, holding it aloft as he made his way to the kitchen. A sense of foreboding overtook him. He had never seen the house so dark and so forlorn. Everywhere was so clean and tidy – and so empty. He lit the gas jet and turned it up, his quick temper rising. He flung open the door which led to the stairs and, stumbling up them, muttering to himself, he yelled: "Hetty! Where are you?" He'd give her what for. What did she think she was playing at?

Back in the kitchen he saw the note. Propped up against the teapot, he snatched it up and read it, swaying on his feet. She'd gone. The bitch, she'd gone! He slumped down into his chair, then got up and with a single massive swipe cleared the mantelpiece. Down went the black marble clock – a present from his grandmother, the pair of vases from Hetty's Mam, the china cow from Dora. Then he attacked the dresser. He cleared one row after another, all Hetty's carefully collected blue and white china smashed to smithereens, lying at his feet. He stared down at the mess as if he couldn't quite make it out, then slumped down into a chair, the tears rolling down his face, his once handsome face bloated, his mouth slack. She'd left him, and there was no food – no dinner. What kind of a wife was she? Good riddance to bad rubbish, he'd say. It was all that bloody Dora's fault. Hetty would never have gone off on her own. Dora had talked her into this. He made as if to get up, but the drink and the shock were too much for him. He began to weep again, maudlin tears. Vida, his little Vida, where was she now? His little bairn . . . He'd kill Hetty when she got back. He clenched his fists, then got up and went out to the privy to relieve himself. Sick to death of everything, he slowly climbed the stairs and fell on to the bed, asking himself what he had done to deserve this. He fell asleep at once, fully clothed.

There being no one to wake him, he slept until ten o'clock the next morning, then collecting his wits about him with one purpose in mind, neither washed nor shaved, made his way to Dora's house. It was bitterly cold and in the harsh light of day what Hetty had done seemed even more scandalous. A murderous rage welled up inside him.

Reaching Dora's little house, he banged on the door in such a fury that it almost gave way under his strength. Dora, unsuspecting, hurried to open it. When she saw who it was, she made to close the door.

"Oh, it's you!" There was undisguised loathing on her face.

"Where is she!" he demanded.

"I don't know – and if I did, I wouldn't tell you."

The look on his face frightened her, but she held her ground, thinking he was about to strike her. "I only know it's you and your drunken ways that have driven her to this, poor little soul!" And despite herself the tears welled up and overflowed. She dabbed her eyes with her apron. "Get off my step," she said, as he made a move towards her. "If you come here again, I shall call the police."

She slammed the door shut and swiftly shot the bolt, then from behind the lace curtain watched him slink away. Look at him, she thought. Who would have believed he would come to this? When you remember how handsome he was, what a catch we thought he was – why, Mam would turn in her grave!

Please, Hetty, she prayed, please let me know soon that you are safe and well.

66

When Pop Collins' front door closed behind Hetty, she knew a single moment of panic, then quickly dismissed it. At least she had a roof over her head. Pop Collins bolted the front door then stood and surveyed the little trio, from one face to the other. Hetty was sure she detected a faint twinkle in his sharp blue eyes.

"Well," he said, "what are we going to do with yer?" He addressed the question to Vida, who regarded him from wide dark eyes.

"Perhaps," Hetty suggested, "you could show us the accommodation?"

"Certainly." And led them down a narrow passage to a door under the stairs. Opening this, he took from a small corner shelf a torch and a box of matches. "I'll lead the way," he said. "Foller me – and mind 'ow you fall." And he took the little girl's hand.

Vida looked up at her mother – she had quickly seen the joke – while Hetty, holding the baby tightly, followed the old man down the stairs. It smelled musty and damp, and she wrinkled her nose. He lit the gas jet, and she found she was in quite a large room, a kitchen with a range and a big table, but all around it furniture was piled high: sofas, chairs, ornaments, clocks, rolled up rugs, boxes; while curtains that had certainly seen better days hung, or rather fell, from the windows. He led the way through to a back room which housed a large brass Victorian bed, piled high with blankets and bedding. There was no way they could sleep down here tonight, Hetty thought, the whole place needed warming up.

"This is the scullery," Pop Collins said, somewhat proudly, entering a small cubicle-type room with a corner boiler and an enamel sink stained deep yellow. "This is the back door," he said. "Leads up to the yard. The lavatory's out there, and ye can 'ang yer washing on the line."

Hetty bit her lip. If it wasn't so awful it would have been funny.

"I'd want six shillin' a week for the rent," Pop Collins said.

"I can only afford five – just a present," she said. "I shall have to find work in any case."

He looked at her shrewdly.

"Ye could cook by that range – it's a good 'un," he said.

"Coal you can 'ave for tenpence a bucket. It's outside in the yard."

Hetty, who was used to coal being almost given away, had a sudden burst of courage. "That's a bit steep," she said. "I think sixpence is enough."

"Oh, yer do, do yer?" he said, as little Vida tugged at her mother's skirt.

"Then again," she said reasonably, "if I work for you, cleaning and cooking, you could either pay me or drop the rent. That's only fair."

"Depends 'ow good you are," he said.

"Oh, I'm a good worker," Hetty said, "and a good cook."

Vida tugged again, "Yes, I know, pet," she said, and made up her mind. She would take it, starting from now.

"Here," she said, giving the sleeping Freddie to Pop Collins, "Hold the baby for a moment – my little girl wants to go outside. I'll borrow your torch."

The old man, his mouth open, looked down at the sleeping baby. Hetty had gone, pulling back the bolt and stepping outside. Shining the torch, she found herself facing a short flight of steps. Taking Vida's hand, she walked up them to the privy.

She held little Vida out high above the wooden seat, almost smiling to herself.

"We're not going to live here, are we, Mam?" Vida asked.

"Yes, pet, we are," Hetty said. "You won't know this place when I've got it cleaned up." I could make a nice little home here, she thought, and he's not a bad old man if I'm any judge of character. She had heard all about the meanness and unfriendliness of southerners, but so far she hadn't encountered it. Anyway, you'd have to go a long way to get the best of a Yorkshirewoman.

Once back inside, she bolted the back door, took the baby away from the old man, and returned the torch.

"First off," she said, "we couldn't sleep down here tonight. It's damp, I'd have to get a fire going for a day or two to air the place out."

He thought for a moment.

"Mmm. 'Ow'd it be if you slept upstairs in my place? There's a sofa, and it's warm. The little gel could sleep in a chair."

Vida turned agonised eyes to Hetty.

"Just for tonight, Vida," she said. "And all this stuff?" She looked around uncertainly.

"It's all valuable" Pop Collins said. "Antiques and that."

Hetty doubted it, although some of the things looked interesting.

"I deal a bit – buy and sell," he said.

"Where would I put it all?" she asked.

"There's a shed in the yard, if there's room," he said. And Hetty thought, I'll deal with that when I come to it.

"First of all," she said, "I need somewhere to feed the baby."

He looked embarrassed.

"We'll go upstairs," he said, and led the way down the passage and into his own room.

His quarters behind the shop looked surprisingly neat and tidy, but Hetty thought they needed a good clean.

"Ye can go in my bedroom," he said. "I'll put the gas on so ye can see." And he led the way, Hetty following, with Vida holding her skirt.

Hetty sat down gingerly in an old cane chair.

"Ye'll be all right in there," he said.

"You're very kind," she said gratefully as he closed the door behind him.

She had a sudden feeling of exhaustion, but seeing little Vida's trusting face turned to her felt a new strength rise within her. She looked down into the blue eyes of the baby, who was gazing around him with interest, and unbuttoned her blouse. He clamped his small mouth over the nipple and began to suck contentedly.

Hetty smiled at Vida. "Do you know what I have got in my handbag?" she said. "A bar of Nestle's chocolate – just for you, because you've been such a good girl."

Vida's lovely dark eyes shone. "Oh, Mam," she said, and made a beeline for Hetty's handbag.

Hetty sighed deeply. Who could ever have imagined that she would land up here in Greenwich, London, in a basement flat? But, at least she was free. If she felt any guilt, it was towards Dora. She mustn't let her sister know – not yet anyway. For if her sister knew where she was and Jack came a-calling, Hetty wouldn't put it past him to attack her, he had such a temper. No, it was better this way.

She put the baby to the other breast, and looked around the room. There was just the bed and a chair, a wardrobe, and a washstand on which stood a beautiful jug and basin. On the mantelpiece was a brass clock, and a pair of vases with glass pendants hanging down all round. Hetty thought they were the prettiest things she had ever seen. They shone in the gas light, showing myriads of colours, and looking at little Vida, Hetty saw that she was watching them too.

"Aren't they pretty, Vida?"

But the little girl's eyes were already closing. She was so tired.

"Come on, lad," Hetty said, removing the baby from her breast. His eyes were already closed and he was sleeping peacefully. She buttoned up her blouse. "Time for bed. Let's see where we can sleep, shall we?"

She turned down the gas jet and went back into the kitchen.

Pop Collins was reading his paper.

"Ah, there you are," he said. "A cup of cocoa, and you'll be ready for bed, I 'spect. All right, gel?"

And from that moment on he never called her anything else.

He found a large drawer from the bottom of a wardrobe for the baby, and Hetty covered him with her coat. There was a large comfortable old couch which she slept on, somehow holding on to Vida for all she was worth.

"Could you leave a lighted candle on the mantelpiece?" she asked him. "I'd feel better if I could see – just in case." She threw him a shy smile. "I'll pay you for it."

"No need for that, gel," he said. And so the night passed.

The candle had long since burned down when Hetty woke and saw that it was five o'clock. She extricated herself from Vida, and tiptoed across to see the baby, who still slept. What a good little soul he was, no trouble at all – Vida had often woken in the night as a baby, but this one never did. She crept silently to the window, and pulling the curtains aside for a moment, saw that a lamp post across the street was still lit. How close the houses were. They stood against the sky at daybreak like sentinels. She crept back to bed for a little warmth, and made her plans.

70

At six o'clock both Freddie and Vida were awake, and she could hear sounds from the old man in the next room. Perhaps, like most old people, he slept little and wakened early. She fed the baby, and as the light came in pulled back the curtains and looked outside. Well, by daylight it was certainly no residential area, there were lights already on behind many windows, but she knew that in a working-class area, hearts were warm.

Pop Collins made them a pot of tea, and they shared his toast which he speared on a toasting fork in front of the fire. "Eat this, gel," he said to Hetty. "Ye'll need some warmth inside yer if ye're going downstairs to see to the fire."

Putting on her coat, she made her way downstairs and, rolling up her sleeves, cleared out the range. Afterwards she unbolted the back door and walked up the steps. She found herself in a fair-sized yard. It was cobbled, and to one side stood a large shed, while facing her was what looked like a small barn. More storage, she supposed, and saw then the straw littered around it at the same time as she heard the distinct sound of a horse's neigh. Her face flooded with colour, almost as she had been found out doing something wrong, and she rushed to the barn door and pulled it open. There, standing on nice dry straw, was a horse! He was a large horse, beside him a cart – and he looked at her with such warmth from his brown eyes, as if so pleased to see her, that she rubbed his neck, and he nuzzled her, and she felt close to tears. "Oh," she said softly, "you beauty. What are you doing here?"

She might have stood like that for ages, everything else forgotten, if it hadn't been for a voice behind her.

"Like 'orses, do yer?"

"Oh, yes." And Hetty, her face flaming, stood back.

What a picture they made, the old man thought. The girl, pretty as a picture, with that cloud of soft dark hair and fresh face, and his Barney, his one and only friend. Why, in the cold light of day she looked no more than eighteen, and her with two young children upstairs.

"What's his name?" Hetty asked softly.

"Barnstaple," the old man said. "That's where I come from, 'cept I call 'im Barney."

71

Hetty patted the horse once more.

"I bet he's a worker," she said.

"Used to be," the old man said. "'E don' get out so much now as he used ter."

"Well," she sighed, "where's the coal?"

"I've brought yer a bucket," Pop Collins said. "'Ere y'are." He handed it to her. "There's wood there in that shed."

"Thank you."

She went back up the steps with the coal and laid the fire, then lit it. What a difference a fire made, she thought, and looked around her with interest. She couldn't wait to make a start on this room – but first things first. Back upstairs she found Vida with a biscuit the old man had given her, while Freddie was trying to sit up in the drawer, looking at her with such a comical expression that she picked him up and hugged him.

Then she smiled across at Pop Collins, who was drinking his tea noisily from a mug.

"I'll need to shop first to get a few things, then I'll tidy up downstairs. It should be warmer by lunch time."

He nodded. "Do what yer want, gel. As long as yer don't interfere with me." He took a gulp. "Rent payable on Fridays."

"Fridays," Hetty said. She had a feeling she was going to settle down nicely – all being well.

Chapter Ten

A sudden burst of wintry sunshine lit up Alderbourne Grange, and David Ogilby, away from home for the last fifteen months, stood back and looked at it. A bit of a monstrosity, he decided, but it was his home, and he had thought of it so many times when he was in Malaya. There, in the steamy heat or fierce sunshine, England had seemed to be light years away, and only the thought of his homecoming had kept him going. There had been so much to do – his grandfather had lived on the rubber plantation for almost fifty years. In fact, David's father had been born there. The old man had never wanted to return to his native land so there he had died, leaving the plantation to his grandson.

David had felt a sentimental streak for the old place – he couldn't let it go now – and had found an excellent manager to take it over, well-experienced and thoroughly trustworthy, as he had discovered in the last six months. Having left everything in order and in capable hands, he finally sailed for home.

He walked on, seeing the trees in their winter bareness; here and there, in this sudden warm spell, a light sprinkling of pale green buds covering the branches. Beneath the avenue of limes the daffodils were in full bud, some almost open. He loved this estate passionately, it was his home. No matter where he went overseas, this would always be home to him. He came to the oak tree, where he and Hetty had lain for that brief moment so long ago. He had put this moment off for too long. He had to see her again. So often, under the canopy of stars out east, he had thought of her and wondered about that

73

husband of hers. Somehow he had suspected all was not well there. Was she happy?

He re-traced his steps and made for the house, calling the dogs to heel.

He found his mother in the library writing letters. She looked up as he came in.

"David, dear, I'm trying to organise the little evening I mentioned to you."

A blank look had come over his face. He couldn't be less interested.

"Now, I am not going to give in to you – you have become so unsociable since your return. I can't understand you. I thought life in Singapore was one long round of parties and balls and soirees."

"It is." David smiled. It was so difficult to thwart her when she wanted something.

"Well, then, everyone has been asking when you would be back, and the girls . . ."

"I know," he said, realising only too well what she had implied. That it was time he married and settled down. Well, he would. All in good time.

"It is a pity that the Grimshaw girl won't be over yet awhile – when did you say she arrives?"

"June sometime, Mother."

"Oh, that will be nice. In the meantime, I'll go ahead with this. What do you think of April the tenth? That's your birthday. Isn't that a nice idea?"

"Yes, super," he said, his mind on other things. "I thought I'd just run down to the village – I think my bicycle needs repairing."

She frowned. "Won't Burney do that?"

"I'm not too sure what's wrong with it," David said. "Probably needs a complete overhaul. I'd rather Joe Enticknap looked at it."

"Yes, dear," she said. "You're not cycling down, are you?"

"I can't, Mother," he said. "I'll take Nelson and the trap."

The bicycle safely on board, he spurred Nelson to a light trot on his way to the village. Calling in to Joe Enticknap's was the best way he knew of finding out about Hetty. Joe had worked up at the Grange before leaving to help his father in the blacksmith's yard, and now he and his father did everything from light engineering to shoeing horses. They had known the Jessops family very well.

David thought about his extended stay in Malaya as he rode down the long drive. If his mother had had her way, he would by now have become engaged to Jane Grimshaw, one of the most sought after girls in the Far East. As she was immensely wealthy, many young men sought her hand in marriage, but she had obviously taken a fancy to him. She was lovely, he had to admit, fair and slim, ultra modern, a bright young thing. She delighted in wearing all the short fashions of the twenties, and in being as lively and fun-loving as all the rich crowd out there.

They had played tennis together, and kissed behind the club house, gone on picnics with a crowd of young people, danced together under moonlit skies – now, in the cold bright light of an English winter, it was almost as if he had dreamt it all.

But this was reality, and as the cob turned into the High Street of Barnsdale, he felt his blood stir, and took a deep breath. There were the pubs, the Crown and the Lamb, looking exactly the same, the cake shop, the grocer's . . . and his mouth set in a grim line as he came to the corn chandler's, for outside stood a swarthy young man, surveying the street. All must be quiet within the shop, guessed David. He knew without being told that the man was Hetty's husband. Handsome devil, he thought darkly.

He drove on, breathing a little faster, until he came to the corner of the High Street and Milton Street and reined the cob to a stop.

"Whoa there!"

He jumped down and walked towards the yard, savourig the familiar smells of leather and hot iron, his boots rattling against the cobbles.

Joe Enticknap the elder was busy shoeing a horse, the animal's great hoof bent upwards against Joe's leather apron. A sizzling, burning smell rose as he banged the horseshoe in, then looked up as the newcomer entered.

Joe the younger had seen David first. "Morning, sir," he said warmly.

75

They looked just the same, David thought. Both with fine heads of ginger-coloured curly hair, Joe senior with a red moustache, and young Joe with a massive red beard. They looked like Norsemen, he decided.

"Welcome back, sir," young Joe said. "It's been a long time."

"Well over a year," David said. "How's business?"

"Booming," Joe said, obviously pleased. "Plenty of work."

"Good," David said. "I've got my old bike outside – something's wrong with it."

"I'll have a look at it for you," young Joe said, throwing down his dirty rag. Probably wanted oiling, he thought. Mr David's sort didn't know much about anything when it came down to it. He walked down the side path. Grown into quite a man, though, he decided. His sister, Vi, had always thought young David the cat's whiskers. If she could see him now. Tweeds, broad shoulders, his face sun-tanned, and an air of quiet assurance about him. Lucky devils, he thought, they don't know they're born . . .

David followed him, and stood by while he got down the bicycle.

"It was a good model, this," young Joe said. "Worth looking after."

"Well, what's been happening in Barnsdale while I've been away?"

"Not much, sir," he said. "Two or three of the old 'uns died this winter – it was rough at the back end of last year."

"So I've heard. Do you ever see anything of the Jessops?" he asked mildly. "Didn't Hetty Jessops marry someone in the village."

Young Joe's face looked grim.

"Yes, she married Jack Maclaren – he runs the corn chandler's."

"I remember," David said.

"Well, she's gone. Left 'im," young Joe said.

David couldn't believe is ears. "Left him? What do you mean?"

"Walked out just before Christmas. 'Course, there are some as say they don't blame 'er, but I dunno – seems all wrong some 'ow."

76

"But where did she go?" David asked, his mind in a turmoil. "Where could she go?"

Young Joe shook his head. "Dunno," he said. "Just took the nippers and vanished – into thin air, as you might say."

"Nippers?" David repeated. "I knew she had a little girl."

Young Joe nodded. "There was a little boy too."

David took a deep breath. "Well," he said, "I'm sorry to hear that. Look, Joe, do you know where Dora lives?"

"Yes, Church Street, number five," he said, and bent down to pick up the bike. His father would have something to say if he stayed out here much longer. "I'll do this for yer, Mr David."

"Thanks," said David, and leaving the horse outside the yard, walked along to Dora's house, waiting for a few moments on the corner to collect his thoughts.

This was the last thing he had expected to find, Hetty – gone. Had no one done anything about it? Where was she? Dora would know. He walked briskly up to her front door.

She answered it to a tall handsome stranger, yet one with a face that looked oddly familiar. The man wore a heavy overcoat and a cap beneath which she could see that his hair was fair and his eyes intensely blue in his tanned face.

Despite the cold air he removed his cap, and she saw his fair shining hair and knew in a flash that it was young David Ogilby from up at the Grange. "Why, it's young David!" she cried, as pleased as punch to see him. "How you've grown – I didn't recognise you!"

He had known all the Jessops except perhaps the two eldest. They had been big girls to him who went to the village school, and big boys who went off to the war.

"Good morning," he said. "Mrs Mason, isn't it?"

"Fancy you remembering me," she said. "Will you come in? It's mighty cold out there."

"Just for a moment," he said. "I expect you are busy."

"No – nothing that can't wait." She suspected he wanted help of some kind or another up at the Grange. "What can I do for you?"

He smiled back at her.

"For the last fifteen months I've been out East in Malaya," he said, "and now that I'm back I've been looking up old friends." He undid his overcoat. It was very warm by the kitchen range.

"Can I get you some tea?" She asked, making for the kettle.

"Thank you, no," he said. "I was down in the village and I thought I'd call in and see Hetty at the shop." He saw a cloud cross Dora's face. "Hetty and I were such good friends. I often thought about her when I was out East." That being, he thought, the understatement of the year.

"I am afraid that Hetty has us all rather worried," Dora said. "She left home just before Christmas, taking the children with her, and no one knows where she is. I've racked my brains to think where she might have gone, but so far — nothing."

"You mean she's just disappeared into thin air?" He asked incredulously.

"It seems so," Dora said miserably.

"Did you inform the police?" David asked.

"Yes, straight away, but all they could find out was that someone answering Hetty's description had bought a ticket for London — but I don't believe that. She wouldn't go to London."

"But why would she do such a thing?" he asked.

"She'd reason enough," Dora said bitterly. "Jack Maclaren drank — and when he was drunk sometimes he beat her. I don't blame her for leaving him, I'd have done the same. I just wish I knew where she was."

"But this is awful," David said, and felt the anger rising in him. "Where could she have gone?"

"I wish I knew," Dora said. "She took hardly anything with her, just what she needed for the children."

"I take it you have asked all your sisters and brothers?"

She sniffed. "Yes, that was the first thing I did. Not that I thought she would go to them, she's too independent.

"What about her husband?" He asked. "Has he no idea at all?"

Dora sneered. "He was drunk for three days, and when he did come round he threatened to kill her if she ever set foot in the place again."

"Poor Hetty," David said, shaken as he had never been in

his life before. "Mrs Mason – Dora – will you promise to let me know if ever you hear where she is?"

Dora nodded.

"You will?" You know where you can find me. Anytime," he said. "Meanwhile I will do everything I possibly can to help trace her."

"Thank you, Mr Ogilby," Dora said. "That's very kind of you." She remembered to address him correctly. After all, he was a grown man and entitled to respect.

She led the way to the front door.

"Are you parents both well?" She asked.

"They are in the best of health, thank you, Dora," he said, and put his cap on as she closed the door after him.

He climbed up into the trap and spurred the cob into a fast pace, not stopping until he reached the stables behind the Grange.

Poor little Hetty – what she must have been through! To be driven to running away, with no one to turn to. And that swine of a husband – he deserved a horse whipping! Had he beaten her savagely before she left? How had she managed? Where would she find the money to feed the three of them? Where would she go?"

He had worked himself up into a fine state by the evening, but at least he had made up his mind.

"Tomorrow, Mother, I have to go into York."

"York, dear?"

"Yes, I've some business I need to do there. I shall leave in the morning and stay overnight."

Very well," Mrs Ogilby said. She had to get used to the idea that her son was a man now. He had matured so much since he had been out East.

Somewhere, David mused, he had heard – or read – of a private detective agency. At all events, he would leave no stone unturned to trace Hetty. He would never rest until he had found her again.

Chapter Eleven

By New Year's Day, no one would have recognised Hetty's basement flat. All the superfluous furniture was piled into the outside shed, while some went into the shop. Hetty kept only what she thought she needed, and by the time she had scrubbed and cleaned, the place looked like a new pin.

None of this would have been possible had it not been for the services of Billy Webb. He was a sixteen year old who lived along Queen's Row. It seemed that Pop Collins called upon Billy every time he needed help, and he was only too anxious to oblige, for he earned a penny or two, and there was nothing he liked more than to accompany Pop Collins on the horse and cart when he made his journeys around Greenwich and up on to the Heath where he collected most of his "good stuff", as he called it. It was quite staggering, Hetty decided, how much nice furniture was disposed of by the occupants of the large houses. One of these days, she thought, when I have time, I'll give him a hand and sort out some of that stuff. Given a good polish some of it was worth a lot more than the few shillings Pop Collins asked for it, she was sure. She had seen similar pieces in the big houses in Barnsdale, especially in the rooms up at the Hall where she had worked as a nursemaid.

Billy Webb gave Hetty her first introduction to some of the other residents of Queen's Row. Billy seemed unable to keep a job because he was not "all there" as Pop Collins said, but it seemed to Hetty that he was a nice enough boy, and not quite as daft as people thought he was. Just a bit backward, she told herself, but so willing and helpful. Young Freddie simply loved him, and his little face broke into smiles whenever Billy appeared. Billy had a way with babies. He was the youngest in a family of five. There was an elder, good-looking brother, and a thin, small, younger one with sleek red hair, and a girl called Doris who worked in a local factory, and wore what seemed to Hetty outrageous clothes. Hetty always made sure she was looking out of the window at half-past five when Doris returned home from work, her red hair fuzzed into tight curls, a bandeau around her head, wearing the shortest dresses Hetty had ever seen and the shiniest, most brillant red lipstick on her generous mouth.

"Hello, Mrs Keane!" Doris would call out, so friendly, Hetty thought. She was totally captivated. The next brother was a handsome young man who was away at sea. Mr Webb was a most imposing figure, a giant of a man, also with red hair, while little Mrs Webb was petite and pretty.

As the days went by, Hetty settled in. She quickly got to know the occupants of some of the other houses, as she pushed little Freddie in a large London pram which had come from someone on Blackheath and had lain in Pop Collins yard ever since. He had cleaned it up for her, and polished the chrome until it looked like new.

Hetty shopped and cleaned for Pop Collins who allowed her to have the coal free. Then he decided that he must pay her for his meals which, he told her, were the best he had tasted since leaving home at the age of seventeen. Hetty saw to it that he had plenty of meat and vegetables – Yorkshire puddings on Sunday with a roast, or a stew made with one of the cheaper cuts of meat, left to braise in the oven sometimes overnight.

"Folk down here in London don't know how to buy meat," she said. "They miss all the best bits."

"Well, you just carry on what ye're doing, gel,' he said. "I ain't 'ad such good food for many a long day."

Hetty knew that the first thing she must do was to get little Vida into school, and after that find a part-time job. It wouldn't be easy with a baby to look after, but she would manage somehow. Her money had almost gone.

"So how are you getting along?" Bill Baldwin asked her one day. He had always felt guilty over sending her to the old man.

"You did me a real favour," Hetty said, her brown eyes smiling at him. That's where the little girl got her looks, he decided. The young woman could be no more than twenty-four or five, and now she looked like a mere slip of a girl, the strained look gone from her face, her hair and eyes shining.

"Is the old chap good to you? We wondered afterwards, Betty and me – he's never had anyone there before, not as I know of."

"Really? Well, he has been very kind. I have the basement to myself, and he's cleared it out and given me some bits and pieces of furniture."

He put her purchases into a paper bag and handed it over the counter. "There you are then, duck, that'll be one and eightpence, please."

Hetty handed over the money.

"Where's your little girl today?"

"She's minding the pram outside."

"Soon be ready for school, I expect."

"Yes, I'm going up there tomorrow," Hetty said. "Once she's at school, I shall be looking round for a job, so if you hear of anything . . ."

"Yes, duck, I'll let you know. Not a lot of work round here."

"No." She smiled. "We'll have to see."

The next day, when the children returned to school after the Christmas holidays, Hetty set off, pushing the pram with Vida beside her. The little girl was excited yet fearful and held on to the pram wide-eyed as her mother pushed it through the gate marked INFANTS and across the asphalt playground of the local council school. The building looked enormous to Hetty's eyes, used as she was to a low, one storey village school sitting in a grassy enclosure.

"Well," Miss Faulkner said, regarding Vida who stood at Hetty's side, while the baby stared around him with wide blue eyes. "So you want to come to school here, do you?"

"Yes, please," Vida said. She had seen lots of children sitting at desks when she came in, and had decided that there was a lot more going on here than at home.

"Very well," Miss Faulkner said. "Since she has gone five, Mrs Keane, there is no reason why she should not start immediately. I will take all the particulars, and then if you would have her here tomorrow at five to nine." Her eyes twinkled at Vida. "And you must never be late, Vida. Isn't that right, Mother?"

"Oh, yes," Hetty said fervently. She had never been late for school in her life; indeed, couldn't imagine such a thing.

The next morning, in a new dress made 'specially by Hetty for the occasion, Vida put on her navy reefer coat, two years old and let down twice, a red woolly scarf and gloves, and walked to the school. Outside the gate was a crowd of mothers and babies, looking through at the children playing in the playground. One mother was holding the hand of a little girl who seemed too shy to let go. The woman smiled at Hetty. "Is your little girl starting today?"

Hetty nodded. "Yes." She looked at the other little child who was taller and thinner than Vida, although about the same age. "This is Vida," she said to her. "Vida Keane."

The children were eyeing each other with interest. One with dark eyes and curly dark hair, the other with vivid blue eyes and a long fair plait, they couldn't have been more different, Hetty decided. They said nothing to each other.

"Tell Vida your name," the woman urged.

"Helen Vincent," the girl whispered.

"Then hold hands, and off you go," Hetty said, and without further ado they clasped hands and walked off slowly into the noisy playground without looking back.

Both mothers looked at each other, and both had tears in their eyes.

Mrs Vincent blew her nose. "You can't help it, can you?" She said. "Poor little things – they don't know what they're in for, do they?"

They waited in silence until the whistle blew and the children formed into lines.

"Oh, look at them," Mrs Vincent said, as at the sound of another whistle the children moved off into the school.

"Well, that's that," Hetty sighed, turning to go.

Mrs Vincent looked at little Freddie, and smiled at him. "What a beautiful baby!" she said. "That lovely fair hair and those blue eyes – he looks like Helen did as a baby."

Hetty braced herself for the words which didn't come:

"He's not mu**ch** like his sister, is he?" So many people said it, but she never got used to it, nevertheless.

As they walked back towards Queen's Row, they talked.

"You're new here, aren't you?" Mrs Vincent asked.

"Yes, I only arrived before Christmas."

"From up north, aren't you?"

"Yes," Hetty said shortly, in such a way that the other woman decided to ask no more questions.

"I've lived here all my life." She sighed. "Wouldn't know anywhere else. Not that I don't long to get away sometimes, but it's home. You know what I mean?"

Hetty did.

"They're a nice bunch of people in Queen's Row – friendly like. Course, some of them you mightn't wish to know . . ." and she laughed.

"That applies anywhere," Hetty said. "It's just occurred to me, since you know the area so well, if you hear of a part-time job going – I need to work, you see, and it's not easy to find jobs these days."

The woman looked at her shocked. However poor, no woman in Queen's Row went out to work. Her husband would never allow it, for a start. And let it be known that he couldn't keep a wife? Not likely! Of course, you might earn a few shillings working at home, like sewing tennis balls, making clothes for people – but not going out to work. Who would look after the children? Then she had a sudden thought. Perhaps this poor young woman was a widow.

"You live along Queen's Row, don't you?"

"Yes, below Mr Collins' shop." And Hetty saw a shut down look come over Mrs Vincent's face.

"Oh."

It had not taken Hetty long to realise that the part of Queen's Row where Pop Collins lived was probably the worst part of the street. This woman probably lived at the other end.

I won't always live there, Hetty thought rebelliously. One of these days I shall move to the other end, where the houses are nicer. And after that – who knows?

"Well, Mrs Vincent," she said, "it's been nice meeting you. I have some shopping to do.

84

Mrs Vincent turned to look at her, and saw a pretty girl, quite young, with large dark eyes that looked sincere, and a cloud of soft dark hair. Her voice was soft and gentle. You can't tell me she's a bad lot, Mrs Vincent decided. She could be a widow, or have a sick husband. It wasn't likely that she was unmarried, with two little . . . She flushed as the word sprand to mind, and took her departure hurriedly.

Hetty, only too well aware of what was going through Mrs Vincent's mind, walked on, head held high. She would have to have some story ready for the future, much as she hated to lie. She would be a widow, her husband having died in an accident, she decided swiftly. After all, she had the rest of her life to live, she might as well get it straight from the start. How to explain to Vida though? She sighed. She would have to worry about that when the time came. Vida mentioned her father less and less now. and Hetty wondered, not for the first time, whether the child had had any idea of what had gone on in that house in Barnsdale.

He is dead as far as I am concerned, she thought grimly. That part of my life is over. Forever.

Freddie was awake, and she sat him up so that he could see out of the pram, tucking the blankets round him. "You and I, Freddie," she said, "are going for a walk in Greenwich Park. And then, if it's not too far, on to the Heath."

He smiled back at her showing his six teeth, his quiff of blond hair sticking out beneath his woolly bonnet. Hetty stood admiringly outside the railings of the Royal Naval College, then walked on up King William Street until she reached Nelson Street. Trams trundled by on rails, looking so tall when you were close to them that little Freddie seemed mesmerised. Hetty waited unitl the trams had gone, then crossed to the other side and continued her walk up King William Street towards the park. Magnificent buildings stood on her left, one day she would find out what they were, and a lovely old church. St Mary's, she read. It must be old. Through the impressive gates, and she was inside the park. A great greensward faced her.

She took a deep breath as she pushed the pram up the hill, for it was quite a climb. The onion dome of the Greenwich Observatory faced her and she began to walk towards it. On the top of Observatory Hill she stopped and looked back at the view. It was magnificent. Imagine, down there somewhere was her home, among all the splendour that was London. She edged cautiously towards the information board outside the Observatory, and saw the Meridian Line. Several people were standing on it and she joined them, it seemed the thing to do. Nearby was another large building, and she walked towards it. Flamsteed House, she saw it was called. An elderly man stood beside her, looking up at the pole and ball on top of the house. Hetty looked at it curiously.

"That's a Time Ball," he explained. "Every day the ball drops at one o'clock – haven't you heard it?"

She shook her head. "What for?"

"It's a time signal to ships on the river – it's been doing that since eighteen thirty-three."

Hetty was impressed.

"The Observatory was built in order to find out the longitude of places."

Hetty wasn't quite sure what this meant, but she intended to find out more about it.

"Not for nothing, young lady, are we the strongest seafaring nation in the world."

"My brother was a sailor – in the war."

"Good lad," the man said, and looked hard at Freddie. "And are you going to follow in his footsteps, young man? Eh?"

Freddie smiled delightedly at the strange man, and banged on his pram cover.

"Good lad," the man said, and touching his cap, walked on.

Hetty turned the pram around. She would not have time to get on to the Heath today – she had been out long enough already. How wonderful it was to have all this on the doorstep. Pushing the pram down the hill and enjoying the view, she made her way home, wondering how little Vida had got on, and conscious that she had stolen some free time in order not to worry about Vida's first day at school. Of course she would be all right.

There were lots of mothers collecting their children, and when they came out, faces flushed, eyes shining, here and there a weeping child, each mother extended a comforting hand. "How was it? Did you like it? Was it nice?"

The two small girls came out together, Helen and Vida.

"Well?" Mrs Vincent said. "How did you get on?"

"It was lovely," Helen said enthusiastically. "I would like to stay there all the time."

Mrs Vincent made a face at Hetty. "What about you, Vida?"

Her brown eyes shone. "It was nice," she said. "And I sit next to Helen."

The two mothers smiled at each other.

"I'll walk along with you," Mrs Vincent said. "Run on ahead, you two – not too far."

They skipped along in front of the pram, while Freddie tried to peer round the shade to see them.

"Look," Mrs Vincent said, turning to Hetty, "come and have a cup of tea with me tomorrow afternoon – that's if you can manage it?" Seeing Hetty's doubtful face.

"Well," she said, thinking of all she had to do. "Yes, that would be nice."

"I live at number seventy-nine." Mrs Vincent said. "Come about two."

How nice it was to have a friend, Hetty thought, and went back to prepare Pop's lunch. She and Freddie would eat later.

She could hardly wait to call on Mrs Vincent. When she did she found the house, with its whitened step and blackleaded coal hole, shining clean in the gloom of a dull day. London, she thought, had a few disadvantages, one of them being the sulphur yellow days, as she called them, days which never seemed to clear, when the skies, heavy as lead, seemed low enough to touch. Barnsdale never had days like this. She pushed the pram up the short path to the front door, then knocked and waited.

Mrs Vincent answered, smiling at her newfound friend. "Oh, bring him in," she said. "Don't leave him out there."

Hetty lifted Freddie out and followed Mrs Vincent into the kitchen, where a fire burned brightly in the range, and there was a strong smell of furniture polish. The large table was covered with a blue chenille cloth, over which Mrs Vincent had placed a snow white tea cloth. The table was laid with china cups and saucers, and a cake sat in the middle of the table next to a bunch of early daffodils.

"Oh!" Hetty said, leaning forward to smell them.

"I'm lucky," Mrs Vincent said. "Ted grows them – he's a park keeper up in Greenwich Park so, of course, our garden is full of things.

She tickled Freddie under his chin. "Well, he is a little love," she said. "Would he like a biscuit?"

"No, he's all right," Hetty said.

"Where does your husband work?" Mrs Vincent said, taking the bull by the horns.

Hetty's eyelids flickered for the briefest moment.

"I am a widow," she said. "My husband died."

Mrs Vincent clucked in sympathy. "Oh! I am sorry. I shouldn't have – "

"It's all right," Hetty said.

"Was it long ago?" Mrs Vincent's blue eyes were sympathetic.

"Last year," said Hetty, and looked straight into the blue eyes.

"Well," Mrs Vincent said, sitting down opposite her, "I tell you why I wanted a word with you. I did hear of a job going – of course, you may not like it. I mean, it's obvious you're not used to . . . I mean, needs must when the – " she floundered.

Hetty looked at her eagerly.

"Where? What is it? I don't mind what it is."

"Well, you don't want just anything," Mrs Vincent said reprovingly. "I'll make the tea and tell you."

She placed the teapot on the table and poured the milk into the cups.

"A friend of mine, a Mrs Gooderson, works up on the Heath in one of them big houses – she's the housekeeper there. Granville Place, it's called. Beautiful gardens – Ted says they're some of the finest in the country. Anyway, my friend Mrs Gooderson has been suffering for some time now with arthritis in her knees – suffers something awful, she does. 'Course, she's sixty nearly, so she can't complain. Still, she can't get about as she used to, and Mrs Harding – she's the lady who lives there – says she must get help."

"I see," Hetty said. Well, it would be something.

"The work isn't heavy, my friend says. It's a big place, but they've carpets everywhere, and lovely furniture, antiques, that sort of thing, and silver – all got to be cleaned, hasn't it?"

She compressed her mouth. "It would be mornings," she said. "Four or five mornings a week."

Hetty looked doubtfully at her newfound friend. "What about the baby?" she said. "I must have him with me."

"'Course you must," Mrs Vincent said indignantly. "What I mean is, if I spoke to my friend, and she thought it would be all right, would you . . .?"

"Of course," Hetty cried. "I should be pleased. I have to earn money from somewhere."

"'Course you do," Mrs Vincent said staunchly. "I think you're ever so brave the way you're managing. "Does . . ." But she stopped. There was something about Hetty's expression that forbade further enquiries.

"Have a piece of my cake?" she said. "I baked it this morning – fruit cake."

"Thank you," said Hetty, accepting a plate.

By the time they were ready to pick up the little girls from school, they were on first name terms.

"I was christened Minerva," Mrs Vincent laughed over her third cup of tea, "but everyone call me Min."

"I'm Hetty."

"Well, Hetty," Min said, "leave it to me."

At the end of the first week of Vida's schooling, Min had some news for her.

"I've spoke to my friend, Mrs Gooderson, and she says she sees no reason why you couldn't take the baby with you – I told her he seems to be such a good baby. So, Hetty, if you'd like to go and see Mrs Harding up at Granville Place on Monday, she'll see you at ten o'clock. I said unless she hears from me, that will be all right."

"I'll be there," Hetty said. "And thank you very much for your help, Min."

"Well, you haven't got the job yet," she laughed, "but I'll tell you how to get there. It's a bit of a walk, up through the park and on the heath, then you follow the wall along until you come to a high gate – you'll see the name over it – Granville Place. You can't miss it."

Pop would know it, Hetty thought. He might even know the people there. He seemed to know everyone, one way and another.

Chapter Twelve

Pop Collins knew Granville Place well. "One of the oldest 'ouses around," he said. "Jorjan." Hetty looked up. "Nice fambly," he said. "You might know 'im – comes from up your way."

Hetty didn't think this likely – she presumed he meant up North.

On Monday morning, after leaving Vida at school, she made her way up through the park and walked on farther than she had been before. She didn't hurry, for she knew she had plenty of time, and eventually arrived at a wide carriage drive, at the end of which were some wide gates. Once outside, she found herself on the edge of a large area of heathland. This then was the famous Blackheath, haunt of highwaymen and robbers, who used to spring out on unsuspecting passengers in the stage coaches plying between London and Kent.

She soon found the gate in the high wall, and pushing the pram through, closed it carefully behind her. An avenue of trees confronted her, at the end of which stood an imposing house. It was of red brick, with many elegant windows. The grounds were immaculately kept. Hetty made her way round to the side of the house where she imagined the back entrance would be.

A high laurel hedge hid what was obviously the kitchen area, for there were two lines of washing out on this Monday morning in a yard holding dustbins and coalbins and various brooms. This must be the right place.

She pulled the iron bell ring, and in answer the door was

opened by a large, comfortable-looking woman who reminded Hetty of her own mother.

"Mrs Gooderson?" she asked.

"Ah, you must be Mrs Keane," the woman said. "Come in. You can bring the pram in – it won't hurt standing on this stone floor."

Hetty wheeled in Freddie, who was asleep, and put on the brake. "He'll sleep for quite a while yet." she said.

Mrs Gooderson nodded approvingly, and glanced up at the big kitchen clock. "We've ten minutes yet," she said. "Time for you and me to get to know one another. Sit yerself down."

Mrs Gooderson liked what she saw. A nice young woman, a cut above the usual cleaning staff – the baby's pram was immaculate and the pillowcase and pram covers snowy white. She approved of that. Min hadn't been able to tell much about the girl though it seemed that she had another child of five. Well, it was none of her business, the mistress would be responsible for looking into that.

"Are you used to housework?" She asked, looking into Hetty's friendly brown eyes.

"Yes. I don't think you would find cause to complain."

Sure of herself, Mrs Gooderson thought.

"It's not hard work," Mrs Gooderson said, "but there's plenty of it. Polishing, silver, stairs – there's three floors in the house – but no basement, thank goodness. I'm not so good on my feet as I was. And, of course, there's the kitchen."

She was interrupted by the bell ringing on the room indicator. The little pendulum swung from side to side above the word "Library".

"Ah, that'll be Mrs Harding now. I'll take you to her. Don't worry, I'll look after the baby."

Hetty followed Mrs Gooderson along a wide carpeted hallway, and up a beautiful staircase and a landing, where she knocked on a door and was bade to enter.

Hetty found herself in a room overlooking the park, where long windows were hung with yellow silky fabric, and the walls lined with books. At a small desk sat the owner of the house, a small, delicate-looking lady, with white hair and a soft pink complexion.

"Good morning," Hetty said. "I am Mrs Keane."

"Sit down, my dear," said Mrs Harding kindly, looking at a paper in her hand. "You have come to help Mrs Gooderson, I believe?" She leaned forward. "I always like to see the people who help to run the house, although I know I can trust Mrs Gooderson to recognise a good worker when she finds one. The question is – how often can you come? Will you be able to manage, do you think? I understand you have a baby."

"Yes, he's downstairs," Hetty said. "Mrs Gooderson is keeping an eye on him. I also have a little girl of five, but she is at school."

"But what happens when the baby is unwell, or your little girl off school?"

"I am sure I can manage," Hetty said, most anxious to get the job now that she had met Mrs Gooderson and Mrs Harding.

The lady of the house appeared to be thinking hard.

"I was a nursemaid before I was married," Hetty volunteered.

"And I understand you are a widow?"

Hetty looked down.

"That's very sad. So you need the job?" Mrs Harding said.

"Could I perhaps," Hetty said boldly, "be given a month's trial? Then if you or Mrs Gooderson found it didn't work . . ."

"An excellent idea!" Mrs Harding cried. She seemed to be relieved that a solution had been found. "Mrs Gooderson will tell you the hours and so on, and the wages – she has been with us so long, I tend to leave everything in her capable hands. But now, poor dear, time is catching up with her. As it is, I'm afraid, with us all. But you are young, and I hope it works for your sake. It can't be easy, with two small children."

"I manage."

"You're from Yorkshire, aren't you?" Mrs Harding said suddenly, and Hetty's heart missed a beat.

"Yes."

"I thought so – I recognised your accent. My husband is from Yorkshire."

Hetty consoled herself with the thought that whatever had happened in Barnsdale, it had been long after Mr Harding's time.

She realised the short interview was over, and rose to her feet.

"Can you find your own way downstairs?" Mrs Harding asked.

Only then did Hetty see the two walking sticks over an adjacent chair.

"Of course." She smiled. "Thank you, Mrs Harding."

After Hetty had gone, Mrs Harding swivelled the chair round to look out of the window. How hard life was for some people. A pretty young woman like that having to go out to work in order to survive. There was something wrong somewhere with the order of things. And she was so lucky herself. She had never known what it was to want for anything.

Back in the kitchen, Mrs Gooderson looked up as she came in. "Well, how did you get on?"

"Mrs Harding is going to give me a month's trial to see if it works out."

"Oh, that's good." Mrs Gooderson said. "I don't mind telling you, I shall be glad of a hand. Some days my back is so bad I can hardly walk. How soon could you start?"

"As soon as you like. Tomorrow?"

"Oh, if you could!" Mrs Gooderson said. "I've to go to the hospital Wednesday morning, and Mrs Wilson doesn't do Wednesday – only Tuesdays and Thursdays."

"Mrs Wilson?"

"She's the woman who does the rough – oh, you won't be asked to do any rough work. Mrs Wilson does the outside lavatories and scrubs the kitchen floor – all the dirty jobs. I'll make a cup of tea, then I'll show you round. You'll soon see just how much there is to do."

"Yes," Hetty said, "but it's a question of how many mornings. I couldn't do five – more like three or at the most four – and I'm afraid I couldn't get here before half-past nine."

Mrs Gooderson clicked her tongue. "'Course, you've got the little girl to get off to school. Do you think you could manage four?"

Anxious to please, Hetty agreed.

Mrs Gooderson made the tea, and Hetty noticed how she walked with difficulty. Her legs were stiff and she was obviously in some pain.

"How long have you been here?" Hetty asked.

"Thirty years," replied Mrs Gooderson. "I come here before I was married, then I lost my husband in the war and came back. They're a lovely family."

"I am sure they are," Hetty said truthfully.

When little Freddie woke, Mrs Gooderson took him out of the pram, despite Hetty's remonstrations, and gave him a rusk. He took to her immediately. "We're going to be friends, aren't we, little man?" She said. "I never had any of my own, but my sister had a houseful. 'Course, they're all grown up now. Well, as soon as you've finished your tea, we'll take a walk round the house."

Hetty was surprised how large it was. Room after room filled with priceless rugs and ornaments, beautiful furniture. The mahogany doors alone must take some polishing, she thought. It was finer than anything she had seen at the Grange or the Hall. She could quite see why it took so much hard work. The sooner she got down to it the better.

It could have all been so much worse, she told herself on the way back. It appeared that she might have fallen on her feet. Little Freddie looked out of his pram, at the great oak trees springing into life, the acres of green grass, but mostly he looked at his mother, at her hair which had escaped from her hat in the breeze, at her soft mouth, her dark eyes which looked at him with such love. He banged his little fists up and down on the pram cover, which so far was the only way he knew of expressing his approval.

When she arrived home, Pop Collins had just come back from his rounds, while Barney the horse stood outside feeding from his nosebag. Hetty wheeled the pram alongside the horse, and Freddie's eyes lit up. Hetty stroked the horse's flank. "There, Freddie, horse." He seemed delighted. Pop Collins appeared from the yard.

"Ah, there y'are, gel," he said. "Ow'jer get on?"

"Got the job, Pop. Starting tomorrow. What sort of day did you have?"

"Not bad," he said, picking up odds and ends from the cart. He held a pair of blackened candlesticks in his hand.

"Why," Hetty said, "they're brass, aren't they?"

"Yep," he said. "D'y wannem?" holding them out to her.

"I'll clean them for you," she said, "but you shouldn't let those go cheaply, Pop. They may be worth a lot of money."

"I dessay," he said, "but I ain't got time to fiddle with stuff like that. You keep 'em."

"Thank you," she said. I will, she thought, they will go towards my collection of antiques – it's a start. They're heavy, they can't be anything but solid brass, and I'm sure they're very old.

"Ere y'are," Pop said, dumping a large carrier bag at her feet.

"What's this?"

"Cookin' apples – the cook at The Gables give 'em me. The end of last year's crop."

Hetty peered into the bag. Large round shiny Bramleys – what a pie she'd make with those!

"I'll make you the best pie you ever tasted!" she cried, and pushing the pram into the yard and under cover in the shed, lifted out little Freddie and carried him down the steps to the basement. She cooked him some potatoes and carrots, which she mashed, and poured over some gravy from the stew. Now that he was weaned, she was giving him all sorts of things. It made life so much easier for her. She warmed his milk, and while he sat in his high chair, sang to him as she prepared the pastry for tomorrow's dinner. She washed and pared the apples, and cut them into pieces, putting them in cold water. She made the pastry and lined the large enamel plate. Dusting the plate with flour, she pared the apples, and covered them with sugar and a dusting of powdered cloves and cinnamon. Placing the covering lid of pastry on the pie, she crimped the edges, made some slits, and brushed the top with milk and sugar.

Carrying the pie to the oven, she opened the door and put in her hand. Like her mother, she had no idea of how to measure temperatures scientifically, using her hand instead to gauge the heat. Just right, she thought, and in went the pie.

"Well, my love?" she asked her son. Lifting him up, she washed and changed him, putting the soiled napkin in an enamel bucket to soak. She cuddled him tightly, then put him to rest by the side of the large brass bed in the cot that Pop Collins had found her. After tucking him in, she went back into the kitchen, where the fire glowed, but she put up the

95

front to conserve the heat for the oven. Then she got out the cleaning box and the candlesticks. Just wait until she got down to these. Glancing up at the clock, she saw there was time before she collected Vida from school. She was sure Min would be pleased when she told her the news. She began to hum quietly to herself as she rubbed away.

The next morning, she arrived at Granville Place just before half-past nine. After wheeling Freddie into the kitchen, she was given an apron and a box of cleaning utensils and a pair of cotton gloves.

"Do you remember the bedrooms on the right of the landing? One with all the Chinese stuff in, and the other done out in blue? Not the main bedroom – that's the one on the left. Well, furniture and doors in both those rooms to be polished. There's the jar of wax polish. And dust the china – but be careful with it."

"Oh, I will," Hetty breathed.

"There's a vacuum cleaner in the cupboard up there. I'd come up myself . . ."

"No need for that," Hetty assured her. "I'll find my way about."

With a final look at Freddie, she made her way up the stairs, and when she came to the top, surprised an elderly man coming out of the main bedroom, a small dapper man who walked swiftly and purposefully. His black twinkling eyes alighted on Hetty as she stood back to let him pass.

"Mornin'," he said gruffly.

"Good morning, sir," she said.

He stopped in his tracks. "Yorkshire," he said. "Am I right?"

Hetty smiled. "Yes, sir."

"We don't have to worry about you, then," he said, and went on his way down the stairs.

Oh, it was grand to hear a Northern voice again, Hetty thought, almost on air as she opened the door to the room with the Oriental china. Her mouth hung open at the sight of so many beautiful things. They must be immensely wealthy to own all this. She wondered, as she hadn't done before, what Mr Harding's line of business was.

Well, it was nothing to do with her. But, oh, Barnsdale seemed so far away. Like another world.

Chapter Thirteen

That winter, Granny Maclaren became ill after influenza. Caring for her took up a lot of Jack's time. What with the shop to look after and the food to get, he was hard pressed to find a moment to himself. In January he moved out of the small house which he and Hetty had shared. He turned off the water supply one freezing January morning, and without a backward glance locked the front door and made his way to the shop.

As the new year wore on, the chances of Hetty returning seemed ever more remote. He drank less, simply because at the end of a long day, and looking after his grandmother at night, he was too tired to go out – all he wanted was his bed to sleep in.

It was a hard winter, with thick snow covering the earth. The little High Street was ankle deep in hard packed snow and ice, the roof tops shining silver and mauve in the winter sun, while a hush lay over everything. Jack was kept busy from morning to night selling animal food stuffs and kerosene and chopped wood and corn meal, medicines for poultry, dog food, and remedies for sick and stranded animals.

He knew his grandmother had not long to live. In her eighties she had been strong, but now, aside from her illness, a new lethargy seemed to have overtaken her, and Jack suspected he knew the reason for it. She was fretting because Hetty and the children had not been to see her, and there was nothing he could do about it. He couldn't tell her Hetty had left him. Her grief and anger over what she had always suspected was his treatment of his wife would be enough to kill her.

97

"I told you, Gran, she's gone to see her sister in Grimsby. Just a visit, she'll be back soon." But he knew she didn't believe him.

"She said nothing to me about going away," the old lady muttered.

"I 'spect she thought it might upset you – she'll be back in a day or two."

But when Hetty did not return, it was almost as if Gran accepted the fact that she would never see her again. She ceased to speak of Hetty and the children, growing weaker by the day. One evening, fortified by a few drinks, Jack made his way to the police station, where he had gone but a few weeks before when Hetty had left him. The constables knew him of old, and when he stumbled into the station, red-faced, his eyes glazed, they looked up from their seats around the stove.

"Nasty night to be out, Jack."

"I want my wife," he said, almost weeping with self-pity and frustration.

"'Course ye do, lad," the sergeant said. He had it in his heart to feel sorry for the man, knowing he was his own worst enemy. The evils of drink, he thought, being a Band of Hope man himself.

"Ye're s'posed to know everything," Jack sneered. "Where is she? 'Ave ye nothing better to do than sit there round a warm fire while my bonny wife and children lie freezing out there in the snow?" And at this sentiment, he openly wept.

The policeman came round to the front of the counter. "There, lad," he said, comforting him. "We've done all we can. All we could find out was that someone like your wife left on a London train with two kiddies, and that's some weeks ago – before Christmas. We don't like it, son, when people go missing – 'specially girls and women. They're likely to get swallowed up in a big place like London." But he saw that Jack was in no mood for soft talk, and tried another tack. "'Ow's about a strong cup of tea, Jack? It's bitter outside."

But he had gone, skulking out into the white night.

"Poor devil," the sergeant said. "You know, it's a funny thing, but I've often thought about it. Where would a young woman go with two young children at this time of year?

Makes your heart bleed to think of it. She must have been at her wit's end, poor thing, and her family say she knows no one down there. I reckon she was desprit, meself."

Jack made his way to the Lamb, to the warm cheering atmosphere of the pub where he was always sure of a welcome from Molly Edwards, who had been a lifeline all during this hard time. He had kept away a bit since his grandmother had been ill, but Molly had pressed him many times to take her home. He knew that one sight of Molly and his grandmother would have had a fit. Well, she wasn't everyone's cup of tea, and her reputation had preceded her, but as far as he, Jack, was concerned, she had been a great comfort to him.

She poured him a whisky, a double, and handed it to him.

"Drink this," she said, "you look as if you could do with it."

He downed it in one gulp. "Thanks, Molly," he said, his speech slurred, but the warmth was coming back now into his icy veins as he looked at her. Through a whisky haze, he saw a warm, plump figure, her breasts appearing invitingly over the top of her white knitted jumper, her hair in corkscrew curls, the red shiny lipstick on her wide mouth, blue eyes which held a gleam – for him.

He leaned forward and whispered. "Tonight we'll go back to yon hoose." She loved the way he lapsed into his Scots accent when he had had a few. She wanted to ask, "Do you mean it, Jack?" because she had never been to his home, but had learned the wisdom of a still tongue in a wise head.

Once she had been to his home, she decided, things would become easier. She knew he had closed it up and moved in with his grandmother, and it would be bloody cold, but she'd soon see to that.

"I'll nip over and see to Gran first," he said, "and when I come back . . . ." He tried to focus his eyes on her, and looked at her meaningfully.

"Sure, Jack," she said. "And you mind 'ow you go." She didn't want any accidents at this stage of the game.

That night she lay awake in Hetty's bed, Jack snoring rhythmically beside her. She was warm enough now, although it had been freezing when Jack opened the door to the house. She had looked around curiously when he lit the gas jet. Nice little place – his wife had got it ever so nice. She smiled to herself in the darkness. She'd got a step inside, and that was half the battle. She turned over and snuggled in to Jack's warm body. She'd soon have a little place of her own, see if she didn't. People would soon get used to the idea of her being Jack Maclaren's woman, perhaps even is wife – life was full of surprises. Who would have thought when she went on duty this evening that this would be the outcome. Jack stirred in his sleep, and she soothed him. Soon he wouldn't be able to do without her.

There was no one more surprised than Jack Maclaren when he opened his eyes and found a sleeping Molly in his bed. Then memories of the night before came flooding in, and he pushed her awake angrily. "Come on, Molly, wake up." She wasn't the prettiest sight first thing, but Jack didn't notice that. "Get dressed and get out of here – quick, before anybody sees ye." And he was into his trousers and shirt almost before she was properly awake. "I've to get going. Shut the door after you."

Realisation dawned, and she smiled to herself. A foot in the door, that was all you needed, she thought, taking her time to dress. She'd be as good as any of these local women, she could hold up her head with any of them. She was sick of sleeping over a pub. If it wasn't one, it would be another . . . When she left she found the key on the inside of the door, and taking her time, locked it from outside for the all the world to see, tossed her corkscrew curls, and with head held high walked back to the Lamb.

Jack found is grandmother looking very frail, and was full of remorse for leaving her. He called the doctor who pronounced her a very sick woman. "Pleurisy," he said. "She'll probably not last through the next twenty-four hours. I can't get an ambulance to the hospital yet – it's full of accidents and pregnant women. You'll have to close the shop and look after her, unless you can find someone."

Jack knew that he couldn't. He would look after her himself. He gave her medicine and warm drinks and sat with her, and when she finally passed away some twelve hours later, wept as he had never wept in his life before. The last link with the past, and she had always been so good to him. Sobs racked his broad shoulders, and tears ran down his face. What a sorry state he had come to. What a mess he had made of his life. And it was all Hetty's fault – Hetty Jessops. He wished he had never set eyes on her.

By March that year, Hetty had been working for the Harding family for three months, and had enjoyed every moment of it. She was used now to the walk, which she did four mornings a week, pushing little Freddie in the pram up King William Street and into the park, and making her way to Granville Place. Mrs Gooderson was pleased with her. She was strong and willing, and polished the furniture and cleaned the silver, taking a special pride in the lovely things that formed part of the Harding menage. Hetty thought Mrs Harding was a lovely person, and had got quite used to seeing Mr Harding about the house on the days when he stayed home from his city office and either played golf or walked in his garden. He seemed to enjoy a little chat with her, liking to hear a familiar north country voice, Hetty supposed. In fact Henry Harding thought she was the prettiest little thing he had seen for many a long day, like the daughter he might have had and who had died at birth.

Most of all Hetty liked the stained glass window on the great landing, where myriads of colours spread over the carpet; it reminded her of the coloured glass candlesticks in Pop Collins' room.

More and more she helped the old man, cleaning and dusting and admiring many of the things he had in the shop. Sometimes she would pick out something and hold it in her hands, savouring its fine workmanship.

"Yer've got an eye for a good thing, gel," old Pop used to say. "Spot a bargain a mile off, you can."

Hetty was pleased. There was nothing she liked more than browsing through Pop's collection of junk, and lately she had taken to walking down to Blackheath Village and looking at the lovely shops. She would look at the wonderful displays in Hinds, the main store, with its expensive merchandise, the polished mahogany doors with brass fittings that shone like gold, and the bevelled plate glass centrepiece. She liked to watch the elegantly dressed customers as they browsed carelessly in the village, small lap dogs at their heels or carried like babes in arms.

She had taken a fancy, too, to a small shop in the Vale where they sold antiques. "Oliver James" the sign over the shop read in impressive gold lettering, while on the bevelled door it said: "Antiquarian Book Seller, Fine Arts, Antiques". Hetty thought it very stylish. How she would love to own a shop like that!

On one wall jewel-coloured rugs were displayed, on another fine oil paintings, while elegant furniture was displayed as though in a room. The fine china was similar to that she cleaned at Granville Place.

There was a lovely baker's shop, too, in the village, where they sold home-made bread. Hetty loved to walk by as it reminded her of home and her mother's baking day. She could make a good loaf herself, but there was never time these days for that, what with working and looking after the children.

She had got to know many of the neighbours in Queen's Row, they were a friendly crowd all told, some of them not much to her liking, but they always had a cheery word for her. It was surprising, she thought, as she pushed the pram homewards that no one ever asked her where she came from, or anything about her background. At home, everyone knew everyone else's business – here, they took you at face value.

In the pram was a remnant of material she had bought for a new dress for Vida. She wasn't as good a dressmaker as her sister Dora, but she did her best. Vida would look lovely in the small print dress – Hetty had seen lots of little girls in the park with their nannies wearing dresses of similar material.

Freddie looked at her, his blue eyes twinkling, his fair hair showing beneath his bonnet. She tipped the pram towards her, and blew him a kiss. He pursed his mouth then chuckled.

"Oh, you are a little love!" Hetty said. He never ceased to give her pleasure. Below her stretched the view right across Greenwich, with the Naval College and its beautiful white buildings. She couldn't have picked a nicer place to live in all the world.

One warm spring-like day, Hetty was feeding Barney, Pop

Collins' horse. Freddie was watching her, blue eyes fixed on her and Barney's reaction. "See?" Hetty asked. "He likes it." And she snuggled her face into the horse's neck. Barney appeared to be smiling, and Freddie chuckled out loud – he just loved these sessions with the horse.

Pop was unloading the cart, and putting some stuff in the shed: a horsehair sofa, which he shouldered as though he was a man of some twenty years, two or three old chairs, and a large wooden box full of oddments. Hetty went over to look at the contents. She was always curious to see what he had picked up.

"Go careful with that clock, gel," Pop said. "It's a good 'un."

But Hetty was lifting out a small brass stool, like a box, with four very elegant legs and two horse's head handles at the side.

"What's this, Pop?" she asked. It was black with age, but despite that the quality of the brass was evident.

Pop looked up. "Stool or summat," he said. "T'ain't nothin' speshul."

Hetty considered it. "There's one like this in that antique shop in Blackheath Village," she said. "Of course, it's beautifully polished. And the Hardings have one in the drawing room." Then she had a sudden idea. "How much would you sell this for, Pop?"

"Couple o' bob," he said. "Why? Djer wanna buy it?" His blue eyes twinkled.

"I'd like to borrow it," she said. "Just for tomorrow."

"If yer like," he said, and later that evening when the children were in bed she polished it until it gleamed. There was no doubt in her mind that it was worth more than two shillings.

The next day, after finishing at the Hardings, she walked over to the village, and leaving the pram outside, took her precious parcel into the expensive shop. It smelled delicious by her standards, of beeswax and polish and lovely old things.

The bell over the door rang as she entered, and as she waited she waved to little Freddie through the window. Presently a tall, good-looking man appeared from the room at the back of the shop. He was in his late thirties, she imagined, with nice grey eyes and a small clipped moustache. He walked with a slight limp, and she guessed him to be a retired army man.

"Good afternoon," he said in a pleasant, cultured voice. "Can I help you?" His tone put her at her ease in a moment.

He saw a young woman with a cloud of dark hair and beautiful brown eyes, who smiled at him shyly before swallowing hard and delving into her carrier bag. He glanced outside at the baby in the pram. She wore no uniform, so the baby must be hers. She didn't look like a nanny.

Hetty withdrew the brass stool, and saw a flicker of interest in the man's eyes. He must be Oliver James, she thought, he looked like an Oliver.

He took it carefully, his fine artist's hands turning it over, then looked at her enquiringly, a twinkle in his grey eyes.

"You would like to know what it is?" he asked.

"Well – yes, please," she said. "I know it's a stool of some sort."

"It is called a brass footman," he said, still holding on to it. "Did you want some idea of its value?"

"Yes, please," Hetty said. "Well," she added, "actually, I want to sell it." His eyebrows went up. "May I ask where you got it?" he said. "Is it yours?"

"Oh, yes!" Hetty said, shocked that he might imagine it didn't belong to her. "I live in Greenwich," she explained, anxious to reassure him of her integrity. "In the basement, below the shop where old Pop Collins lives. Pop keeps a second-hand shop." And she saw the flicker of interest re-kindle in the man's eyes. "Sometimes he brings things home that I am sure are too good to sell cheaply, and it seems a shame."

He looked outside at the pram where little Freddie was sitting up and taking notice of everything around him.

"Is that your baby?" he asked.

"Yes, that's Freddie."

"I see," he said gravely. He regarded her for a moment or two. "Do you know anything about antiques?"

"No, but I'd like to learn."

"Well, I will give you a pound for the footman." And he pulled open a desk drawer, hearing Hetty's intake of breath, and saw the brown eyes shine with pleasure. He handed her a pound note, and saw her cheeks flush with excitement as he began to write out a receipt on his letter heading. "And, of course, you must sign this receipt as proof that it belongs to you." He handed her a fountain pen, and saw the slightest hesitation before she wrote: "Hetty Keane".

Well, if he was any judge of character, she hadn't stolen it. She looked as honest as the day was long, and it wasn't every day that you became the owner of a Georgian footman.

"Thank you," Hetty said, placing the money in her purse and preparing to go.

"Perhaps," he said to her, "if you find anything else that might be of interest, you could bring it over for me to see?"

"Oh, yes," she breathed, agog with excitement. "Yes, I will."

"I am Oliver James," he said. "And you are – Mrs Keane?"

"Yes," Hetty said. How she hated lying, especially to someone as nice as this man.

"Very well, Mrs Keane, I look forward to seeing you again."

"Thank you, Mr James. You have such lovely things."

"And I am sure you understand that I am only interested in very fine, unusual pieces."

"Oh, yes, I do." And outside the shop she put her purse into her handbag. Wouldn't Pop be pleased.

When she arrived home, she dashed upstairs to find the old man. "Look, Pop, I took the brass stool over to that expensive shop in Blackheath Village and Mr James gave me a pound for it." She thrust the note into his hands.

He looked down at it, speechless at what she had done.

"It's called a brass footman," Hetty said. "Mr James told me, and he said – "

"'Old on," he said. "You mean that bit o' brass . . .?"

"Yes."

"Well, I'll go to blazes!" he said, and looked down at her smiling face. "It's yours, gel." and he made to give it back to her, but she put her hands behind her back. "No. I just wanted to find out what it was worth."

"I can't take it all," he said. "Bizness is bizness, gel. We'll split it two ways, eh?" Even then I've made a profit." And he handed her a ten shilling note.

"All right," Hetty said. "Thank you, Pop." And tucking it into her skirt pocket, she went down the stairs humming to herself.

She was still humming as she prepared the children's tea.

Vida sat up at the table, her mop of dark curls tied back in a ribbon, her lovely violet brown eyes watching Hetty intently.

"Helen's mother said I could go to tea there on Saturday," she said. "It's Helen's birthday, and she has a new frock."

"Well, I must see if I can finish yours in time," Hetty said, looking at her daughter's upturned face. She was growing so pretty, she thought. "I shall be seeing Mrs Vincent tomorrow, so we'll talk about it then."

She must cut out the material this evening if she was to finish it in time. She sighed, thinking how beautifully Dora would have made the dress, and how much she would have enjoyed making it, with no daughter of her own. But she mustn't think about Dora. She had such feelings of guilt. One day, she promised herself, she would write to Dora. But not yet. It was too soon, much too soon.

Chapter Fourteen

One day in June, Dora made her way down the High Street in Barnsdale, and stood stock still on the corner, astonished to see that Maclaren's shop was shuttered, with a large "Closed" sign across the door. Well! What was all that about?

She made her way to the newsagent's along the street and went inside. She didn't beat about the bush. "Well, Mr Morton, what's going on at yon shop – at corn-chandler's?"

"Oh, aye," Mr Morton said. "Chap's gone – done a flit, I reckon. Stuff was moved out on Saturday, and according to some the place is empty."

"Well!" Dora was flabbergasted, and sat down on the seat by the counter. She was short of breath normally, but given a shock, needed time to recover herself.

"Wa'nt 'e your brother-in-law? Married your young sister?"

Dora nodded grimly. 'E was – not as I'm proud to admit to it."

Mr Morton nodded. "After the old lady died, he went to pieces – out drinkin' every night as God sent."

Dora sat tight-lipped.

"And that – well – woman I s'pose she calls 'erself, she didn't 'elp. I reckon she was after his brass, what little 'e'd got."

Dora listened until she got her breath back, then she stood up.

"Well, Mr Morton, I'll be away – it's been a terrible business, but I for one am glad to see the back of 'im. Good riddance, I'd say."

"Good day, Mr Morton."

Walking through the side way to the shop, she peered up the iron staircase towards the flat. She'd not get herself up them, they were too steep to climb, but she could see a few empty cardboard boxes soaked by the night's rain, and there were no curtains up at the windows. Oh, he'd gone all right, she thought grimly, and it was to be hoped that he hadn't left a trail of debts behind him. She walked along the High Street to the greengrocer's. Well, it was no business of hers. It wasn't as if she could even write and tell Hetty, and a lump came in her throat as it always did when she thought of her young sister. Sometimes she could hardly bear to think of her out there somewhere fending for herself and her two bairns, but as Tom said, it really was none of their business, and Hetty was sensible enough to know what she was doing. But it was a hard pill to swallow all the same. Dora blew her nose and walked on.

When she had finished her shopping, she made her way to the little house where Hetty had lived with Jack. She had been made aware by neighbours only too soon that Molly Edwards from the Lamb had moved in, and had been torn between anger at such a woman taking over Hetty's little home and a strong desire to keep out of trouble. Now she could see that the little house was empty. No curtains hung at the windows, there was no need even to walk up the narrow path, but she did so out of curiosity. Peering through the glass, she could see that it was indeed empty. Nothing remained, not even the lino on the floor.

She bit her lip, and walked slowly home. What a sad state of affairs. Thank God her Mam had not lived to see the day. They had all had such a wonderful childhood at Alderbourne Grange when their father was alive. And Hetty and young Master David – what a grand pair they had been. She had caught a glimpse of him only the other day. He had called at her house soon after Hetty went. She'd had no news for him then, no more than she had now, but it had been kind of him to ask after young Hetty.

She walked down the narrow hall and into the kitchen. A nice cup of tea was what she wanted.

Tea was also being served at Alderbourne Grange where Mrs Ogilby, her smooth white forehead now creased into a frown, was holding a letter, written on stiff vellum paper, the contents of which were obviously causing her some anxiety.

"It is such an awful thing to have happened," she said quietly, gently biting her quivering lips to hold back a sob. "Just two weeks before the wedding."

Her son David stood with his back to her, looking out of the window to the smooth lawns beyond. It was indeed sad, he reflected, to learn that the young man, Henry Armitage, who had been betrothed to Dorothy, the daughter of his mother's distant cousin who lived in Vermont, New England, had been killed in a motor car accident just two weeks before the wedding.

"Poor girl," Mrs Ogilby said. "What a shock it must have been. And for his parents – he was an only son, I believe."

Colonel Ogilby, who had just returned from a drive round the estate, held out his hand for his cup of tea.

"It won't make any difference to your visit, Ethel, my dear," he said. "Tassie will be more than glad to see you – it will help to take her mind off the tragedy."

"I wonder," Mrs Ogilby said. "We could put it off until later. It seems such a pity, though, with everything being reserved for us, our cabins, the – "

"Exactly," the Colonel said. "What do you think, David?"

"I'm quite happy to let the arrangements stand," he said, "but I think I'll leave the decision to Mother."

"All those wedding preparations!" Mrs Ogilby said.

"They do things in such a big way in America."

"Why not telephone her, my dear?" the Colonel said. "She may be very glad of your moral support, and I am sure the girl will be pleased to see David. She hasn't seen him since they were over here – when was it? About ten years ago?"

Mrs Ogilby looked a little brighter. "Yes, I'll do that, Gerald," she said, and glanced at her watch. "Now, we must get the timing right, and put in a personal call."

David sauntered out into the garden. He had not been all that keen on the proposed trip to Vermont to visit his Aunt Tassie when it was first mooted. After a long sojourn in Malaya, he was quite pleased to be back in England.

Ethel Ogilby came from an old Suffolk family whose for-bears had been among the earliest settlers in New England, and his parents had spent their honeymoon in the ancestral home. David himself had never been there, although his mother visited Vermont every few years, and the American cousins came to England from time to time. He consoled himself with the thought that it would be a change from his mother's everlasting matchmaking efforts.

At the end of the day David was pleased when they kept to the original plan and sailed for New York, and was more than pleasantly surprised on arriving in Vermont to find himself in a home from home, except that the countryside seemed to have been set of fire, so vivid were the trees in their riotous colours.

It was harvest time, and the autumn sun shone down on golden cornfields. As far as the eye could see there was bright yellow gold, while the backdrop was an artist's palette of green, orange, scarlet, red and yellow.

The Strafford residence, too, was something of a shock, being rather grand, and at the same time gracious, which somehow he had not expected. It sat in a golden valley, sur-rounded by the home farm and small cottages, while the grass was lush and a rich green. Looking at the horses who grazed in the September sun, he thought the setting could not have been more perfect.

They were met at the station in a horse drawn wagon, and driven through the delightful village with its white houses and picket fencing, evocative of all the films David had ever seen about the United States. The Straffords themselves were soft-spoken, gentle people, whose one interest in life after their daughter was the land and their home.

He found himself in a large hall of exquisite proportions, with polished floors covered with rich rugs and some fine pieces of furniture. A scent of apples and candles pervaded the house.

In his room, which held a large Colonial bed, there were wide wooden floorboards, again polished like glass, heavily draped cotton curtains and wire screens over the windows. The air coming in through the open window was warm and scented and outside he could hear the humming of bees, and the songs of birds that were new to him. Far in the distance he could see that astonishing backdrop of brilliant colour. How sad, he thought, that this should be a house of mourning, and had to admit that he was not looking forward to meeting Dorothy in her bereavement. Aunt Tassie had thanked him for coming: "You are just what she needs – someone young in the house . . ."

Wheh he was showered and changed, he made his way downstairs to the drawing room, and saw her sitting there alone, her hair shining against the light of the window.

She was lovely, he had to admit. A shy, pretty girl with excellent manners and a gracefulness about her that he had not hitherto connected with young American women. It had, he thought, to do with her background, and her parents, but now she was saddened by the sudden death of her fiancé. She was in mourning and so wore black, but it suited her soft fair beauty, although her blue eyes, which were made for smiling, were now sad and thoughtful.

Mrs Strafford was delighted that they had not changed their plans. They were more than welcome, and helped to minimise the shock of recent events. A young man like David, and from England, helped to take her daughter's mind off the tragic event which had resulted in the death of Henry Armitage, and the realisation that but for his untimely demise, she might now have been on her honeymoon.

Being in mourning, there were no social events for Dorothy to attend, and the famous hospitality of the New Englanders was naturally restricted to formal invitations in order to introduce the visitors from England to the local community. After that first evening under the anxious eyes of both parents, the young couple grew slowly used to each other and began to relax.

They rode a lot, spending most of their time with the horses, beautiful creatures in their natural setting, and David found himself in the company of an excellent horsewoman for Dorothy rode as to the manner born.

He encouraged her to talk about her dead fiancé, and as the days wore on she was able to do so more and more in a relaxed manner which pleased Mrs Strafford who had feared that the girl might retreat into herself with no young people around her to help minimise the shock of Henry's death.

One lovely evening, David and Dorothy took a walk around the lake, then sat on a grassy knoll watching the sun sink low behind the mountains. David thought he had never seen anything more beautiful than the colours of the sky reflected in the clear cool waters of the lake. It was a quiet, intimate time for confidences, and he was not surprised when one day Dorothy turned to him, her blue eyes regarding him curiously.

"What about you, David?" she asked. "I have talked so much about myself and Henry."

He smiled and shrugged his shoulders. "There's really nothing to tell."

"I don't believe that," she smiled. "Sometimes you have a faraway look, as though you are thinking or remembering something – or someone."

He made no answer.

"Were you ever in love, David?"

"Yes," he said.

"Can you talk about her?" she asked gently.

"It's not quite how you think it was," he said slowly. "We were boy and girl sweethearts, grew up together."

"That's the best kind," Dorothy said.

"Her name was Hetty, and she was the daughter of our groom – the family lived on the estate, or did until she was about fourteen when her father died and they had to leave and move into a cottage in the village. I lost touch with her then, in a sense."

She was silent, waiting for him to go on.

He was thinking, as he spoke, that he had never spoken of this to anyone before, and realised what a relief it was to put it into words.

"Tell me about it, David," Dorothy said.

"Well, after that we lost touch. She had to go out to work, and I left school and eventually went to Oxford. Then I heard she had married – a local chap, the owner of a village store, and that she had a small daughter."

He turned his head and looked straight at her. "I am not sure I should tell you what came next."

"I think you must," she said gently.

112

"One day I saw her again, unexpectedly. It was the day of the September Fair, and there she was."

She waited.

"I don't know what came over me. At least, I do. I knew then that I loved her, that she meant more to me than anything in the world. When I looked at her, it was like coming home. She was everything I ever imagined a girl would be. Everything that I wanted. She was lovely, pretty, and warm, and I felt I had to see her again, even though I knew it was pretty hopeless."

"And did you?" she prompted.

He was silent for a while.

"I was going abroad for a year two days after that, and I knew that I had to see her before I left. She told me she had a little girl, and I asked her if she was happy – and she said she was. Finally, when I begged her, she agreed to see me the next day for old times' sake. It was my fault – I made her come, she really had no choice, although I knew in my heart she felt the same way."

"You mustn't reproach yourself, David."

"I do, and have done a thousand times since. I make no excuses, but it is something I shall never forget. She made me promise to forget that it ever happened – that we must never get in touch with each other, ever again."

She reached out and covered his hand.

"And you never have. Poor David."

"But that's not all!" he cried suddenly, startling her with his vehemence. "When I got back from Malaya fifteen months later I went down into the village – oh, I don't know why. I only knew I just had to see her again – and she had gone. He buried his face in his hands, while Dorothy's hand flew up to her face in shock.

"Gone? Gone where?"

"She had left him, taking the two children with her. No one knew where."

"But this is dreadful," Dorothy said. "Why did she leave him?"

"I spoke to her sister, and she said the husband was a drunkard and beat her."

"Oh, David! How sad. And children, you said?"

113

"A girl and a boy – where could they have gone, Dorothy? Just to disappear like that? I am sure she had no money."

Her face was very pale. He took her hand.

"I'm sorry, I shouldn't have told you like that. It was unforgivable. It's just that I've lived with the knowledge for so long."

Dorothy's face was very drawn.

"What I can't understand," she said at length, "is why you have never found anyone to take her place. Did you love her so much that no one can replace her?"

"At first," he admitted. "Though I knew nothing could ever come of it. I hope now she has settled down somewhere and is making something of a life for herself."

Presently she asked, "If you found her, would you marry her?"

He shook his head. "No. She wouldn't marry me anyway. And it wouldn't work, I know that now. Hetty was always more sensible than I was, even as a child. She knew that, and she is fiercely independent."

"Father knows one or two eminently respectable private detectives," she said thoughtfully. "Have you thought of that?"

"Yes, I engaged a man. In fact, I also went to the police, but nothing came of it. She has obviously changed her name. I need hardly tell you that my parents would be shocked and horrified if they knew."

Dorothy's blue eyes looked troubled. "I can understand that, can't you?"

"Yes, of course. But it has become a kind of obsession, and one that I can't throw off. To find her."

"Do you believe in fate, David?"

He frowned. "I've never given it much thought. No, I don't think so. Do you?"

"Yes, I do," she said firmly. "I believe what is to be, will be. Like Henry being killed. It was ordained. And if you are to find her, then you will. Sometimes it's hard to come to terms with, but that is what I believe."

"A rather fatalistic attitude."

"Yes, if you like. But it does make it easier to accept things."

114

"I'm not sure that I go along with it," he said. "I think I like to believe that I am in charge of my life." And she laughed out loud, for the first time since he had arrived.

He saw that the sun had finally disappeared behind the dark hills, and rose to his feet. "It's getting chilly," he said, holding out a hand.

"You know," he said as they walked slowly home, "for a pretty girl, you are jolly sensible." And she smiled.

"I take that as a compliment, sir," she said, and together they walked back to the house, unaware that the two mothers were watching their progress from an upstairs bedroom window.

"Oh, wouldn't it be wonderful, Ethel?" Tassie Strafford said softly as she straightened the long curtains.

They moved back into the room.

"It would indeed," Ethel Ogilby replied.

Chapter Fifteen

Summer arrived in June that year, all the more welcome after the long hard winter. Along Queen's Row there were lines of washing in the tiny backyards, and the front doors were opened to the street.

The fat family at number twelve pushed up the sash windows and you could hear their laughter all the way down the street. They were always laughing, but now you could hear them as they eased themselves out of the windows and overflowed on to the window sills. From the Widow Haughton's flat came the strains of an Indian love lyric, while Betty Baldwin, the grocer's wife, exchanged greeting with Paddy MacNeill, the manager of the off-licence on the opposite corner, who was now preparing to open the trap door to take delivery of the new Kent beers. Upstairs, over the off-licence shop, the widow Donaghue dreamed over her jewel case, and her fabulous collection of earrings.

After hanging the clothes on the line for an airing, Hetty went over and had a sweet word with Barney, who was always delighted to see her. Young Billy Webb was coming to take him out today, for Pop Collins was getting over a cold. All through the winter Billy had helped Hetty carry coals into the house; there was nothing he was not prepared to do. He was glad of odd tasks, for he seemed unable to keep any job for long, and spent most of his time at the local Labour Exchange.

Back in the kitchen, Hetty put the finishing touches to Freddie's birthday cake. One year old, she thought. Already he was taking a few faltering steps when he'd a mind to, but loved to crawl just everywhere.

Today was Friday, her day off, the day she reserved for doing all the odd jobs, and there was always so much to do that she didn't know where to begin. Before she went to the shops, she would call in on old Mrs White whose elderly husband had recently died. Twice a week she collected a crusty cottage loaf for Mrs White who was unable to get out because of her bad legs.

Mr White had been an unusual character, known to everyone, for the Whites had lived in Queen's Row as far back as anyone could remember. He was a massive figure in his ginger-coloured suit, and sported a heavy gold watch chain and albert across his vast chest. He always wore an expensive velours hat and had the finest white curled moustache to be seen anywhere. No one could remember if he had ever gone to work, or if he had, what he had done for a living. He left the house every morning for his daily constitutional and returned at lunch-time.

It was the daughter, though, named Charity, who excited the most interest, and many were the jokes that abounded about that. For Charity was a hospital sister, a fine figure of a woman with enough curves to turn any man's head. People remembered her as a girl, her black flashing eyes, black tumbling hair, beautiful complexion, and the devil in her, they said. She had left home to train as a hospital nurse, and before two years had gone by, there was much coming and going at her parents' house, and after a time a very nice pram stood outside the front door, a baby boy inside it. Charity White went back to nursing, and the grandparents brought her baby up. He was now almost twelve years old, a handsome auburn-haired boy whom everyone liked for his good manners. It was obvious, the inhabitants of Queen's Row decided, that he was the son of a doctor or surgeon. But now, in the last year, and after all this time, again there had been much coming and going by the handsome Charity White, now a nursing sister in a voluminous cloak which hid a multitude of sins. A woman in her prime, thirty-eight or so, she had produced another son, and this time a very expensive, very shiny, London baby carriage stood outside the front door for all to see, while Mrs White with her bad legs once more set to looking after a baby. Trevor was his name, and the only comment Mrs White ever made was that Charity had been a naughty girl again.

Hetty knocked at the door and waited, hearing Mrs White's heavy step coming along the passage. The door opened and she stood there in her voluminous black dress covered by a snowy white apron. She never wore anything else, and people suspected that the aprons were ex-hospital issue. Her eyes were red from weeping.

"Come in, Hetty, it is good of you to call."

"I won't come in," she said. "I was on my way to the shops and wondered if you wanted your bread."

"Bless you," Mrs White said. "You're a good girl, Hetty. But come in – just for a minute. I've something to show you."

Hetty manoeuvred her way past the large empty pram in the hall and into the front room.

"I won't be needing the loaf any more – not now that Mr White's gone," said his widow, dabbing her eyes with her apron. "Oh, he was that fussy about his bread – liked it home-made – but the baker who calls will do me. Look, what do you think of this?"

Hetty stood in astonishment, her mouth open, hardly believing her eyes. For the room was stuffed full of furniture, like a storeroom, and unless she was very much mistaken most of the things were valuable antiques. On the far wall stood a large wardrobe, heavily inlaid, reaching to the ceiling. In front of it was a large curved cabinet, elaborately painted and edged with brass. On it stood several pairs of Oriental vases. In another corner stood a handsome grandfather clock, with the date 1690 in painted figures. Letting her eyes wander round the room she saw walls lined with dark oil paintings, delicately made chairs, an intricately carved Chinese flower table similar to one she admired in the Hardings' house. The room was a treasure trove, she decided, and looked at Mrs White whose red-rimmed eyes obviously saw no beauty in any of these things.

"Goodness!" Hetty said, at a loss for words.

"It belonged to Mr White. He brought it all from his mother's home when she died. He wouldn't get rid of it, although as you can see we needed the space. But he wouldn't part with it. Of course," she went on, "he married beneath him when he married me. Still, he never had cause to

118

complain, and I don't think he did. Except, of course," she confided, "for our Charity . . . Still, you can never be sure how they're going to turn out, can you?"

But Hetty was still looking at the fine pieces of furniture.

"Mr White was a surgeon," Mrs White went on. "Famous, until – well, it's all water under the bridge now. I want to get rid of it. I can't be doing with all this stuff. And Charity – well, she's not interested, she's got her life at the hospital. And to tell you the truth, I could do with the money. I've had my doubts about calling in your old man, Pop Collins. I don't much care for him, he frightens me sometimes."

Hetty smiled at her. "He's really very nice," she said. "He has been very kind to me. But . . ."

It wouldn't be fair, she was thinking. Pop would give her nothing, or hardly anything, for all of this, and it deserved a better home. Since working for the Harding family she had grown used to nice things, and knew an antique when she saw one. Far better to ask someone with more knowledge to look at this. She knew that this was a situation that called for Oliver James' expert opinion.

"I think," she said to Mrs White, "that this is too nice for Pop to deal in. He is really a second-hand dealer. If you will leave it to me, I will ask Mr James who has a shop in Blackheath Village to come and look at it. I don't know if he will, mind, but I will ask him. I could always take some of the smaller things over for you – we'll have to see."

"Oh, bless you, Hetty," Mrs White cried gratefully. "I can leave it to you then?"

"Yes," she said confidently. "I'll let you know what he says."

After lunch, she wheeled little Freddie over the heath and down into the village. Leaving the pram outside, she pushed open the door of the elegant shop.

Oliver James recognised her instantly. "Good afternoon," he said, his grey eyes contemplating her. He thought not for the first time what a pretty little thing she was.

"Good afternoon," Hetty said, and taking a deep breath, told the story of Mrs White's treasures. She saw the grey eyes liven with interest.

"And you think these things could be of interest to me?" he said thoughtfully.

Hetty nodded vigorously. "I'm sure of it," she said. "I have seen a lot of things like it in the house where I work on the Heath."

"Oh," he said curiously. "And where is that, may I ask?"

"At the Harding residence, Granville Place," Hetty said, and saw Mr James break into a smile, his eyes twinkling.

"As well you might," he said. "Many of those things Mr Harding has bought from me – he is a collector, and only the finest things interest him.

"Please sit down." He indicated a chair, and Hetty glanced outside to where Freddie sat quietly contemplating the scenery. He opened a small book and picked up a pen. "Now, if you will tell me where it is . . ."

"Greenwich," she said. "Number forty-three, Queen's Row." And saw the merest flicker of his eyelids.

"Mrs White – that's her name – is a very nice lady," she said. "She's not – well, like some of the people who live there."

"I am sure she is," he said reassuringly, and looked up at her. "Is she likely to be there if I call on Monday morning?"

"I am sure she will be," Hetty said. "I'll tell her you are coming." Making for the door, she turned. "If you are interested, you will give her a good price, won't you?" she asked earnestly. "She needs the money."

"You can trust me," he said stoutly, his lips twitching. "Of course," he said seriously, "in the event that I do business with her, you will be entitled to a commission." And he saw the look of horror come over Hetty's fact.

"Oh, no!" she cried, her cheeks rosy.

"Of course," he said mildly. "That's business. No one does anything for nothing in business."

"Oh, but – "

"That's lesson number one," he said kindly, escorting her to the door. "Come and see me next week," he added. "Good afternoon."

Hetty pushed the pram back home, delighted with her efforts and thinking that perhaps there might be another future in store for her. If she could find nice things and let Mr James know, and she got paid, she would be learning all the time, for there was nothing that interested her more. She had no desire to go on cleaning houses all her life, she wanted something better for the children. Freddie and Vida deserved more than she was giving them. Just keeping her head above water was not going to be enough. And what better opportunity could she have than living in the same house as the second-hand furniture dealer? Not that Pop got much in the way of nice things. Still, you never knew. There had been the footman, and the brass candlesticks.

Vida was waiting at the school gate with Mrs Vincent and Helen. In the six months they had been in Greenwich, Vida and Helen had become very close friends, and liked to do everything together. The mothers were pleased, for they knew they were not going to be influenced by some of the rougher elements in the school.

"Hello, Hetty," Min Vincent said as the two small girls ran ahead. "How are you getting on with Mrs Gooderson?"

"Oh, she's nice," Hetty said. "I get on with her very well. It's such a shame about her rheumatism, she is in such pain some days. Like Mrs Harding herself, she's crippled with arthritis."

"Makes you think," Min said. "All that money, living on the heath, and what's it all for? I'd rather have my health, wouldn't you?"

Hetty nodded vigorously. "It's everything," she said.

"You look strong," Min said, eyeing her. "For such a dainty little thing, I mean."

"Me? Dainty?" Hetty laughed. "Well, I've never been called that before!"

"Young Doris Webb gets married on Saturday," Min said, "Billy's sister."

"Does she?"

"Yes – six bridesmaids, and she's got the most beautiful dress, white satin. Mrs Webb showed it to me. 'Course, it's a bit of a laugh, Doris getting married in white – she's been around, our Doris."

Freddie used this moment to shout at a passing motor car. "Oh, he loves motor cars," Hetty said.

"And what it must be costing!" Min said. "No expense spared, from what I hear. You wouldn't mind, but he's a bus conductor – the 53 run."

"Well, she's the only daughter with four brothers. I expect they want to make the most of it."

"I expect you're right," Min said moodily. "Hetty, why don't you let Vida come along to us on Saturday, then she could see the wedding? They would both like that."

"Thanks, Min," Hetty said, as they reached her front door.

"Coming in for a cup of tea?" Min asked.

"No, thanks. I must get back. I promised Pop I'd give him a hand. He's a bit under the weather just now."

"You spoil him," Min said. "Waiting on him hand and foot."

Hetty laughed. "He wouldn't let me do that," she said. "And he's been very good to me. I'll see you on Saturday, Min."

On Monday morning, when she took Vida to school, a smart motor car stood outside Mrs White's house, and Hetty had a shrewd suspicion that it might be Mr James'. A motor car, unless it was the doctor's, was not too common a sight in Queen's Row. He's not wasted much time, Hetty thought, and was pleased.

Mrs Wilson who did the rough work, the washing and the scrubbing, was already there when she arrived. She usually started work at eight. Mrs Gooderson came down with a breakfast tray. "The poor mistress," she said. "She didn't have a very good night."

The back door was open and Hetty left Freddie outside.

"He'll sleep presently," she said. "He was awake so early this morning."

"We'll have to do the china room today, Hetty," said the housekeeper. "I never did get around to spring cleaning it — but now that I know you are careful, I can safely leave some of it to you." Hetty wondered where the china room was. There were several rooms she hadn't been inside yet.

"Don't worry about the lad," Mrs Wilson said. "I'll keep an eye on 'im."

Upstairs at the end of the landing was a room that was kept locked. Now, armed with her basket of cleaning materials and dusters, Hetty unlocked the door to allow herself and Mrs Gooderson in. The housekeeper went straight over to the windows and pulled back the curtains.

Hetty gasped as she was the shelves and the wonderful collection of china they held.

"We don't wash this, Hetty, but once a year, though of course it has to be dusted regularly for it don't do it no good to absorb the dirt nor the light. This is Mr Harding's collection of old china – I expect you've noticed a lot of things downstairs. Sometimes he'll put a piece out for a change, but mostly he keeps it locked away. E'll spend hours up here looking at it and cataloguing it. It's 'is 'obby, you might say."

Hetty devoured it with her eyes. Such beautiful things, delicate eggshell china, too frail almost to touch. She looked apprehensively at Mrs Gooderson.

"You'll get used to 'andling it. It's a bit nerve-racking at first, but you soon get used to it. Now start on the top shelf and do each piece carefully.' She smiled at Hetty. "You're a careful girl," she said. "You won't break anything."

There was a rap on the door, and Mr Harding looked in. "Ah, there you are, Goody," he said. "Go along to the mistress's room, will you? I think she'd like a hot drink and another blanket – she seems to be so cold, and it's really a very warm day."

"Of course, sir," Mrs Gooderson said. "Now get on with it, Hetty. Don't stand gawping at it or you'll never get round to it."

She swallowed as Mr Harding came into the room, his small brown eyes twinkling at her. "Given you the job of dusting it, has she?" he said. "Well, what do you think of it?"

"I have never seen anything so beautiful in my life," Hetty said. "It's, well – "

"I am glad you approve," he said. "It has taken me a long time to achieve this. I inherited some from my father, he collected Chinese porcelain, but I like the French – and the English. What do you think of this?" he said, taking down a hexagonal vase painted with exotic birds. "That's a Chelsea Vase – or do you think these prettier?" And he pointed to a pair of Coalport vases, exotically coloured with sprays of flowers which were very ornate.

"I like the Chelsea better," Hetty said truthfully.

"So you prefer the simpler style," he said. "That's the bit of Yorkshire in you. Ah, well," he said. "I must be on my way. Be careful with them, lass."

123

On the way to the City in his chauffeur-driven car, Henry Harding opened his paper, but he wasn't reading. He was thinking of that young woman, and the way her face lit up when she saw all that china. Nice little thing, pretty as a picture with that cloud of soft dark hair, the way her brown eyes smiled. He couldn't help thinking that she looked just like the daughter who had died at a few days old, yet he had no way of knowing what she would have looked like had she lived. Perhaps because she looked a little like his wife when they first met. Laura had been petite, and dark, and pretty . . . Sighing, he opened his paper and began to read.

Hetty rolled up her sleeves and got down to it, looking underneath each piece to see the maker's name. It was fascinating. When she had finished one shelf, she went downstairs to give Freddie his milk and get her morning cup of tea.

"You locked the door after you, did you?" Mrs Gooderson asked as she poured the tea.

"Yes," Hetty said, her eyes still full of the colours she had absorbed. She stirred her tea. "I never knew there were so many beautiful things in the world."

"Some people never see 'em," Mrs Gooderson said laconically. "In this house there are lots of lovely things, just because Mr Harding likes them and collects them. Mrs Harding, bless her, has no interest in that sort of thing whatsoever. She used to be a well-know lady golfer you know," she said as she drank her tea.

"Really?" Hetty was amazed. To think of that frail white-haired elderly lady playing golf was almost unbelievable. "What sort of business does Mr Harding do?"

"He has an import and export business in the city. The boys work there too – well, I say boys, they're both young men now and married."

Hetty stood up. "I'd better get on," she said, and saw that Freddie still slept peacefully outside in the kitchen garden.

"It'll become more difficult as he gets older," Mrs Gooderson said. "It's all right now, but you wait until he's walking everywhere."

"I know," Hetty laughed. "I'd best make the most of it."

If, one day I had a small shop, she thought as she continued the dusting, then I could buy and sell nice things, and make

124

enough money to send the children to decent schools. 'Specially Freddie. It's important for a boy. Vida will get married one day, it isn't the same for a girl. Of course there was a lot to learn, buut she could do it. She could do anything if she tried. It wouldn't be like Pop's shop, but something more like the shop in the village, only not as grand. Once Freddie was at school, perhaps she could get a job in an antique shop and gain experience.

Her head dancing with plans, she made her way home.

On Thursday she made her way to Oliver James' shop in Blackheath village, and was surprised to find a removal van outside unloading Mrs White's furniture.

She waited until the van had departed before entering the shop.

She saw immediately that the huge wardrobe had pride of place on the straight wall, while the grandfather clock stood in the corner.

Oliver James followed her eyes.

"That," he said "is a French armoire – and a very fine example if I am any judge."

Hetty mouthed the word, and Oliver wrote it down for her.

"Armwar," he said. "Say it like that."

"I thought it was a wardrobe," she said.

"Well, it is in a way. Would you like to see inside?"

"Yes, please."

He opened one of the doors with a key, to expose the satin-wood lining, the drawers with their gilt handles, the hanging space inside, all polished like silk.

"Oh, it's beautiful!" Hetty said. "Just imagine – it's stood all that time in Mrs White's tiny room."

"That's part of the excitement in this business," Oliver James said. "You never know what will come to light next."

He opened a drawer and took out a crisp note. "This is for you," he said. "It is your commission."

Hetty blushed crimson. "Oh, I couldn't," she gasped. "That's much too much."

"Take it," he said. "You've earned it. And don't worry about your Mrs White. She's more than pleased with what I gave her. She had no idea the stuff was so valuable, so you have no fears on that score."

Hetty looked down at the note. Her very own money.

"Thank you," she said.

"And if you find anything else, let me know."

"Oh, I will!" Hetty was not sure if she was standing on her head or her heels. Dashing out of the shop, she hurried back over the heath and through the park into the lower road to collect Vida from school.

Chapter Sixteen

When Vida brought home her hand-made Christmas cards from school, Hetty knew it was time to prepare for the festive season.

She had been in Greenwich just twelve months, and an eventful year it had been. Freddie was eighteen months old and walking everywhere on his sturdy little legs, while Vida at seven was growing prettier every day, and so much like her father that sometimes the likeness caught at Hetty's throat. She still worked up at the Harding house, although sometimes she wondered how long it would go on, for there had been talk of them moving away to a warmer clime which would be beneficial to Mrs Harding's health. Henry Harding was due to retire and leave the business in the hands of his two sons.

Hetty spent more time in the shop, usually in the afternoons, and this way she got to know more and more people. Its was surprising that some of Pop's best customers were from the big houses on the heath, ever anxious to find a bargain. Sometimes they were lucky, but not often. The stock mainly consisted of ugly Victorian furniture that young people threw out when parents died.

She had discovered, quite by chance, that Mr Harding owned quite a lot of property in the district, not the least of which were several shops, one of them being Oliver James' antique shop. One day, clearing out some of Pop Collins' boxes, she discovered a vase whose obvious quality made her realise that she had a find. It was similar, if not the twin, to one Mr Harding had in his china room. She washed it carefully, and the next morning took it with her to show him.

She had seen the mark, Royal Worcester, and saw that it was signed "Freeman," while the glorious colours of the painted fruit took her breath away.

Mr Harding recognised it at once. "Hetty," he said, "you're a marvel." And he squinted at it through his magnifying glass. "And not a chip on it, nor a crack, I do believe. Is it for sale?"

"I expect so," she said. "I'll ask Mr Collins, but I'm sure he'll agree."

"You're not going to carry it back again in that pram, are you?" he laughed, his merry brown eyes twinkling.

She smiled. "All right, it will be safer with you. He knows where it is."

Pop had made quite a bit of money on that, and had given her some. He had never enjoyed life as much as since Hetty came to live in his house. She was the best thing that had ever happened to him, and he blessed the day that she had stood there, facing him squarely in her dignified way, and he hadn't had the guts to turn her away.

Now she kept the place clean and helped in the shop, and as for her cooking . . . It was out of this world. No wonder they said Yorkshire cooking was the best. And if he was honest, he had a soft spot for the kiddies, especially the little lad. Having no children of his own, they were special to him in his old age. He wasn't quite at ease with the little girl, but the boy . . .

One day, when she called in at Oliver James' shop, Hetty was met by a pair of quizzical grey eyes. "So you've set up in competition with me, have you?"

Hetty looked puzzled.

"Mr Harding showed me the exquisite Worcester vase he bought from you. You didn't bring it to me," he chided with mock severity.

Hetty blushed. "Well, I knew Mr Harding had the other one," she said.

Oliver laughed. "My dear, that's good business! I didn't mean it, you mustn't mind me."

He looked down at Freddie who stood beside Hetty holding her hand. "My word, but he's growing a big boy, isn't he?"

Freddie rewarded him with a delightful smile, at which Oliver rummaged in his drawer and came up with a small silver teaspoon. He eyed it through his eyeglass. "London, seventeen fifty-eight," he said. "English silver, hallmarked. This is for you. It will be worth something one day."

Freddie took it and regarded it.

"Say thank you" Hetty urged.

He made an effort and smiled at Oliver, holding tight on to the spoon. When she tucked him in his pram, he was still gripping it, and when he got home insisted on using it to spoon up the apple puree she had made for his tea.

When he was in bed, Hetty took it and put it away safely in a drawer. He would appreciate that when he was older.

She began to plan for Christmas and went out into the yard to find the tiny foot-high Christmas tree which she had bought last year. She had watered it every week and saw that it had even grown a few inches.

She pulled open the drawer at the front of the wardrobe which contained all her personal possessions. She opened the shoebox and took out the few faded photographs. Here was her mother, standing outside the cottage with Hetty and her brothers and sisters, then herself on her wedding day. She sat back on her heels. She couldn't think why she kept that. Perhaps the thought that one day Vida would ask questions about her father. How handsome Jack looked then in his unaccustomed suit. herself in a white wedding dress with a wreath of orange blossom in her hair. Here was a pair of Freddie's baby shoes, the pair he had worn when they first came to London, yellowing now. And in an envelope, wrapped in tissue paper, was her engagement ring with the seed pearls. "Unlucky" Mam had said. The tears sprang to her eyes and she brushed them away angrily. She had got over that, put the past behind her. No one here knew where she came from or who the father of her two children was, not even Min Vincent, her closest friend.

She opened the envelope containing Vida's christening certificate with its blue and gold decoration. St Luke's Church, Barnsdale, nineteen twenty-three – how long ago it seemed.

She replace the contents of the box and closed the drawer. She must put her house in order. Preying on her mind was the long overdue letter to her sister Dora. It hadn't mattered much about the others, but Dora was special. Bad enough that she had left Barnsdale the way she had, no matter her strong reasons at the time. Now, a year later, it didn't seem to matter that much if Dora knew her whereabouts. A lot of water had passed under the bridge since then. Today she would buy a Christmas card, a pretty one with robins and holly and mistletoe – Dora would like that – and send her the long awaited letter.

Holding the tiny Christmas tree and the Christmas fairy, she made her way to the kitchen, Vida would be so excited to see it when she came home from school, and would love to decorate it.

That night, after the children were in bed, she sat down at the plush-covered kitchen table, a very white sheet of paper in front of her, and began to write, slowly and thoughtfully.

21, Queen's Row
Greenwich
London, S.E.10

Dear Dora,

I know it will come as a shock to you after all this time to receive a letter from me. As you will see from the above address, I am living in London where I have been all this time. When I left home I only knew I had to get away, and I am sure you can guess the reason. I didn't want Jack to find me, and I thought if you knew he might become violent and force you to tell. I knew in my heart that I had to make a fresh start where no one knew me, and I have never regretted it – although I have sorely missed you at times. I shall always be a Yorkshire lass at heart.

I often wonder how you are – all the family, and the boys – they must be growing up. Vida is six, she will be seven in March, and Freddie is eighteen months and walking!

No one here knows anything about me, they just take you as you are – not like a village where everyone knows your business. A kind old gentleman who has a shop took me in as a sort of housekeeper, and I work up at a big house most mornings and sometimes help in the shop. There is always plenty to do.

130

I would love to see you again, Dora, but I don't know when that would be. Perhaps one day you will come to London to see me. You and yours are always welcome.

It's a bit late now to say I am sorry for the worry I caused you, but I am, just the same. You can always write to me at the above address if you want to. Love to everybody.

Your loving sister,
Hetty

P.S. I forget to tell you – I took Mam's maiden name, and I'm Mrs Keane. Please don't tell anyone about this.

Dora would understand what she meant, she thought, and blotting the letter, read it through a mist of tears. Oh, why hadn't she done this before – she had been so unkind to Dora who had only ever helped her when she could. She sighed, and slipped the letter with the Christmas card inside the envelope, sealing it down. There, that was done, and about time too. She felt as if a great weight had been lifted from her heart. She posted it on Saturday morning in the bright red pillar box on the corner of Nelson Street.

"What's G.R. mean, Mummy?" asked Vida, looking at the embossed lettering below the time table.

"George Rex," Hetty said. "It means King George – our King, because all the letters and parcels that are sent through the post are Royal Mail, under the protection of the King."

"Oh." Vida was impressed. She had a mental picture of a rosy-faced king in a scarlet cloak with white fur and wearing a golden crown, beding down to unlock the pillar box and taking out the letters.

"Who were you writing to?" she asked as Hetty continued along to the market.

"Your Auntie Dora," Hetty said. "I don't expect you remember her."

"Yes, I do," Vida said. "A fat lady. She was nice – she used to cuddle me."

"Fancy you remembering her," Hetty said thoughtfully. It was a long time since Vida had mentioned her father. What else did she remember?

When the postman slid the letter through the letter box,

Dora walked slowly to the front door. She was a large woman, much like her mother had been, and suffered acutely with weight problems, but that had never prevented her from being cheerful. It took a great deal to upset her sunny disposition.

With difficulty she bent down to pick up the letter, and seeing the Londn postmark, her curiousity knew no bounds. Then the handwriting – and her heart began to beat faster. Surely this was little Hetty's writing? She walked back into the kitchen to get her breath, tearing the envelope in her haste to find what was inside. It couldn't be – after all this time – but it was. A Christmas card and a letter. She began to read avidly, line after line, until when it was finished, she went back to the beginning again and read it through once more. Her eyes were wet with tears, and she dabbed them with her apron. Fancy, after all this time . . . But Hetty was safe and well, and the two children. Fancy, the baby eighteen months and walking and little Vida nearly seven. Who said there wasn't a God above?

Dora sniffed and put on the kettle for a cup of tea. There was nothing like a cup of tea to pull you round. Then she sat down, she felt quite shaky, and read the letter again, absorbing everything until she almost knew it by heart. She couldn't wait for Tom to come home, and she must write to the others and let them know, and answer Hetty's letter straight away. She made the tea and let it brew, then poured herself a strong cup and sipped it while it was piping hot. Nowadays she thought of Hetty every so often, but as time passed memories of that awful time diminished in their intensity. It was true, she thought, time heals. Now she re-lived the events leading to Hetty's sudden flight to London and thought what pluck she had had. With two small children, Dora herself never could have done it.

She would wait until Tom came in, though, best to ask him what he thought she should do about the newspaper cutting she had kept since last August. Getting up, she went to the mantelpiece, where from under a large black vase painted with vivid exotic flowers she took a yellowing scrap of newspaper. She opened it to read once again the report of what she imagined to be Jack Maclaren's death. She had seen it quite by chance in the *Yorkshire Post*, a report of the inquest held on John, otherwise Jack, Maclaren, who had been run down by a car in a village just outside Leeds. He was aged thirty-two, which would have been about right, and owned a small shop in the village of Farmoor End near Leeds. Evidence was given that he was drunk at the time and a verdict of Accidental Death was recorded by the coroner.

Dora sighed, and put the scrap of paper back in its place. Hetty would have to know, it was only right, and if she wanted to investigate further it was up to her.

"Best news you could send her," Tom said when he came in and read Hetty's letter.

"Oh, don't say that, Tom! Poor man – I wouldn't have wished that on anyone."

"I daresay," Tom said, "but he was a drunk, and she did well to leave him when she did. Mind you, I still think she could have told you. But it'll give her a chance to start again, as a widow. She might even marry again or come back up here."

Dora looked up hopefully. "Oh, Tom, do you think she might?"

"You never know," he said, sitting back in his Windsor chair and lighting his pipe. "You never know, Dora."

When the postman arrived with Dora's letter on Friday, Hetty's heart leapt with excitement. She put the letter in her apron pocket to savour after breakfast. Freddie sat in his high chair while Vida fed him spoonsful of porridge, her own breakfast of a boiled egg finished, the empty shell placed upside down so that it looked uneaten.

Freddie's eyes watched Vida roguishly as he waited for the next mouthful, and he made faces at her and reached out to grab her hand.

"Come on – last one," Vida said, scraping the bowl, "then you can have some toast."

"Toast," said Freddie, "and 'made."

"Marmalade if you're a good boy," Vida said. "Are you a good boy?"

He nodded his head vigorously.

"Right, then," Vida said as she spread the home-made marmalade over the toast. "Here you are."

Hetty came in from the scullery and looked at Vida's plate. "Oh, you didn't eat your egg!" she said reproachfully, and Vida, eyes down, joined in the game.

"No, I wasn't hungry."

Hetty went to the table and turned the egg over, pretending shocked surprise. "Oh, you rascal – it's empty!"

Both children joined in the laughter that followed.

"Now get your satchel and your coat – Mrs Vincent will be here in a moment." They sometimes shared the school walk, which was only five minutes away.

When they had gone, she put Freddie in his playpen and settled down to read the letter, savouring every word, and discarding for the moment the enclosed news cutting. As she read on, her face paled. She smoothed open the cutting and read, then buried her face in her hands, the tears falling unbidden and despite herself, sobs shaking her, from pity and shock and sorrow – and a kind of relief. Poor Jack.

She got up and splashed water over her tear-stained face. It was the last news she had expected. The joy of hearing from Dora was quite overshadowed by the sad news the letter contained. For Jack to die so young . . . All her fear and disgust at him paled into insignificance. She could only remember the good times: Jack as a handsome young lover, his recklessness, his wonderful eyes and brilliant smile.

Freddie looked up at her and she smiled at him. He mustn't see that she had been crying.

She began to wash the dishes, worrying as she did so. Vida would have to be told, and Hetty dreaded it. Her eyes clouded over.

Suddenly she was still, staring out into the yard.

I am a widow, she thought. No need for any more deception. I am a widow.

Chapter Seventeen

"This is a beautiful spot, Henry," Laura Harding said to her husband as he sat in a cane chair in the garden of their home in Cornwall. In the distance foam-lapped waves splashed into a little sandy cove. Palm trees and cordylines lent an air of exotic splendour to the well laid out gardens, with roses in full bloom, and geraniums and petunias vying with each other for pride of place.

"Everything is so far ahead down here," she said, "and it is wonderful to feel the sun on my creaking limbs."

"That's the point of it, my dear," Henry Harding said.

He had brought this house over a year ago, for retirement and for his wife's failing health in order that they could escape from the harsh winters in London and enjoy long summer vacations. This was their second visit, and the more they went down to Cornwall, the more they liked it. He would himself have preferred to buy something abroad, in Italy perhaps or France, but Laura had a strong aversion to travelling and Cornwall was the farthest place from London she could consider.

He put a hand over hers. "As long as you are happy, my dear," he said. "I have to say it is a lovely spot, and I think we were lucky to find it."

Laura Harding lay back and closed her eyes. "I can imagine getting so used to it down here that I won't want to come home," she teased.

"Yes, you will," he said. "You wouldn't like being down here on your own. And until the boys are ready to take over, I shall have to put in an appearance at the office occasionally – these things take time."

"Of course, Henry." She was silent for a few minutes. "I've been thinking . . . about Hetty Keane. You know, while we are away down here she won't be necessary. And it occured to me – "

"Yes?"

"Well, she's going to miss the money."

"Oh, she'll find another job. Still, I know what you mean. She's a nice little thing – and wasted, I always think, on house-cleaning."

"That's exactly what I thought," Laura said eagerly, determined to strike while the iron was hot.

"What did you have in mind?" Henry asked, for he knew something was coming.

"I wondered whether Oliver would be prepared for her to work in the shop sometimes – you know, for experience – it would be good for her. And as you say, she is quite a good judge of antiques."

Henry Harding was thoughtful. He never liked to give an answer until he was sure of his facts.

"Yes," he said slowly, "I agree with you. If Oliver is agreeable, I can see Hetty being very useful to him."

"The first thing is to get him to agree. I feel responsible for Hetty somehow. with those two darling children. Life hasn't been very kind to her. Sometimes, Henry . . ." she glanced at him shyly ". . . I wish they were my grandchildren."

"Oh, the boys will start families when they are ready," he said. "I don't know what's the matter with young women today that they don't want babies as soon as they are married. All they think about is tennis parties and bridge and gadding about the countryside in sports cars – to say nothing of night clubs."

"They're nice girls, though, Henry," Laura said.

"Oh, they're nice girls," he agreed, and was silent for a moment. "I'll have a word with Oliver," he said at length.

"Thank you, Henry." And having got what she wanted, Laura closed her eyes against the sun.

Hetty stood in front of her latest acquisition, a cheval mirror which stood in her bedroom in all its glory. Early Victorian, it was painted a greeny-grey and decorated with stylised flowers, and Hetty had fallen in love with it when Pop Collins brought it home.

"Five bob to you," he said, although he would have given it to her gladly, but knew how independent she was.

It was so long since she had had a new dress, that Hetty stood entranced, looking at herself in the mirror. It was a straight dress, reaching just below the knee, with a round neckline and short sleeves. It was in palest pink silk, which suited her dark colouring, and she couldn't imagine when she was going to wear it. True, it was only new to her, not new from a shop. She had bought it at the local Greyladies jumble sale for the church, as well as a few items for the children. The clothes were hardly worn and looked expensive and she couldn't resist the dress. Two shillings was a lot of money, but it was the prettiest dress she had ever seen, and even if she didn't wear it, it was lovely to hand in the wardrobe. You never knew. Sometime in the future she might just wear a dress like this. She so seldom indulged herself that she felt quite guilty. It looked new, anyway, and she turned to the label: Molyneux. It meant nothing. Still, it really was pretty. She put it on a hanger and covered it with a pillow slip – she had more than an ample store of linen, for Pop Collins bought it up by the cartload, and the good pieces she washed and ironed until they looked like new. In the big old wardrobe she had a store of embroidered linen sheets, lace-edged pillow slips, to say nothing of finely worked table cloths.

Which reminded her . . . she must lay the table for little Freddie's birthday party. He was having three of his friends to tea for his birthday, and Hetty had made a cake. It sat on the dresser with three white candles waiting to be lit.

Freddie was outside in the yard on this lovely June day, watching Pop Collins grooming the horse, who though old, was still able to do his job. Pop had found a three-wheeled tricycle for him, which after cleaning and painting looked like new. There was nothing Pop would not have done for the little lad.

Hetty busied herself until Vida came in from school, she was eight now and such a help around the house. She and Helen were as different as chalk from cheese. Helen, an

137

extrovert, never stopped talking, saying the first thing that came into her head.

Vida was different. She was quiet and reticent with strangers, and Hetty sometimes wondered how much she remembered of her life in Barnsdale, and whether she had overheard any of those scenes when Jack had arrived home the worse for drink; if she had ever been aware of the real reason for Hetty's bruises, whether she known that Jack laid out with his fists when drunk, and the real reason behind their flight to London.

One day, if she does know, Hetty thought, it will come out.

Hetty waited until Tom had verified Jack's death before telling Vida, but once she received legal confirmation, had wasted no time telling her that her father had died as a result of an accident. Vida's lovely eyes remained on hers until she finished, then she had turned away.

"May I go and play?" she asked, and that was that, leaving Hetty to wonder what thoughts were going on in her daughter's pretty little head.

Hetty changed into her navy and white dress, ready to receive the small visitors, and sat in the window sewing until Vida came home, her thoughts full of the future. She was twenty-seven and it was high time she got on with her life. When Freddie was three, he would go to morning school from nine until twelve, which would make life easier.

One morning, Mrs Harding called Hetty into the library. The elderly lady was in a wheelchair, and sat facing the garden, looking out at the roses that grew beneath the window.

"Come in, my dear," she called, hearing Hetty's knock on the door. "Sit down. I want to have a talk with you."

She had grown fond of Hetty in the time she had been at Granville Place, and often asked her to bring in little Freddie to see her. She thought he was a lovely child, as indeed was the little girl, who was going to be a real beauty when she grew up. Often, with time on her hands, she sat and thought about Hetty and her children, and felt certain that there was a story there, a mystery to this young woman who worked with dignity and a quiet resolve. But it was none of her business. Now she smiled at Hetty.

"Now that we are going to be away so much," she said, "Mrs Gooderson tells me you are only going to do one morning a week while we are in Cornwall."

"Yes, Mrs Harding."

"Have you found other morning employment?" she asked. "I know as a widow with young children you must need to replace the wages you receive here."

"I haven't yet," Hetty answered, "but I will – as soon as Freddie starts morning school which will be in September."

"Well," Mrs Harding went on, "my husband and I have had an idea. He had a word with Mr James who runs the antique shop in the village – he is an old friend of ours – and suggested that you might like to work for him in the shop on the mornings you don't come here."

Hetty's eyes were shining with excitement. "Do you mean it – to work in the shop?"

"Yes, as I say, we talked to him and he thought it was an excellent idea – if you would like to do it. He will pay the same wages and the hours would be the same, but the work would be more congenial, my dear. More importantly, you would be learning and gaining experience. I know you are interested in antiques, and I thought – "

"Oh, Mrs Harding, that would be wonderful! I should love it – to work in a shop like Mr James! Of course, I do help Pop Collins sometimes, but it's not exactly the same thing."

"No, so I gathered" Mrs Harding smiled. How wonderful to be the age of this young woman, and to see the enthusiasm on her pretty face – it was time life was a bit kinder to her.

"As long as you don't entirely desert us," she chided. "We don't want to lose touch with you. You have been such a help to Mrs Gooderson.

"I like working here," Hetty said. "There are so many lovely things."

"You may thank my husband for that," Mrs Harding said. "Now run along, and tell Mrs Gooderson I am ready for my morning coffee. I think I'll have a cold drink as well this morning, and before you go, Hetty, you might open these French windows for me. I am going to sit in the garden for a while."

Hetty walked home that day delighted with the turn of

events. Who would have thought it? That she, Hetty Jessops, would be working in such a lovely shop as Oliver James'? This would be something to write to Dora about.

When the three small boys arrived for tea, Hetty and Vida set about keeping them occupied. They played in the yard for a time, each of them fascinated by Barney, whose head appeared over the stable door. Then there was tea with cakes and jelly, and the cake whose candles were blown out by Freddie with much help from Vida and Hetty.

Hetty was surprised when a knock came at the door and Pop Collins stood there, his baby-like pink skin scrubbed clean, his white hair silvery in the light as he stood with his cap in hand.

"Come in, Pop," she cried. "Freddie's having a birthday party."

He entered the room gingerly. It was clear he felt he was intruding. Freddie's eyes lit up. He simply adored the old man. "'appy birthday, son," Pop said awkwardly, and from behind his back brought out a cardboard box. It contained a shiny locomotive and three carriages, and Freddie was beside himself with excitement.

"Pop, Pop!" he yelled. "Is it for me?" For my birthday?"

Pop nodded, pleased as punch.

Hetty looked at the old man. The train set was new. He must have gone out and bought it. A lump came to her throat.

"That's very kind of you, Pop," she said. "It's beautiful. What a wonderful thing for a boy to have."

Pop Collins looked pleased. "Well," he said, and turned away.

"What do you say to Pop?" Hetty asked Freddie.

For answer, the boy ran to Pop and threw his arms round the old man's knees.

"'Ere," Pop said, embarrassed, and trying to keep his balance, and in a flash Freddie was sitting on the floor surrounded by three admiring and envious small boys.

"I'll be off then," Pop said, but Hetty called him back.

"Sit down," she said. "It's your turn for a piece of cake."

Not long after that, when she was helping him in the shop one day, the old man looked at her long and hard. He had never, in all the time she had been there, questioned her as to her background or where she came from.

"Come from up North, don'tcher?" he asked now.

Hetty was surprised.

"Me?" she said. "Yes, Yorkshire." She no longer minded answering questions about her past.

"Widow, are yer?" And Hetty, flushing to the roots of her hair, nodded. "Yes."

He said nothing for a while, until she, as honest as the day was long, felt constrained to speak. "I wasn't always," she said. "My husband died last year. He was killed in a road accident."

He nodded, as if she had confirmed what he had already suspected.

"Left, 'im, didjer?"

She nodded, "Yes."

"You got some pluck."

He continued to sit, staring in front of him, until Hetty got up, and as she passed him, patted his hand. She had grown so fond of him, he was like a grandfather. It had indeed been a lucky day when she knocked at his door.

After the summer holidays, the days settled into a pattern, with Freddie at morning school, and Hetty either working at Granville Place or in Oliver James' shop. There was no need to ask her which she preferred. Every day in the shop was a delight, and as the weeks flew by and she became more and more experienced, Oliver was more disposed to leave her alone in charge of it.

This was something Hetty liked best of all. To be in charge, to dust and arrange the objets d'art, to shine the mirrors and straighten a picture. To welcome a customer, to help him choose, to air her knowledge which was growing every day she was there. Sometimes she sat and daydreamed in the large wing chair behind the big mahogany desk. She was always sorry when the session came to end, although she looked forward to seeing the children after school.

When Christmas came round that year she wrote as she did every few weeks to Dora, telling her all about the job and how much she liked it. How the children were growing and about her life in London.

That Christmas Dora wrote back to say that her eldest boy, Charlie, had started work at the local farm, and that she was

141

enclosing a picture of David Ogilby and his new bride which had appeared in the local paper.

Hetty felt her heart turn over at sight of the picture.

Mr David Ogilby, of Alderbourne Grange, Barnsdale, and his bride, Miss Dorothy Arlington, from Vermont, New England, after their wedding on Saturday at St Luke's church, Barnsdale. The couple met . . .

Hetty put the paper down, staring unseeing for a few moments, then picked up Dora's letter.

Lovely girl, isn't she? I knew you would be interested to see it. I remember you and David as children – you got on so well together. He came here after you left, asking about you. Of course, I said I didn't know where you were, but wasn't that kind of him? They were a nice family. Pity that the mother died suddenly one day last year. I tell you who else died – old Sarah . . .

Hetty sat lost in thought. She was pleased for David, very pleased, and the girl looked nice. She hoped they would be happy. It was all for the best. Imagine David coming to ask after her, proof that she was right not to let anyone know where she was. Another chapter in her life had closed as it had with the death of Jack Maclaren.

She brushed away the memories. No good came of indulging in those. She had to get on with her life and that of her children.

142

Chapter Eighteen

As Hetty gained more experience in Oliver James' shop, so she grew more confident. She bore little resemblance to the girl who had arrived in Greenwich almost five years before. With Freddie starting day school in September, and Vida almost nine years old, she was filled with a consuming desire to get away from Queen's Row and all that life there entailed. Despite her fondness for old Pop Collins, she knew he could not go on forever. He was ageing fast and although she had never known how old he was, she suspected that he must be in his eighties. Barney the old horse had died the previous year, and Pop had not replaced him. It seemed to Hetty that from that time Pop deteriorated, as if a lot of his reason for living had gone, and he called on Billy Webb more than ever for assistance.

Her loyalty to the old man was strong, yet she knew she had the children to think about, and the more she saw of life in Blackheath, the more she realised that she wanted better surroundings for them. Somehow or other she was going to get them.

Her feelings were compounded by the news that the whole of the area in that part of Greenwich was to be demolished. "By the end of the 1930's it will all be gone." they said, "to give way to gracious walks, new housing schemes. The area has long been a black mark on London's landscape . . ."

Well, parts of it were, Hetty had to agree. She had never imagined that such places existed, or that people could live in such poverty in such mean dark streets, in hovels infested with rats. But it was a city and very old, some of the streets had been there since Elizabethan times.

143

Hetty knew she must get out and the sooner the better. Nowadays, especially in the summer, she felt stifled in the heat, and longed to get out and walk in Greenwich Park, to wander round the rose gardens with the children, to take them to the Observatory, to sit on the plateau and look down over the river and the view. Sometimes they walked on the heath itself, where harebells grew beneath their feet, and Freddie sailed his boat on the Prince of Wales pond.

Sitting in the shop, she was writing a letter to Dora, taking advantage of the quiet afternoon. Oliver was at an auction in town, and there were few customers. A gentleman who wished to dispose of a collection of snuff boxes – she knew Oliver would be pleased to hear that – and a lady who purchased a delicate porcelain teapot.

Now she continued her letter to Dora, and sat immersed in memories of Barnsdale, seeing her sister and the children and the little High Street, and Tom, and Mam . . . She read her letter through, then took out the photograph of the children, the first one she had taken on the new Brownie camera she had bought for Vida's birthday. How pleased Dora would be to see it, she thought. She bit her lip, looking at Freddie in the picture, for his likeness to David Ogilby was unmistakable to her, his fair good looks just like his father's. She smiled wistfully. Only I would recognise that, she thought, and slipping it inside the envelope, sealed it down.

On a warm sunny day in September, Hetty's letter arrived in Barnsdale, and Dora picked it up from the doormat and tore it open where she stood. A photograph! She scanned it avidly. Oh, what a pretty girl Vida was and how like her father, while the boy – how fair he was beside Vida, as sturdy as a young tree. She sat down with a brew of tea. A handsome lad not in the least like his father, but by heckie young Vida was! The same eyes and eyebrows, that dark, curly hair.

She opened the letter and read it. Hetty – working in an antique shop! Well, good for her! She was a cut above housework, she had always been the prettiest one in the family, the most ladylike – she might even have a shop of her own one day. Dora returned to the photograph. Taken at the top of some steps, the children looking into the camera. There was no sign of a garden – perhaps it was the front of the house? A puzzled look came over her face. The boy reminded her of someone, but she couldn't think who.

She folded the letter and put it back in the envelope, gave the photograph one last look and put it one the mantelpiece for Tom to see.

She was at the sink, her arms covered in suds washing the boys' jerseys, when she stopped suddenly and stared out into the garden, unseeing. The boy, Freddie – it came to her now. He was the spitting image of David Ogilby at that age! She moved slowly from the scullery into the kitchen and sank down into a chair, her heart beating fast. She knew she was right. She picked up the letter and examined the photograph again. With a sudden thought, she lifted down the box from the top of the dresser where she kept odds and ends, and raking through a few things discovered what she was looking for. From a brown envelope she took an old photograph, sepia-coloured, a group of the family outside the cottage they had lived in at Alderbourne Grange. It was the only photograph they had ever had taken. There they all were: Mam, Father, two of her brothers, her sister Eva, herself – she must have been all of thirteen there – and young Hetty aged about eight. She was sitting on the ground in front of the standing group, one hand on the dog's head – while next to her was David Ogilby. Dora's heart began to pound. It could have been Hetty's son, little Freddie. She put the photographs alongside each other. It stood out a mile – the boy was the image of him. She could see him now, playing with young Hetty – and she buried her face in her hands. Oh, Hetty! She had never dreamt, never imagined. And Jack Maclaren – had he known? Was that the reason he beat her? Because if it was, she deserved it.

She sank down into a chair. And yet, she knew Hetty like the back of her hand. She couldn't have been carrying on with young David Ogilby – when could she have found the time? He never could have visited the house without someone seeing him. Her face flushed with colour at the shame of it all. Oh, Hetty! All these years, and I never guessed. And there was no one else she could ask. Tom never knew any of the Ogilby family.

She made herself a strong pot of tea, and sipped it slowly,

feeling the strength coming back into her as she re-lived those dark weeks after Hetty's departure and the memories came flooding back. After Hetty had gone, David Ogilby called at the house and asked after her! No wonder he wanted to know where she had gone. Had he known . . . but then if she recalled aright, he had said he had been abroad for a long time. Flushed now and thoroughly uncomfortable, she got up and went back to her washing. She would put the whole thing behind her. Poor Hetty, what she must have gone through. No wonder she ran away. Yes, after telling Tom, they must forget all about it. No good came of re-hashing old wounds.

But she thought of David Ogilby throughout the rest of that day, and when Tom came in handed him Hetty's letter together with the photograph.

He studied it. "They're bonnie children," he said admiringly. "Don't seem as if they've gone hungry – look at this young fella." He turned to Dora, seeing the grim look on her face. "What's wrong?"

"Look at yon lad," she said, pointing to Hetty's picture. "And now look at this."

She gave him the other picture, stabbing her finger towards David Ogilby. "Look," she said. "Can't you see?"

Gradually his face darkened, and he stared down into the fire. "So that's what it was," he said softly. He looked up into Dora's stricken face. "Now listen to me," he said. "Not a word, You're not to mention this to Hetty or anyone, you get me?"

She nodded miserably.

"You don't know," he said. "You know nothing."

It seemed a long time before Hetty heard from Dora, who usually answered quickly, and when the letter finally came, it was something of a disappointment. It was short, Dora simply thanking Hetty for the "lovely photograph" without even mentioning the children at all. Hetty put the letter away, feeling that something was missing. But she had little time to brood for events took over.

Pop Collins had walked that morning to Ship Dock, to see his friend, David Noakes, who ran a coal depot and a hay and straw business. He had always bought Barney's hay and straw from Noakes, their friendship was of long standing. Sometimes they talked of Noakes' slide projector, the

"Noakesascope", and his successful magic lantern shows at the Albert Hall. Noakes was old now, like Pop himself. Sometimes they watched the skiff owners dredging coal from the river which had been dropped by barges, selling the sacks at one and eightpence a time. Sometimes they walked along the water's edge, smelling and savouring the sights and sounds of the river.

Pop hadn't done this walk for a long time, and Hetty was a little concerned for him, since he had been tired lately and not himself. When he returned, she insisted that he get to bed early after she had given him some hot broth.

It was in the morning that she knew something was wrong, for he was usually up and about by seven o'clock, even in these last few months when he had not been himself. At eight o'clock she took him a cup of tea, climbing the stairs and knocking on his door. When there was no reply, she opened the door fearfully, half knowing what she would find.

He was in bed, his blue eyes turned sightlessly to the ceiling one hand caught in his nightshirt at his chest, as though he might have struggled for breath. Hetty sank to her knees and wept. If he had called out, she would not have heard him in the basement. She touched his forehead. He was ice cold, and must have been dead for some hours. She dried her tears and sent for the doctor.

He had died of heart failure, and the doctor said there was nothing she could have done. Pop Collins was eighty-six and had had a good life. Hetty was astonished that he was such an age. He had been so active until a year ago. After his death, there was much to do.

First there was the confrontation with the landlord, for she paid her rent to Pop Collins who in turn paid the landlord every Monday. She just hoped that he didn't turn her out before she had put her house in order.

After the funeral, she began to clear away the contents of Pop's flat, and it was there, in Pop's private tin box, that she found the will. Handwritten and witnessed by Mr Noakes, in it Pop left everything to Mrs Hetty Keane. Her eyes filled with tears. She had ample cause to be grateful to the old man; people who thought he was an ogre would have been surprised to learn the truth about his kindness and generosity.

147

"Well?" The landlord asked her, a squat, round man who live in a small modest house in another part of Greenwich, but who owned half of Queen's Row. "Do you want to keep the shop on – and the rest of the house? He rented it all, you know, from the basement to the top floor, though I believe it's mostly empty."

"Yes, it is." Hetty said.

"Perhaps you'd like to move up into Mr Collins' flat – it's better than the one you've got."

Some time ago Hetty would have done just that, but now her ideas had changed. There was no point in moving upstairs – she wanted to move out altogether, but not yet. Not until she had found somewhere else to live, something she could afford. At one time, the renting of the shop would have been attractive, but now she knew that she would never get on in life if she stayed in this area. Besides, who knew how long these places would stand? They would probably pull them down before long.

"I don't want the shop, Mr Ferris," she said, "but I'd like to stay on in the basement for a while. I shall be moving away shortly."

"I see," he said. She was certainly not like most of the residents in this area. Smart, well-spoken – and the neighbours had told him that the old man had left her the contents of his flat and shop. Well, he didn't imagine that would amount to much.

"I can let it easily," he told her, "I've a waiting list for these places."

"I am sure you have," Hetty said, confident now that at least she had security of tenure, for a time at least.

She got Billy Webb in to help her, and had a sale. Everything was sold off at half price or less, and the local people flocked to find a bargain. In no time the shop was empty, with Billy carrying the furniture around to the purchasers. She didn't know how she would have managed without him. When the shop was empty, she whitened the windows and swept the floor, dusted and cleaned and locked the door. Then she tackled the flat.

The things she loved the most were the beautiful lustres which had stood on either side of the mantelpiece in Pop's tiny bedroom, and she recalled the day when she arrived and he had told her she could feed the baby quietly in there. She had sat looking at them, the way the gas light had flickered and send myriads of brilliant colours round the room. They had always fascinated her. But now she found other things, small treasures he had collected over the years, some worthless, some valuable. She stacked and stored them away for the future. She got rid of his bed and the old deal kitchen table and chairs, and the wardrobe which had stood in his bedroom. It was while she was clearing that out that she found the box. A shoe box, and inside it a hoard of golden sovereigns – nearly two hundred of them. The flush spread from her cheeks to her neck. Two hundred pounds – it was a fortune. She was rich.

"My word." Min Vincent said when she brought Vida home from school. "You've had a clearout." She surveyed Pop's empty flat. "It must have been in a state – I should think he had collected things from way back."

"Yes. I have to give the key to the landlord when he comes on Monday."

"What will you do, Hetty? Move up here? I don't know how you've stuck it in the basement all this time."

"No, I don't think so, Min. I'm going to try to find something nearer the shop."

"What? Blackheath, you mean? That'll cost you a bit, won't it?"

I don't know until I look around," Hetty said. "Anyway, I shall try."

"Yes, well," Min said grudgingly, "I hope you don't move too far away from us – Helen would be broken hearted if Vida left the school."

"We'll see," Hetty said.

The following week, when everything was finished, the rooms and the shop empty, she spoke to Oliver about her problem.

"Yes, I can see you want to get away from there," he said in his practical way. "Now that he old man has gone, you are free." He was thoughtful. "Well, as a matter of fact, I do know of something. It's in Blaize Park, a ground floor flat of three rooms and kitchen in a large Victorian house with a bit of garden, at the top of village, only two or three minutes' walk from here."

"Oh, Mr James, really? Do you think – "

"I wish you'd call me Oliver, Hetty," he said. "After all, if we're going to be neighbours . . ."

"Neighbours?"

"I live next door but one, that's how I know the flat's going. The people are going abroad."

"When could I see it?" she asked.

"No time like the present," Oliver said. "Pop round now. Go on – it's a Mrs Daly. You'll like her."

Hetty put on her coat, and her best hat bought in Glover's.

"Thanks, Oliver," she said, and her face flushed with suppressed excitement, made her way down into the village and up the other side towards Blaize Park.

On the way she thought hard. Now that she was about to start a new life, she had best put some things straight. Like her real name. No need to hide it now. In the future the children might need their birth certificate or even she her marriage lines – you never knew. The time had come for honesty and truth. She would explain to Oliver what she had done, but he wouldn't mind. Keane or Maclaren, it would be all the same to him.

When she arrived at the semi-detached Victorian house with its small green lawn and laurel bushes, its solitary laburnam tree, the porch with its pitched roof and black and white tiled floor, she knew that unless it was simpy dreadful inside, or the rent was too high, she would take it. It was everything she had ever dreamed of.

The middle-aged woman who opened the door gave her a welcoming smile.

"Good afternoon," Hetty said, and explained the purpose of her visit.

"Do come in," the woman said. "What is your name?"

"Maclaren," she said. Mrs Hetty Maclaren."

Chapter Nineteen

When Hetty left the shop in order to find new accommodation, Oliver sat, with his elbows on the desk and his fingertips pressed together, thinking hard. Why on earth had he recommended Hetty to the flat so near to his? Wasn't he making things harder for himself?

For he knew now, without a shadow of a doubt, that he loved her. It had been growing since that very first day when she had arrived at the shop, her pretty face flushed with excitement at the prospect of what she was about to do, her warm brown eyes looking expectantly into his. The way she looked at the boy, her smile . . . he had been drawn to her even then.

It was all a nonsense, he told himself, but from that first meeting he had hardly been able to get her out of his mind, and when she came to work in the shop it made things even more difficult. Not for her, of course. She was so wrapped up in the shop and her enthusiasm, to say nothing of the love she obviously bore her children, what room could there be for an old soldier like himself – a man with a limp?

He had been eighteen when he went into the army straight from his OTC, the year that the war ended. He had received his leg injury on the Western Front in the battle which had seen the end of the war in 1918. As a captain in the Royal Artillery, he received his discharge, and like thousands of others joined the great army of civilians trying to get work.

He had been one of the lucky ones, going to work for his uncle who owned an antiquarian bookshop in Oxford. It was there that he met Isabel, the daughter of an Oxford don, and they had married two years later.

Looking back, they had been happy, but the marriage was of such short duration. Isabel had never been strong – it had been her waif-like appearance, her helplessness which had drawn him to her in the first place. When she had died from meningitis after three years, his grief had been over-whelming. It was then that he decided to branch out on his own, removing himself to Blackheath to begin his life all over again. Always interested in antiques, he had added them to his business interests, and until the arrival of Hetty on the scene, had been content enough as a widower.

Now . . . He took a deep breath. They were both casula-ties, he and Hetty. For there was an element in her that led him to believe that behind the outward appearance was some-thing of a mystery. He knew she was a widow, perhaps she had never got over the death of her husband? Whatever it was, there was something about her that defied the asking of personal questions. He respected that – it was something he disliked himself.

He was thirty-eight years old, approaching forty, perhaps that was why he sometimes fantasized these days about Hetty being part of his life, apart from the shop, where the two children came to him for guidance and advice and he could watch them grow – a ready made family.

He was interrupted by a customer, a woman with a small dog, who had had her eye on a Chinese vase in the window for some time. Presently she pushed open the door and came in.

By the time she was gone, the precious vase now in her pos-session, Hetty had returned, her eyes shining, looking as pleased as punch.

"Oh, Oliver, thank you! The flat is simply lovely! So conve-nient, and Mrs Daly was very nice."

The die is cast, he thought. Now I shall see more of her than ever, and if I am honest, I couldn't be more pleased.

"I'm glad, Hetty," he said. "I had an idea you would like it."

"I should think so!" she laughed. "After Queen's Row, it's like a palace."

A month later she moved in, and was overjoyed to do so. The area was so handy for the shops, and the rent was reason-able for what it was, part of a Victorian house in a prestigious road. Her furniture fitted in well, with space to move about, and the lofty ceilings and decorated plaster work, the marble fireplaces and solid mahogany doors, gave her endless pleasure.

The new home had resulted in the children moving to schools nearby, much to Vida's disappointment, for she missed Helen. But Hetty asked Helen up to play at weekends, which pleased the girls no end.

Working longer hours now for Oliver James, the time had come, Hetty felt, to leave the Harding household, and she had given in her notice. One morning she made her way across the heath to Granville Place.

"Ah, it's you, Hetty," Mrs Gooderson said, as Hetty pushed open the back door and went into the kitchen.

"I thought I'd call in and say goodbye to Mrs Harding," she said, closing the door behind her.

"Oh, she will be sorry to see you go," Mrs Gooderson said, "and so will I." She was sitting down to iron, since her back was giving her so much pain.

"I'll be sorry too – in one way," Hetty said. "I always enjoyed coming here to work. How is Mrs Harding?"

"Not too good." Mrs Gooderson clicked her tongue, and looked up as the indicator bell rang.

"Ah, I expect she saw you coming up the drive, Off you go, Hetty."

She climbed the wide staircase with the beautiful landing window and its stained glass, remembering the day almost five years ago she had first done so. She had thought the house beautiful then, and still did. Past the marble bust at the top of the stairs, and the illuminated cabinet containing oriental china. She tapped on Mrs Harding's door.

"Come in."

Hetty closed the door softly behind her, and Mrs Harding regarded her with sheer pleasure.

What a pretty young woman she was with that soft dark hair gathered into a knot at the back of her head, the brown eyes always so warm and friendly. She was petite and slim and today wore a cream silk blouse and a soft green suit. The neckline of her blouse was fastened with a large cameo brooch – one of her finds, Mrs Harding suspected. Had she but known, it was the only thing left to Hetty by her mother.

153

She reached out a hand and took Hetty's. "My dear, I am so glad you came. Time hangs very heavily sometimes. Sit down. So, you are about to leave us?"

"Yes," Hetty said, "Sadly – I always enjoyed working here – but now . . ."

"My dear, it is time you move on, from your own point of view," Mrs Harding said. "We are very sorry, but you are young, with your whole life in front of you, and I am delighted to hear that you are going to work almost full-time of Oliver James. He is such a nice man. Are you happy in your new home?"

"I can't believe I was lucky enough to find it," Hetty said.

"I'm so glad. I have some news for you, too. We are moving down to Cornwall in September." And Hetty had a sudden sense of loss. It was hard to say goodbye to old friends.

"My husband finally leaves the business in August, and our eldest son John will be coming to live here. They have a baby now, I have a grandson, so of course I am very pleased."

"And you love it down there," Hetty said.

"Yes, I do. We more or less decided during the Munich crisis, thinking, well, if war comes, we shall want to be well away from London. But as luck had it . . ."

"Yes, we all gave a big sigh of relief," Hetty said. "There was talk of evacuating the children down to Wales – but I was so busy that I have to admit I didn't have much time to dwell on it, which perhaps was just as well."

Mrs Harding smiled. "Well, in the event, nothing came of it, and let's hope it stays that way. War is something we can all do without. Now, my dear, you must come down and see us. I really mean it. We should love to see you."

How kind they were, Hetty thought. They had done so much for her since she began to work for them.

"And how are the children? That small boy of yours tugs at my heart."

"Mine, too," Hetty laughed. "He is five now, you know."

"Seems only yesterday I first saw him," Mrs Harding said. It had been on the tip of her tongue many times to ask Hetty about her background, but she never had. It was Hetty's business. But she had always been curious about this reserved young widow who found the time to stop and chat to an old woman like herself.

"Can I get you anything?" Hetty asked.

"Just my morning drink, and if you wouldn't mind bringing it up for me – poor Goody is almost past coming up those stairs, to tell you the truth. When we leave she is going to live with her sister in Sussex – and I think she is more than ready for the move."

It was the end of an era, Hetty thought as she walked back over the heath towards the village. Tomorrow was her birthday and she would be thirty. A milestone! Ten years since Vida was born, and what a lot of water had passed under the bridge since then. Whoever would have thought that her life would change so much? She had been lucky. Leaving Jack Marclaren was the best thing she ever did.

Calling into Hind's the draper's she bought some cotton and buttons to sew on Vida's new dress. It was such a nice store, she always enjoyed seeing the local people shop there, sitting at the counters while the assistants waited on them; the way the floor walker in his frock coat stood at the top of the three carpeted steps, hands behind his back, obsequiousness in every inclination of his head, his centre parting gleaming white in the well Bryl-creamed black hair, black moustaches stiffened and waxed.

Tomorrow she was going to an auction in town. Nowadays Oliver insisted that she play her part in buying stock. "It will do you no harm to gain experience."

Armed with her marked catalogue, items pencilled with the maximum sum she was to bid, Hetty had made several of these excursions and enjoyed them enormously. She took advantage of the train journey to study from Oliver's quite considerable collection of reference books, and read them avidly.

On this occasion she managed to secure two out of three items she had bid for – a terracotta bust and a French carved ivory plaque. Oliver always had clients waiting for this sort of thing. The Fine Arts sales were slightly different from ordinary sales since there were always fanatical collectors prepared to pay the earth for what they wanted. Today she had been lucky.

"Well done," Oliver said when he heard the news. "You did well. What was the bidding like? Fierce?"

"Not really," Hetty said. "One or two of the usual collectors weren't there."

"I know why that was – there's an important sale on today in Sussex. I expect they were there." He sat back and regarded Hetty. "You, my dear, are going to have to learn to drive."

Hetty didn't know whether to be pleased or petrified. "Drive? Oh, Oliver, I couldn't!"

"Of course you could – you are never going to be able to run a business if you can't drive. You will need it for buying and deliveries. Not everyone can supply removal men like the big auction houses. Besides, how do you think I manage to get around to the local people?"

"Oliver, I know, but I never . . ."

"All the more reason," he said firmly. "I suggest we start on Saturday afternoon. Can you get someone to look after the children?"

"I suppose Miss Swinnerton upstairs would keep an eye on them for me. How long would I be gone?"

"Just an hour at first, you need that to get to grips with it. Shall we say two o'clock on Saturday?"

"Well . . ."

"Good. Then that's settled. I will telephone the driving school. I've already booked you in."

She looked at him, eyes wide. "Oliver! You've already organised it!"

"Had to," he grinned. "You'd only have argued otherwise."

He had left no room for argument, and in a way she was pleased. Unless she was thrown into the deep end, she would never do it.

Fortunately all the shops in Blackheath Village closed on Saturday afternoon, which gave her time to herself. Oliver also closed on Mondays, unlike the rest of the shops. He needed that time, he said, to buy stock and deliver.

One morning in October, Hetty saw that the small shop next door to Oliver's was having a sale. It was an exclusive dress shop, the sort of establishment with one model dress in the window, and an expensive handbag and shoes to match. Now there were several dresses in the window, and a large sign pasted outside: "Closing Down Sale". The owner, Betty Simpson, was an elegant woman in her mid-fifties who often came into the shop for a chat.

Hetty hurried into the antique shop and found Oliver in the office at the back. She hung up her hat and coat.

"Good morning, Oliver. Did you have a nice weekend?"

"Yes, thanks, and you?"

"Thank you, yes. Did you see the sign next door?"

"Yes, Hetty I did. Sit down, I'd like to talk to you."

"Weren't you surprised, Oliver?" She sat herself down in the large mahogany chair. All Oliver's chairs were man size.

"Yes and no," he said. "I've known Betty Simpson ever since I came here. Her mother is bed-ridden as she may have told you, and she is giving up the shop to look after her. In view of this, I've been doing some thinking, Hetty."

Looking across at her, seeing the dark lashes on her cheeks as she looked down and straightened her skirt, at the brown eyes which regarded him steadily when she looked up at him, he was more than ever sure that he wanted her. Not for what he had in mind first, a business partnership, but more than that.

He cleared his throat. "How would you like to go into partnership with me?"

A look of complete astonishment came over her face, and it was a moment or two before she could answer him.

"A partnership with you? Oliver – are you serious?"

"Deadly serious," he answered. "But let me explain. The lease has run out next door, and as I expect you know, Harding owns the freeholds. I intend to ask him to let me take a new lease. I am sure he will let me have it."

"But, Oliver, how do I fit in with this grand scheme of yours?" There was amusement in her eyes at the very idea.

"Well," he said undaunted, "if you came in with me we could expand the business, my books in one part of the shop and antiques in here. There would be more room. And I have to admit, Hetty, I do quite well on the books side. I am well known now, people come to me, and that's the side of the business I am more interested in. On the other hand, I wouldn't like to let go the goodwill I have built up as an antique shop."

157

"But, Oliver," she said gently, "Much as I would like to – I don't think I could afford to take over the antiques part. How much money would I need?"

"No, let me put your mind at rest," he assured her. "The only thing that might be difficult for you is the extra time involved. Do you think you could work full time four days a week and every other Saturday morning?"

"Not at the moment," she said. "It would mean getting someone in to collect the children from school in the afternoon, and to see to the flat if I was out all day. After all, we don't close until five."

"Do you think you could find someone to do that? Would you be prepared to enter into a partnership agreement?"

He could see the idea appealed to her. Perhaps it wasn't fair to put too much pressure on her.

"Look, Hetty, I don't want to rush you, there's plenty of time, but I'll outline the plan. I take over the shop next door for the books. You work longer hours at an increased salary – you will draw your wages as a salary if you become a partner. We will take an inventory at the start of the partnership, and from that date on you receive a quarter of the profits."

"I don't understand – all the stock is yours. Why would you give me some of the profits?"

"Because you would be a partner, sharing the business and the responsibility. It would leave me free to concentrate on the books, and I have every confidence that you could do it."

Seeing the doubt mixed with excitement on her face, he wanted to take her in his arms and comfort her, explain to her that there was nothing to worry about.

"Well!" she said at last. "It sounds like a wonderful opportunity but I'm wondering where the snag is. I'm from Yorkshire, you know, and we tend to look carefully before we leap." And she gave him a rueful grin.

"And quite right, too!" he said. He decided he had said enough for the time being.

"Think about it, Hetty," he said. "There's no hurry and I know you have some problems to sort out first, but come to me if you have any doubts."

She looked at him warmly. "It sounds wonderful. I do

thank you, Oliver. After all, where would I find another opportunity like this?"

When she closed the door behind her, her heart was beating fast with excitement and anticipation. She could do it, she knew she could. There was nothing you couldn't do if you had a mind. Now she saw the shop from a personal angle. It would be up to her to make a profit, above all to know what to buy to please the customers. She had a long way to go and a lot to learn, but knowledge came through experience.

Between them, Oliver James and Pop Collins had taught her everything she knew about buying and selling, both in their different ways. The answer was knowing a genuine article when you saw it, being able to spot the fake. It was not going to be easy; she had so much to learn, it might take a lifetime. "Always buy what you like," Oliver had taught her. "That way you can't lose, for if you like it and get stuck with it, then it doesn't matter."

She spend that night thinking hard, but when she finally slept knew what she was going to do. She would take advantage of Oliver's offer, and throw her lot in with him. It was a chance that might never come her way again.

In the morning, she found the children waiting for her, eyes sparkling, just waiting for her to make a discovery. She always laid the table for breakfast before she went to bed, and now she saw two small packages by her plate, and two birthday cards.

"What's this?" she asked, pretending surprise.

Opening the cards, she saw that they were both hand made, highly coloured and festooned with flowers, birds and animals – both wishing her a Happy Birthday. In one small parcel was a bar of chocolate and in the other a pretty embroidered hankie.

"Goodness!" she cried. "What lovely presents. Oh!" She looked crestfallen. "You must have spend all your pocket money."

"I made it at school," Vida said proudly.

"I gave Miss Swinnerton my pocket money and she bought it for me," Freddie said.

"Oh, you are kind children. Come here." And enfolding them in her arms, Hetty hugged them. "Thank you." She looked at them both, seeing Freddie's incredibly blue eyes, then Vida's dark ones. How pretty Vida had grown. At ten years old she had Jack's colouring, a mane of chestnut curls, lovely violet-coloured eyes and the longest lashes. "Listen, tomorrow we'll go to the pond with Freddie's boat – would you like that?"

They both squealed with pleasure at that. They loved going on to the heath. Later, when Freddie was in bed, she would tell Vida what she was about to do. She was an intelligent child, and old enough to understand.

"Also – " she added slowly, as they waited " – we are going to have tea in Jobson's. Would you like that?"

"Oh, Mummy!"

Bless them, she thought. They both deserved the very best that she could give them.

On recommendation from Miss Swinnerton, she was put in touch with Lilian Macdonald, a Scotswoman who had come down from Aberdeen before the war to work as a cook-housekeeper with a local family. When they had moved away she had found a room in the village, and now did odd jobs cleaning, nursemaiding, in fact anything that she could find to do.

Interviewing her, Hetty felt sure she would suit, and put her on a month's trial. The children took to her, and it was arranged that she would be on hand to look after them after school until Hetty came home. She was also not averse to doing the odd Saturday. If it worked, Hetty thought, it would be a miracle.

When she told Oliver of her decision, he felt a glow of satisfaction and promised himself that she would never regret it.

"Then it's agreed?" he asked.

"Agreed," Hetty smiled, and he held out his hand. A nice reassuring firm grasp, Hetty thought.

"I'll have my solicitors draw up the agreement," he said. "Leave it all to me."

When all was ready, and the agreement signed, Oliver decided to give a small Christmas party.

"To launch our new partnership," he said. "Besides, it's good for business."

Having arranged for the children to be looked after for the

evening, Hetty studied her wardrobe. She was not in the mood to buy new clothes, and possessed very few old ones. She needed every penny, what with the shop and Christmas coming on for the children, and then she had a brainwave.

The pink dress! It had been hanging in its cover ever since she bought it. Now she took it out and looked at it. It was still as pretty and not at all out of fashion, with its short length and straight style. Of course, it was lightweight, thin, of pure silk. Was it too summery?

Determination won the day, and when she was dressed she regarded herself in the mirror.

"Oh, Mummy!" Vida breathed. "You look lovely! So pretty. And the dress . . ."

Her lovely eyes were full of admiration.

"Really, Vida? Shall I wear it?" Hetty's own dark eyes were a perfect foil for the delicate dress.

"Oh, yes, you must!"

"Very well, then, I will."

She clasped a long row of pearls around her neck, artificial pearls, but that didn't matter in electric light, she told herself, and put on her pale-coloured stockings and best high-heeled shoes.

"There – what do you think?"

Vida's eyes glowed with admiration. "You will be the prettiest lady there," she said, and Hetty had to remind herself that her young daughter was growing up fast and would soon be someone to contend with.

She put a shawl around her shoulders and walked the short distance to the house next door but one. She could hear the noise and laughter going on and the sound of music coming from inside the house. The inner door was open, and Betty Simpson stood waiting to welcome new arrivals. She bent and kissed Hetty.

"My dear, you look lovely." She bent low, "Where did you find that lovely dress?"

Hetty smiled, and gave a huge inward sigh of relief. Everything was going to be all right.

Betty took her hand. "Now come along, and I'll introduce you to the others."

They entered the drawing room, which was warm and cosy

and full of cheer. There were low lamps, and flickering firelight on the walls. She might have known that Oliver would have a room like this.

There were welcoming sounds and smiles from all round the room as Hetty shook hands, not really seeing anyone until she came to the tall figure of the man standing by the fireplace. He held out his hands, "Hetty, my dear."

She went towards him, noticing again that firm handshake, and felt herself tremble slightly, not with trepidation but with a new and overwhelming feeling.

But Oliver seemed unaware of any of this as he drew her to his side.

"Everybody, hush! Silence, please. I want you to meet Hetty MacLaren who is going to help me run the shop from now on. Will you drink to the new partnership?" The rest of his words were drowned by the cheer that went up and the cries of congratulations.

Oliver bent down and gave her a chaste kiss on her cheek. It seemed to Hetty that she could feel the imprint long afterwards. "Let me get you a glass of champagne."

It must have been the dress, Hetty decided, as exhausted with the evening's festivities and the wine, she fell asleep as soon as her head touched the pillow. But in the morning her thoughts flew to the man who had been her escort for most of the evening. She could not deny the warmth of her feelings for him, and it was wonderful to receive compliments after all this time, to know that she was still attractive. She was drawn to Oliver, but supposed it was natural enough. He was the only man in her life. She shouldn't confuse the kindness he had shown her and the success she was having in business with something deeper.

It's time you got up, Hetty Jessops, she told herself sternly. There's work to be done.

Chapter Twenty

Alderbourne Grange lay bathed in sunshine on this spring morning as David Ogilby cantered over the fields surrounding the house. To the north lay the Yorkshire moors in all their glory, while to the east the sheep grazed with their new lambs. He rode towards the stables, pulling up by the fence to watch the new mares he had added to the stable in the past few weeks. His father had always employed an estate manager, but for the past three years David had managed the estate himself, and it was a full-time job.

He trotted over to the stables, having a chat to the groom on his way back to the house, past the row of cottages that housed the estate workers, scaring a cockerel out of his path and hearing the clucking of the hens which the tenants kept in their small back gardens.

Nearing the house, he stood stock still, surveying it in all its glory. Alderbourne Grange and its hundreds of surrounding acres meant more to him than life itself. It was in his blood, he felt passionately about it, as his grandfather had before him. His father had opted for life in the army, but David was like his forebears. The thought of his heritage was enough to send the blood racing through his veins. He could never live anywhere else.

Spring came late to Yorkshire, but now the copse was alive with daffodils, and in the beds around the house tulips in pinks and red vied with the wallflowers for colour. It was a bright scene, David thought, and it livened his heart at this sad time.

For the funeral had taken place the day before of his father,

Sir Frederick Ogilby, knighted for services to his country and honoured for his outstanding contribution to the armed services. David often wondered if his father was disappointed that he himself had not wanted to follow him into the army, but he had seemed pleased that his only son had chosen to manage the estate.

David couldn't have been more proud of his father, nor of the Ogilby name. His one sorrow was that there was no son to follow him, thus perpetuating the line. The family went back hundreds of years – there had always been a son. It was the one thing that marred his marriage to Dorothy.

He found her now in the drawing room, thumbing through a gardening catalogue. She looked up as he came in, smiling warmly at him.

"David, I wondered where you were."

"I've been riding round the grounds. I must say, Dorothy, you've done wonders round the lake. All that planting – what are they? Such colours."

"Rhododendrons and azaleas," she said. "Don't the azaleas remind you of my home?"

"I can't remember," he confessed. "I think I was too busy looking at you."

"Flatterer!" She smiled.

"You know I've never been a gardener."

"But you like to see a garden," she said. "Well, how about some tea? And I thought perhaps we'd go for a drive – take your mind off things."

He knew to what she referred. The age old problem, the one that had reared its ugly head every so often, after the first miscarriage, then the second – and worst of all when she had learned after stringent tests that she would never be able to bear a child. This was the hardest blow of all. For Dorothy but even more for him, for he had the lineage to consider, whereas Dorothy just wanted a baby – any baby.

He had steeled his heart against it. Wanting to please her, to give her what she wanted, yet knowing that he hated the very idea of adoption. It went against all his principles. A baby who wasn't an Ogilby – it wasn't the same thing at all.

"David," she had said, so often, "I am thirty-four – how long do you intend to wait? I want a baby while we are still reasonably young enough to enjoy her." For she wanted a girl.

"You know how I feel," he said stolidly.

They had reached an impasse, and she sighed. "I think we'll sit in the garden."

Once they were settled on the terrace, David looked out at the acres of land surrounding Alderbourne Grange. A man had to be proud of it, it had been in the family for almost three hundred years.

"I sometimes wonder if you realise how I feel," Dorothy said. "Unable to give you a son, a child of your own, sometimes I think it might be better . . ."

He put down his cup and took her hand. "Dorothy! You mustn't talk like that."

"I've been doing some thinking myself, David," she said, wondering what his reaction to her idea would be. "I long to see Mother and Father again – it's been quite a time – and I feel the break might do us both good. What do you think?"

"How long would you be away?" he asked quietly.

"About a month, I thought. It's not worth making the journey for anything less than that. It's two years since I saw them, and although I love living here it's not the same."

"Of course, darling, of course you must go home. I understand. that."

"Thank you, David." And he saw the relief on her face.

"I have to go to London shortly, to see the solicitors and so on – order some new suits, that sort of thing. I might as well take advantage of the time that you're away – unless of course you'd like us to go down together? You could do some shopping. It's a long time since we went to London."

"No, thank you, darling. Thanks all the same. I'll set about planning for the trip now that I know you don't mind – I do feel that the short break will be good for both of us. Get things in perspective, as it were. I'll get a letter off to Mother this evening.

"Some time in May, then, I imagine," David said. "Incidentally, I am thinking of engaging another farm manager – I don't know what your feelings are, but all this talk of war does make one wonder."

She looked up, startled. "You don't think there really will be a war?"

"I wouldn't be at all surprised. Rumours are one thing, but if you read between the lines, this chap Hitler is playing a very nasty game. Not one, I'm afraid, that we can allow him to get away with."

"So much for your pacifist attitude," she said drily.

"There are limits," he said, "even to someone of my temperament."

"Would you go? I mean, if there were a war? Enlist?"

"Of course, Dorothy," He looked slightly shocked at her question.

"Don't let's talk about it – I can't bear it!" She shuddered. He smiled at her fondly. She was an ostrich, he thought, like so many people. But there came a time when you had to face the writing on the wall. Bitter regrets at not having a child didn't help. Some time or other he was going to have to make a decision about adoption, whatever his feelings might be, if only for Dorothy's sake. Like most normal women she wanted a baby, and he owed her that much. He wouldn't like to see her going through the rest of her life without a child, it would be cruel.

He got up and sighed. Well, he didn't have to make the decision right now.

Hetty looked up as the elderly actor came in with a newspaper bundle under his arm. He was a frequent visitor, but she never enjoyed his visits. For inside the parcel would be yet one more treasure that he was selling in order to buy drink. He had first appeared on the scene a year ago when Hetty had helped in the shop, bringing in a beautiful Georgian tea service of solid silver. Oliver had sent him to the silversmith's in the village.

"I like to play safe," he told Hetty then. "Silver is such a specialised subject, and since the time I undervalued a piece of Paul Lamercy, I get cold feet! After all, I wouldn't expect a silversmith to spot a first edition of Browning's poems."

He had explained later how recent marks could be taken out and earlier ones put in, so professionally that it would take a real silver expert to spot the difference. Now Hetty felt the same way. It was bad enough to have to learn about china marks and furniture; she could not afford to take chance on

166

something as valuable as silver. One day, when she had time, she would take in silver as a subject – but one couldn't do everything at once.

The time it was a pair of vases, very ornate.

"What do you want for them, Mr Baker?" she asked, knowing that all he wanted was the price of a bottle of whisky and she could have robbed him easily of what was rightfully his.

"I leave it to you, my dear," he said, his once handsome face familiar to thousands of matinee fans, that wonderful voice roughened by drink. Drink, Hetty thought, it's a curse, as she knew from bitter experience.

She gave him her considered valuation, entered the purchases in her stock book, giving them a number, then priced them on a shelf. She had been so lucky since taking over the business. Everyone had rallied round.

This morning being a Saturday, the shop was due to close at one, and she looked forward to her free afternoon. She stood back and considered the beautiful piece of furniture which had just been delivered from a big house on the heath. She had taken a chance and given the owner what he asked for it, though not before looking up the price of comparable pieces. It was a gamble, she had to find a buyer, but that was what the business was all about. More of a gamble than anything else, a little knowledge, and a great deal of luck.

She preferred to buy small items which were harder to find – there was always a market for those, and the shop was not large enough to accommodate large pieces. There had hardly been room to move when the French armoire was there, but now luckily she had sold the Coromandel screen newly purchased and the cabinet stood in its place.

It had been well looked after, an eighteenth-century oystershell walnut and satinwood cabinet on chest. The patina was wonderful, and she had examined the drawers and with a torch looked underneath as Oliver had taught her to do. By now she had learned the feel of well-made furniture, the way the drawers slid on their runners, the hallmarks of a skilled craftsman. She followed Oliver's advice to the letter: that if she admired something herself and would have liked to own it, she couldn't go far wrong. Well, she would give her eye teeth for this little gem. The question was would she be able to sell it and make a profit? It was the most expensive item she had ever bought.

She ran a soft duster over its surface, and edged it into position, then stepped outside to see the effect. Yes, it looked very well. She didn't imagine she would have much difficulty finding a buyer.

Now that she had been in the shop some time, she could quite see why Oliver had been glad of her help, for a shop like this was almost impossible to run on one's own. You couldn't be everywhere at once – buying, delivering, attending auctions – and the fact was that once you had a superior piece in the shop, someone bought it, thank goodness, and you had to replace it. Lovely things didn't just grow on trees, they had to be found. But she loved it all. The quest, the finding, just having the shop and dealing in beautiful things.

Presently Oliver came in, through the archway that they had made in order to join the two shops.

"I won't be a moment," she said.

"Take your time. I wanted to ask you if it is still all right for – my word!" as his eyes fell on the new acquisition.

Hetty blotted her entries and closed the small book.

"Do you approve? Did I do well?"

He bent to examine the desk then looked at the unobtrusive price tag.

"Well done," he said. "That should sell like a hot cake. Where did you find it?"

"Telephone call from someone in St John's Park."

"Nice to know there is still stuff like this around."

He watched her as she put the finishing touches to closing the shop, straightening an ornament, putting a vase of silk poppies on a small side table. She had given the shop what it lacked previously – a feminine touch. Now she switched on a Chinese lamp with a pink shade which sent a warm glow over the interior.

She locked the door, and as they walked home together through the village, thought, as she had so many times before, how different things might have been. Being with Oliver like this was sheer contentment, and she wondered how he would react if he knew how fond of him she had become.

No – fond was hardly the word, she was in love with him. In

love as she had thought she never would be again. A quiet, lasting, strong kind of love. It had been her misfortune to fall in love with men above her station, for despite the improvement in the quality of her life, she could never, ever be more than a business partner for Oliver James. With his education, his background, she must seem like a simple country girl, for all she was a good business woman, and she wondered again what his first wife had been like. The daughter of an Oxford professor, he had said. Well, then . . .

There was no photograph of her anywhere, not even in his flat, where she had been many times with the children. They loved Oliver's home, his books, his garden where there was a small pond with frogs and tadpoles and minnows. He was a keen gardener, and taught the children so much. About wild life and about history. He had taken them into Greenwich Park and shown them the Observatory and Queen's Oak, taken them to Greenwich and brought its history to life.

"All right for me to take the children to the fair on Monday?" he said now. "Give you an hour or so at home to yourself."

"You are good to them, Oliver," Hetty said. "You know they simply love you to take them about."

He wanted to say: "You come too, Hetty please," but as always something prevented him.

If ever there was the slightest chance, he thought, he would take it. But it wasn't now. Perhaps it could never be.

The heath looked totally different on Monday. As far as the eye could see there were stalls: hoop-las, roundabouts, whirligigs and coaster rides, dodgem cars and coconut shies, and blatant strident music. The sweet sickly smell of Indian toffee and roasting chestnuts hung over everything, the cries of excited children; the screams of those riding on the daring machines rent the air.

The children held on to Oliver, each with a hand in his, their faces rosy from the cold air, the excietment of it all shining in their eyes.

Oliver was enjoying it hugely. It was years and years since he had been to a fair. "Come on – the dodgems," he said. He felt like a boy again as he asked for a car for three, and soon

169

they were sitting in it and bumping into everyone amid shrieks of laughter.

Breathless at the end of the ride, they dismounted. Afterwards they rolled pennies down a slide, and Freddie won a Dinkie car, while Oliver won a set of spoons.

"We'll give these to Mummy," he said. "She'll like them," putting the thin tawdry things in their velvet case safely in his pocket.

Then on the hoopla stall Vida won a small doll, a black doll which fascinated her.

"It has probably come all the way from Africa," Oliver said, and saw her look up at him to see if he was serious.

Vida put it in the crook of her arm. "I never play with dolls much," she said, "but I like this one."

"That's good," he said.

"Once, when I was very little, I went to a fair with my father," she said, and Oliver looked at her sharply.

"Did you, Vida?" Freddie asked. "I don't remember that."

"You weren't even born," Vida said with the authority of her extra years.

"What was he like?" Freddie asked, and Oliver saw Vida's lovely eyes darken, and she frowned. "I don't remember," she said shortly. "But I remember the fair."

Freddie lost interest. It all seemed so long ago.

After the fair had gone, and the heath returned to its normal green state, the summer holidays arrived, and with them, talk of war. The children had brought home notes from school with plans for evacuation outlined. In the event of war being declared during the summer holidays, all children should report to their school from whence evacuation would take place. There had been some evacuation of children the previous year during the Munich crisis, but later they returned. Now it was as if everyone realised that there was no escape. War seemed inevitable.

Hetty began to sleep badly. Uppermost in her mind was the thought that the children would be taken away from her and sent to places considered safe.

"It is a sensible arrangement, Hetty," Olvier said reasonably, hating to see her so worried. "After all, if the raids did

170

start, you wouldn't want them to be in London – in fact, I hope you would all three go to a place of safety."

"And what about the shop?" she asked.

"I am afraid that would lose its importance," Oliver said. He recalled the Great War, and knew that anyone who hadn't been involved in it had no idea of the grim reality of being at war.

"I don't want to go to Wales," Freddie said, and Hetty hugged him.

"I expect it's jolly nice," she said, just in case. "They've got mountains and rivers . . ."

"And coal mines," Vida said. She was always practical.

"Why don't you take them away for a few days, before they go back to school?" Oliver suggested. "You can leave the shop to me – take them up to Yorkshire."

"No" Hetty said swiftly. She wasn't ready for that yet.

"Then may I suggest something else? How about leaving them with me or Miss Macdonald and going up to town for the day? There's a viewing at Sotheby's on Thursday – you do that, and then take in some shopping. Buy yourself something nice, a new frock or a hat. Wouldn't you like that?"

Her eyes shining, Hetty was completely taken out of herself.

"Could I?"

At that moment, Oliver almost took the plunge – to take her in his arms and fold her to him.

Their eyes met, and the look held for what seemed like an eternity, but was probably only a few seconds, before he looked away and laughed.

"Why not?" he asked.

171

Chapter Twenty-One

All the way up in the train to London, Hetty thought of the look that had passed between herself and Oliver. What had they been trying to tell each other? Had he seen by her expression just how deep was her regard for him – that she loved him? Had he been embarrassed, laughing it away like that? "Why not?" he had said.

By the time she reached London and made her way to Bond Street, the incident had been forgotten. It was a day in late August, an air of autumn all around them. The biggest shock were the sandbags, mountains of them, outside buildings, shops and offices, while new notices everywhere showed the way to shelters. Some shops even had strips of sticky paper across the windows to strengthen them against blast. Altogether it made a depressing picture.

In Sotheby's she went upstairs to the Fine Arts section to find the Italian carved wooden figures which so interested Oliver. Her knowledge of the subject was almost nil, but on seeing them she could understand their appeal. They were small, a matched pair, a boy smiling and a boy with a frown. She found herself smiling too as she looked at them, feeling the old Flemish oak beneath her hands, seeing the artistry that had gone into the carving of them.

Of course she could tell him how beautiful the figures were, and their condition, but she suspected he had used the viewing at Sotheby's in order to give her a day out. Rather than shop at the large stores in Oxford Street, she decided to browse along Bond Street, window shopping. Such lovely things to see. She could spend a whole day and never get tired. Even Bond Street itself seemed to smell of French perfume, as she walked towards the Piccadilly end.

At that moment, David Ogilby was leaving the Burlington Arcade where he had just bought a cashmere sweater for Dorothy in palest blue, which was her favourite colour. He glanced at his watch. Ten-thirty. He had one hour in which to get to Lincoln's Inn for his appointment, and decided to stroll down the rest of Bond Street before hailing a taxi. Already this morning he had been measured for suits at his Saville Row tailor's, and this afternoon promised himself a visit to the Royal Academy.

Afterwards, he couldn't have said how far away from him Hetty was when he first recognised her. He only knew that at first he thought he was dreaming, for this pretty young woman was coming towards him, looking just like Hetty, and yet nothing like. For this Hetty was dressed elegantly and walked with an air, her smart hat of pale straw sitting on a cloud of dark hair. She was wearing a gold-coloured suit of some soft material, and a cream blouse. He watched mesmerized as she came towards him, her skirt blowing in the breeze, not seeing him, engrossed in what she saw around her.

He knew of course by now that it was she, and stopped abruptly a yard in front of her, raising his hat. He couldn't believe it was happening. He almost blocked her path. She stopped to look up at him, momentarily taken aback, and then the colour left her face.

"Hetty," he said softly.

She reeled slightly, and caught her breath. "David!"

He took her arm to steady her. "Hetty, I'm sorry."

"Oh, David, how you startled me!"

"I saw you from way back," he explained, "and I couldn't believe it."

The colour was coming back into her cheeks now, and she gave him a tentative smile, gaining courage with every second.

"Goodness! I can't believe this – what are you doing in London?"

"Several things." He smiled. "But first, before you disappear again, tell me where you live. Up here? In London?"

"No," she answered, "I'm up here for the day. On business," she added.

"Business? Hetty, what is all this?"

She looked delicious, pretty enough to eat, he told himself. Although she hadn't changed physically, there was an air about her of someone who had found her feet. At least he need not worry now that she hadn't managed all this time.

He led her gently under a large awning, out of the way of passing shoppers.

"Hetty, I am due at my solicitor's at eleven-thirty. But now that I've found you, I'm not going to lose you again. Will you have dinner with me this evening?" Then seeing her doubtful face: "Please?"

She smiled. "I'm afraid I can't, I don't live in town."

"Then where? Where do you live? I promise you, you won't get rid of me so easily this time!"

Her thoughts were racing. She knew that he wouldn't give up now, and after all, where was the harm? He was married, an old friend – that was all.

"I live in Blackheath," she said, "that's south London. And I work in an antique shop in the village."

"Did you get married again?" he asked her. "I know your husband died."

She shook her head. "No."

"And the children?"

"Very well," she said swiftly, and preventing further questions about them, returned one of her own. "And your parents?"

"My mother died three years ago, and my father just six weeks ago. That's one of the reasons I'm in London."

"Oh, I'm sorry, David. And your wife?"

"Visiting her parents in America. Look, Hetty, I must see you again. Have dinner with me this evening? I'll come down to Blackheath."

"Oh, no!" The words escaped from her in a sudden rush of panic.

"Why not?"

"Well . . . She could think of no good reason to give him, but had plenty of her own. She was terrified to think he might see Freddie, and recognise him for his son. But perhaps she was exaggerating the risks? And she would never stop him now. If she showed too much concern to prevent him he might think there was a reason.

174

"Hetty, I shall come down to Blackheath this evening and take you out to dinner. I won't take no for an answer. Give me your address."

He had changed more than somewhat, Hetty decided. Gone the rather shy, wistful young man. Now he was a man of the world, well able to stand on his own two feet. She was surprised at herself too, that she could stand and talk to him so easily – on a par, almost, as if she had never been a farm worker's daughter. All that was in the past, she had no qualms on that score.

"Hetty?"

She gave him her address, watched him write it in his diary, and thought: The die is cast now. And knew a sense of relief mixed with fear.

"I'll call for you at seven-thirty," he said, taking both her hands in his. "Is there a good restaurant nearby?"

"The Heathside Hotel is supposed to be very good," Hetty said, still not believing that this was really happening.

"Leave it to me," he said. "Until seven-thirty then."

Hetty watched him go, seeing his tall figure mingling with the crowds until it vanished from sight.

What had she done? She must have been mad. But she consoled herself with the thought that Freddie would be in bed by seven-thirty. And what on earth was she worried about? No one could harm her now, certainly not David. And it was nice to see him again, her childhood friend. To meet each other just like that in the middle of Bond Street was surely fate.

She walked along Piccadilly until she came to Swan and Edgar's in Piccadilly Circus where, determined to make the most of her shopping day, she bought a dress for her evening date. It was in green, a colour which suited her, and had a matching jacket which would be useful.

Happy with her purchase, she made her way back to the station. There was no point in hanging about now, she might as well get back. Somehow, the day in London had lost its purpose. There was a much more eventful evening awaiting her at home.

She came out of Blackheath station at four-thirty and made her way to the shop, where she found Oliver sitting at her desk.

175

He looked up when she came in, and noticed straight away that something had happened to her.

"How did you get on?" he asked. "Was it pretty awful in town? I have the feeling that we are in for a momentous weekend."

"Really, Oliver? In what way?"

"They've announced that the Prime Minister is to make an important speech."

"Oh, no, Oliver! You mean . . ."

"I'm afraid so. Still, that's enough of that. What sort of day did you have?"

She hesitated, and he prompted her. She seemed nervous he thought, but it didn't seem to be the war scare. "Did you go to Sotheby's?"

"Yes, I did. And I saw your two carvings. They were beautiful – I could quite see why you might want them."

"In good condition?"

"As far as I could see," she said, drawing off her gloves.

"And you did some shopping?" He smiled, glancing down at her carrier bag.

"Yes, I bought a dress. As a matter of fact, something rather strange happened. I met an old friend from Yorkshire I haven't seen for years, not since I came to London years ago."

The words came tumbling out as if she couldn't get them out fast enough.

"He's staying in London, and has asked me out to dinner this evening."

He felt a pang of jealousy. So it was a man?

"What a nice surprise," he said, noting her jumpiness. She was usually such a calm person. What had happened to shake her equanimity?

"I'll put the kettle on and we'll have a cup of tea," he said. "Then you can get home. No need to hang about, I'll be here."

She had just poured the tea when a shadow fell across the window and they both looked up. A man stood outside, a pleasant-looking man, and he was smiling at Hetty. Looking at her, Oliver could see she had gone deathly pale.

The man pushed open the door and came in, closing it after

176

him. "Forgive me, Hetty – I just couldn't resist coming down early. I wanted to see you and your shop."

Then his blue eyes looked candidly into Oliver's, and he held out a hand.

"David Ogilby," he said. "I am an old friend of Hetty's."

"How do you do?" Oliver said coolly. "Oliver James."

"Ah, the name over the shop," David said. "Perhaps Hetty told you – we met quite by chance in London today?"

So he was part of Hetty's background, Oliver thought. He had not imagined someone quite like this, and by the way Hetty reacted he had quite an effect on her. Her brown eyes were warm when she looked at him and she was not her usual composed self. Where did this man fit into her life? he wondered. How important an old friend was he?

"Staying in London long?" he asked courteously.

"A few days," David said. "Now that I've found Hetty again I'd like to stay longer, but I rather think I'll have to get back. The news isn't so good, is it?"

"No." Oliver said, glancing at Hetty who was biting her lip. He didn't quite like the effect this man was having on her. Was she afraid of him?

"Hetty, my dear, you get along now," he said kindly. "I'll lock up."

"Thank you, Oliver."

And was he married, this man? Oliver asked himself. Where was his wife? Was this the secret in Hetty's life?

He watched them go, Ogilby lightly holding Hetty's arm, her Swan and Edgar's bag in his gloved hand.

Whoever he was, he had given Hetty a bit of a shock, that was clear. He had never seen her so disturbed. He seemed a decent enough chap. How important had he been in Hetty's past?

Meanwhile, Hetty had walked round to the back of the shop, and had got her small car out of the garage. David sat beside her on the short journey through the village, marvelling at the change in her, her hands on the wheel, her profile with the short straight nose, the thick dark lashes and deep brown eyes, but most of all her self-assurance.

As she turned into the short tree-lined avenue, he looked at the large houses, some Georgian, some Victorian, and to his

177

surprise she stopped the car outside a cream-painted house, a large residence with gables galore.

"Is this where you live?" he asked her.

"I have the ground floor flat," she said. "This way."

Into a wide hall and through to the dining room which led to the kitchen, and there were the children, and Lillian Macdonald sitting by the fire, knitting. She got up as Hetty came in, rolling up her ball of wool and sticking the knitting pins into it.

"Ah, there you are, Mrs Maclaren – they've had their tea."

"Thank you, Lillian. This is Mr Ogilby, an old friend of mine from Yorkshire. Children, this is David. And this is Vida, and this Freddie."

Had David been looking at Hetty he would have seen the pulse beating rapidly in her throat, but he was too busy looking at her two delightful children. The girl was a beauty and he imagined took after her father, with those gypsy dark looks and lovely eyes, while the boy was of a different mould, slim and fair. There was an angelic look about him, but judging by the train set on the floor, he was a real boy.

David held out his hand. "Hello, Vida, Freddie."

"Hello, Mr Ogilby," Vida said. "Have you come from Barnsdale – that's where my mummy comes from."

"Yes, Vida, I have," he said. "It's a very long way from London."

"Did you come on a train?" Freddie asked.

"Yes, on a steam train," David said.

Freddie was impressed. "I'm going on a steam train one day," he said.

"I'm sure you are," David said. How lucky Hetty was to have two such beautiful children.

"I'll just see Miss Macdonald to the door, and then I'll be with you," Hetty said.

Closing the door behind her, she stood still and took a deep breath. Lillian could manage to look after the children this evening. She glanced in the hall mirror and patted her hair before returning to the dining room.

"Shall I make a cup of tea, David?" she asked, going into the kitchen.

"Lovely idea," he said, busily turning the key of Freddie

clockwork train. "You're quite near the shops here, aren't you?" he asked.

"Yes – at the corner of the road."

"Then if you don't mind I'll just pop out for something," he said. "Don't bother, I'll find my way."

He returned with sweets for the children and flowers for her.

"Oh, David, you shouldn't have!" Hetty protested.

"My pleasure."

Later, when she was getting ready for the evening, he read Freddie a story while Vida listened. When Hetty came downstairs and saw them, her heart was in her mouth. She felt more guilty than she had ever felt in her life. Her cheeks flushed a rosy red, and she felt her hands shaking. She was glad when Lillian re-appeared to look after the children for the evening.

David was open in his admiration of Hetty in her new dress.

"You look wonderful," he said. "This is one of the happiest days of my life."

She crossed her fingers behind her back. Please let it work out all right. Oh, Oliver, I need your wisdom, your kindness. If I could only tell you all about it.

She smiled up at David.

"Shall we go?"

179

Chapter Twenty-Two

Hetty faced David across the table, not quite sure if she was dreaming or if it was real. He smiled at her, his grey eyes complimenting her, coupled with an air of achievement, as though he was experiencing a wish fulfilled.

There was no denying the pleasure she felt at seeing him again – and now that she had got over the hurdle of him actually seeing Freddie without the slightest sign of recognition, she settled down to what promised to be an enjoyable evening. It was nice to be here with him, a long-lost friend from childhood, and if the memory of that day long ago thrust itself to the forefront of her mind, she pushed it back again. Now, it was hard to believe that it had really happened like that. Of course, she loved him, would always have a special place in her heart for him, but people changed – he had changed – he was no longer the boy she had known, and she was sure she appeared vastly different to him.

David handed the menu back to the waiter, and looked at her approvingly.

"Hetty, did I tell you? You look simply wonderful! You always were the prettiest girl in Barnsdale."

"Thank you, David." She had to keep things on an even keel. "I was sorry to hear about your father."

"He died peacefully, I'm glad to say, although he had suffered a lot in the last few months . . ." Then his face brightened. "Tell me about the work you do in the shop. It isn't yours, is it? Although nothing would surprise me!"

"I used to work there odd days, that sort of thing. Now Oliver and I are in partnership."

Oliver, he mused. He hadn't missed the way the fellow had looked at Hetty. Protectively.

"And doing well?"

"Up to now," Hetty said, "although if there is a war, I'm not quite sure what we would do. I don't suppose there would be much of a market for antiques."

"It may not happen," David said, but sounded doubtful. "And you never thought of marrying again?"

"I've been too busy to think about it," she said.

"What about Oliver James?" he asked. "Is he married?" And saw her blush.

"Oh, no!" she said swiftly. "Oliver is a widower – I don't think he'll ever get over the death of his wife."

David waited while they were served the first course. That situation had not been quite the way he had interpreted it. Still . . .

"Well, Hetty my dear" he said, "let's drink to the future, shall we?" Her deep brown eyes looked into his, as candid as a child's, and he felt a moment's sadness, regret for something that might have been.

"Tell me about your wife. Where did you meet her?" Hetty asked.

"Dorothy? I met her in Vermont – her mother and mine were distant cousins several times removed. Anyhow, she was engaged to a chap and about to marry him when he was killed in a motor car accident."

"How sad, David." Hetty had wonderfully expressive eyes. Now they were full of compassion and pity.

"Yes, it was. We were going over there to see them, Mother and I, when the news came. Aunt Tassie thought we should keep to the arrangements, it might be a good thing for Dorothy – take her mind off the whole affair."

"So you went? That was nice."

"Yes, and we liked each other, but I have to admit that at that time marriage could not have been farther from my thoughts. Dorothy talked a lot about Henry, her fiancé, and as a matter of fact, I told her about you."

Her face flamed and she put down her knife and fork. "David, you didn't!"

"I did. Why not? You were very close to me – I – "

181

She looked down.

"I'm sorry." He took a deep breath. "Well, anyway, we corresponded for a year, and then I went over again and proposed to her, and we married, and came back a month later."

"Very romantic." She smiled up at him.

His face clouded over. "Hetty, how did you manage when you first came down to London? You did come straight down here, didn't you?"

"I went first of all to Greenwich, and all I can say is that I did manage – but I was lucky, people were very kind, and an old man gave me a home. I've come up in the world, as they say, since then." And she gave him a mischievous smile.

"I thought about you so often. I went to see Dora . . ."

"Yes, she told me, that was kind of you. I didn't let her know where I was for ages." She stopped as the waiter prepared to serve the next course.

When he had gone, she raised her eyes, pleading with him. "Don't let's talk about it, David. It's past now. I just want to look forward to the future."

He raised a glass of red wine. "To us, Hetty."

She sipped the wine carefully, unused to drinking.

"Dorothy sounds nice. Does she like living in England? I should think she must be very impressed with the Grange."

"Yes, although she had a lovely home in New England." His eyes clouded over. "She is there now, as a matter of fact, visiting her parents." Then he looked at Hetty thoughtfully. "She had had rather a rotten time of it in the last couple of years."

"What do you mean?"

"She has suffered two miscarriages – " Hetty bit her lip " – only to be told now that she can have no more children."

"Oh, David!"

She put down her knife and fork, and dabbed her mouth with her napkin. Suddenly the food seemed tasteless, David couldn't have told her anything more calculated than that to reawaken her guilty feelings. How devastating for his wife, and perhaps worse still for David. Especially now.

"Are they quite certain of that?" she asked gently. "So much can be done."

"Oh, yes, quite certain," he said, almost bitterly.

There seemed nothing she could say to liven the conversation. Thank heaven he had no idea about Freddie. She swallowed hard.

"It does sometimes happen, even after being told that."

David shook his head. "Dorothy has been to the finest specialists, she had had every test it is possible to have. You may be sure that we have left no stone unturned."

Hetty thought she had never heard anything so cruel – when you were fortunate enough to have children you didn't realise that for some women it wasn't so easy. She felt she wanted to get home and see that they were both safe and sound and tucked up in bed.

"You see, Hetty," and David sighed, "from my point of view there is the question of succession – no one to carry on after me. And there have been Ogilby's for four hundred years."

Hetty could hardly bear to listen, she felt like a rabbit caught in a snare, trapped with her guilty conscience.

"The problem at the moment – in fact we have been living with it for the last six months – is that Dorothy wants to adopt."

Hetty heaved an inward sigh of relief, and grabbed at this solution as at a lifeline.

"Ah, well," she said brightly, "isn't that the answer? After all, then you can choose what you want."

"A son," he said shortly, "no doubt about that – although Dorothy would like a daughter."

"Well, both then," she said, feeling as inadequate as she would ever feel. ·

He shook his head. "No, I can't, Hetty," he said. "It's not the same thing at all."

"Aren't you being a little selfish, David?" she asked gently.

"I don't see it that way," he said. "I have strong views about it."

"Do you love her."

At that, he looked straight at her, his honest grey eyes showing no doubt at all.

"Yes, I do, Hetty."

"And I should think there is no doubt that she loves you, so you have much to be thankful for."

He put out a hand and covered hers.

"We were always good friends, weren't we, Hetty?"

The waiter reappeared with the menu, but she shook her head.

"No, thank you, David. Let's walk slowly home. It's a nice evening, and the air will do us good."

"No coffee?" he asked.

"No, we'll have it at home, then you'll be in good time for your train."

He linked his arm in hers as they walked home, like two lovers on an evening stroll.

"That's really why she has gone home – we were both a bit het up, and I think the change will do her good. As for me, it was a tonic finding you after all this time."

She glanced across the street to the shop.

If war came no lights would be allowed, and they had already ordered a black out blind, but from here it looked like a haven, a refuge.

They turned into Blaize Park, and following her up the short path, David waited as Hetty inserted the key in the lock.

"Come in here, David," she said, opening the door to the drawing room. "I'll have a word with Lillian and put the coffee on. Make yourself comfortable."

He took off his coat and draped it over a chair, hearing Hetty say goodnight to the nursemaid then close the door.

He looked around him at the tastefully furnished room with its cretonne-covered sofa and chairs, the few nice pieces of furniture, at the table by the marble fireplace on which stood a silver-framed photograph. He got up and went over to it, picking it up. It was of the two children, taken recently he would imagine. They were lovely children. The little girl was a lot like Hetty, while the boy . . . He frowned and looked closer at it, then his heart began to race. The boy was like him – pictures of him as a child looked just like this. Could it be? Was it just possible . . .

Hetty had just been setting the cups when the thought came to her. Oh, what a fool she had been – the picture! She hurried into the drawing room and stood there, her face as white as a sheet, as she met David's accusing eyes over the photograph in his hand.

184

"How old is he?" His voice came out harshly.

"Freddie?" She cleared her throat and swallowed. "Six – almost seven."

"Born when I was in Malaya?"

"Er, yes, I think he was." Now that it was out she felt a flood of relief. She had been wrong to keep it from him. "David – "

"He's my son," he said. "Isn't he, Hetty?" He griped her wrist. "Please, tell me the truth."

She drew her hand away, and took a deep breath. "Yes," she said, her hands hanging weakly at her sides. No point in denying it now.

"Why didn't you tell me? Why?"

"David – let me get the coffee. I think we both need it."

He was staring at the picture when she came back, and looked up at her with eyes full of tears. Then he put it down and blew his nose.

"You can't imagine what this means to me," he said. "To have a son."

She handed him the coffee in silence.

"What you must have gone through," he said. "You poor little thing – and on your own."

"It wasn't because of Freddie that I left Jack," she said. "He had no idea at all the baby wasn't his. I left him because he drank, and because I'd had enough . . . no, don't say anything." She brushed his hand away. "I was glad about the baby, I really was. I knew right from the beginning he was yours, and I have never told a soul – until now."

"Hetty – "

"No, let me finish. I wanted to bring him up myself, and I knew it wouldn't be easy, but I managed." She allowed herself a small smile. "Are you pleased with what you see?"

"If I had ordered a son to my own specifications, he would have looked just like Freddie," David said. "But now your troubles are over."

She frowned. "What do you mean?"

"I can give him everything, Hetty – education, background, his rightful inheritance."

"David!" Her eyes were blazing. "How dare you!" she stormed. "How dare you suggest such a thing! He is my son,

185

too, you know, and he belongs with me. You have no right to him."

"Oh, Hetty, my darling. I don't want to take him away from you!"

She looked at him suspiciously. "Then what do you want?"

"I want to be responsible for him, for his education – "

"I shall give him the best education money can buy," she said. "You can rest assured of that."

"Hetty, listen."

"He is my son – only yours by accident of birth. You have no claim on him."

He might have been talking to a stranger. "Hetty, I don't want to take him away from you."

"You had better go," she said, leading the way to the door. "I hope you are satisfied. Now perhaps you will leave me alone."

"Hetty, I can't leave you like this," he said. "I don't want to upset you – "

"Then please go," she said. "You have done enough damage for one day."

He found himself on the other side of the front door with it firmly closed in his face.

Back in the house, Hetty subsided in a flood of weeping, unable to control herself. It was if the strain and torment of the last few years had finally come to a head and she wept as if her heart would break, unaware that Vida, in the next room, had heard every word.

186

Chapter Twenty-Three

In the morning, Hetty dragged herself out of bed feeling drained and weak from lack of sleep.

How could she have spoken to David like that? He was her friend, her childhood sweetheart. Of curse, he was overcome to learn that he had a son – it was only natural, the more so since he could have no children from his marriage. She had shown lack of understanding, had been almost cruel to him, so fearful was she that Freddie would be taken away from her.

She splashed her face with cold water, and brushed her hair, wondering all the while what David would do now.

When she was ready, she went to the kitchen to put on the kettle. Thank goodness she had this Saturday free. It was Oliver's turn in the shop, and she could not have been more grateful.

She opened the door to the children's room, which they shared, and was surprised to see Vida still in bed. Freddie was sitting on the floor playing with his toys.

She attempted a smile, "Come on, lazybones, aren't you going out with Helen and Auntie Min this morning, Vida?"

Her mumbled reply came from beneath the bedclothes. "Not until half-past nine."

"Well, you'd better get up and have some breakfast. It's almost eight-thirty now."

She went over and hugged Freddie, giving him an extra kiss this morning. How David hadn't spotted the likeness to himself in the first place, she'd never know. But it was obvious that she could never have got away with it for ever.

She went over and kissed Vida's curls. "Come on, pet."

She put a hand to the girl's forehead. "Do you feel all right, Vida? You're awfully warm."

She wriggled beneath her mother's hand. "I'm all right," she said irritably.

"Get dressed, then," Hetty said, "and you too, young man."

By the time she had cooked the breakfast, made the toast and tea, they were both sitting up at the table, Freddie with his Shredded Wheat and Vida with an empty plate in front of her, her glass of milk untouched.

"Not hungry?" Hetty asked, looked at the flushed face and bright eyes and hoping that she was not coming down with anything. "Have some toast, poppet," she said. "Just a small piece – otherwise you'll feel hungry when you go out."

But Vida wouldn't look at her, and now Hetty felt almost sure there was something wrong.

"Hurry up, Freddie. Wash your hands, and go into the garden."

When she was sure he had gone, she began to clear away the breakfast dishes, then returning from the kitchen sat down opposite Vida and waited.

She could see the misery in Vida's lovely eyes, the doubt and suspicion, and had a sudden cold feeling in the pit of her stomach.

She got up and went round to her daughter, putting her arm around her shoulders, but Vida shrugged it off.

"He's not my father – that man – is he?"

Hetty almost gasped with shock, although she had been half expecting it. She sat down abruptly, looking at Vida's face and seeing the anguish there.

"Oh, Vida, you heard us," she whispered, her hand over her mouth as though she would bite back the things she had said the night before. Now, she knew, the time had come for the truth – she owed Vida that much.

She sat up straight. "Of course he's not," she said gently. "You remember your father, don't you?"

Vida nodded miserably.

"Well, then," Hetty said. "But your father is not Freddie's father – it is something you will understand when you are older."

"I understand now," Vida said coldly. "I know about babies and how they come, they talk about it at school, and I know that Mr Ogilby is Freddie's father, and you were not married to him. That's why my father sent us away!"

Hetty's face was stained scarlet, while her heart was pounding in her chest.

"That isn't true, Vida," she said, with a calmness she didn't feel. "I left of my own accord – I am not saying that to excuse what I did, but at the time I thought it was the right thing – for all of us. I was very unhappy."

Vida seemed not to be listening. "I remember sitting on my father's knee, and he took me to the fair."

Hetty herself was near to tears. "Can you remember anything else about our life in Barnsdale?"

"Yes, I remember school, and Auntie Dora, and Granny Maclaren."

Hetty was shocked. All this time, and the child had never said anything.

"You never talked about them," she said.

"I thought we came away because my father hit you," Vida said.

"Vida!"

"He shouted when he came home, when he looked horrid, and smelled nasty. And after he hit you and you fell down, your face was all bruised. We left home after that – and came to London.

Hetty was horrified. "You saw all that? Where were you?"

"At the top of the stairs."

"Oh, Vida!"

"But we didn't leave because of that, did we? It was because of Freddie, and my father not being Freddie's father."

"No, it wasn't because of that," Hetty said. "Your father didn't know that Freddie was not his son."

Vida turned accusing eyes to her mother's pale face. "That's wicked," she said. "And cruel. I don't wonder he stayed out and drank."

It was as if she had slapped Hetty's face.

How had she ever thought the past was dead and buried? Hetty wondered. She must have been living in a dream world.

"I can only hope that you will understand one day," she said gently.

"Will you tell Freddie?" Vida asked, calmer now that it was all out in the open.

Hetty shook her head. "Not yet," she said. "He's not old enough to understand. But I will one day, when I think the time is right."

"Mr Ogilby wants him, doesn't he?" Vida said. "I heard him say so."

"I think you overhear too much, one way and another," Hetty said wryly.

"You did shout," Vida said. "I'd never heard you shout like that – you woke me up."

"I sorry, I was beside myself – with anger, with being found out. Mr Ogilby didn't know until yesterday. He saw the photograph in the other room."

"You won't let him take Freddie away, will you?" Vida pleaded.

"Of course not," Hetty assured her.

"Will he try?" Vida looked fearful.

"There's nothing he can do," Hetty said, with a confidence she was far from feeling. "Freddie belongs to us. He's my son, and your brother."

Vida got down from the table, and looked straight at Hetty.

"I wish Mr Ogilby had never come here," she said. "He's spoiled everything."

Hetty put her arms around her, feeling the resistance in the young shoulders, but not relaxing her hold.

"We grew up together, David and I," she said. "Ever since I can remember, he was there."

"Then why didn't you marry him?" Vida asked scornfully.

"That's something else you will understand when you are older," Hetty said. "Now forget all about this, and hurry up and get ready. They'll be here soon."

Children were resilient, she thought. When Min came with Helen, Vida kissed her goodbye and danced off as though nothing had happened. Who knew, though, what was going on in a child's head? Parents were responsible for a lot more than they thought.

Tidying up the flat and washing up, she watched Freddie in

190

the garden playing with his tricycle, round and round the small lawn, as happy as a sandboy. The pleasure he had given her was worth all the heartbreak. She fell to wondering about David. What would he do now? For she hadn't seen the last of him. Now that he knew he had a son . . . and back came all the doubts and fears, interrupted by the sound of the front door bell.

Drying her hands, she hurried to the door. She opened it and saw David Ogilby standing there, a newspaper under his arm.

"David!"

"Good morning, Hetty. May I come in?"

She looked over her shoulder, then at him again. What else could she do but invite him in?

"Of course. But what are you doing here? I thought you – "

"I got a room at the Heathview – I couldn't possibly have gone back to Yorkshire last night, Hetty. I was much to excited, and worried about you as a matter of fact."

Hetty led the way into the drawing room. "Sit down, David."

"Where is he?" The longing to see his son again was unmistakable.

She led the way through the dining room to the French windows which were open. They watched Freddie riding around, and a look of pride came over David's face.

"He looks like me, doesn't he?" he asked. "I mean, he's an Ogilby, Hetty, say what you like."

"Oh, he's an Ogilby all right," she smiled, "but that's not what we're talking about, is it? He's my son. Freddie!" she called, and he rode over to them, smiling up at David.

"Hallo, Mr Ogilby."

"Stay with him," Hetty said, "while I put the coffee on."

When it was ready, and David came in, she could see he was as pleased as punch. Now, she thought, for the battle.

"By the way," he said, indicating the newspaper headlines, "it looks as though we are to be at war any minute now."

Hetty's brown eyes were troubled. "So this is it," she said. "After all the scares and denials, it's finally going to happen."

"What will you do?"

"I haven't thought much about it," she said. "I know the children should be evacuated. What will happen about the shop, I really don't know."

"Hetty, don't take this the wrong way – but I really mean it – I could do so much for Freddie, send him to my old school to start with. My dear, I know you will do a grand job – I never doubted that for a moment. But he is an Ogilby, and his rightful place is as my heir. He will be inheriting everything when I am gone."

"But, David, how is that possible? What would your wife say? And what about me? We are a family, Vida and me and Freddie. You can't expect to come here and disrupt our lives."

"I'm talking of the future, Hetty. Freddie's future. Wouldn't you like to know that he'll inherit Alderbourne and all it stands for? After all, he has every right to."

"Do you mean to tell me you are going home to tell Dorothy that you have a son, after all this time, knowing that all she longs for is a child of her own? You are being very selfish, David. Think of her."

"I am thinking of her. She will understand – and she will be able then to adopt her little girl, whatever she wants, as long as Freddie is my heir."

The family, Hetty thought, the family name, the inheritance. Was anything more important to him than that?

"David, you would be breaking up a family. Who knows whether what you wish to do for Freddie would make him happy?"

"It's not a question of that, Hetty, it's a question of what is right, his due. He is the eldest son of an Ogilby. The family is four hundred years old – it is his whether you like it or not."

"Yes, I understand. I do know that," she said. "But it isn't legal, is it? It's only something you would like to happen. Without my consent, you can't have him."

"That's what I am asking you for – your consent," David said. "Please, Hetty. I could legally adopt him, and send him to my old school at thirteen – then on to university, Oxford, like me. Oh, Hetty, you can't refuse him that!"

"And where is he up to that time?" she asked coolly.

"With you, of course."

"I see. And at thirteen, he goes away to boarding school."

"Of course."

"And when you do see him? You are not going to settle for my having him all the time, surely?"

"Sometimes, perhaps, in the holidays, he could come up to Yorkshire and stay. Bring Vida."

"Oh, David, stop! Please! I've heard enough. I can't bear any more. It's been such a shock, for you as well as me. Please go."

He took both her hands in his.

"Will you promise to think about this, please, Hetty?"

She nodded, and he bent and kissed her cheek lightly.

"Thank you, for everything. And he went outside to the garden, lifting little Freddie up high, then hugging him tightly. Hetty felt her throat constrict as the tears came to her eyes.

David put down his child and hurried through the house and out of the front door, before Hetty had a chance to say anything else.

His eyes blurred, he hurried to the station, in his haste passing Oliver James on the other side of the road, who taking advantage of the lull in trade on this quiet Saturday morning, had returned to the house for a book.

Oliver turned and watched him go. So that was it! Ogilby had stayed overnight. He felt a surge of jealousy he hadn't thought himself capable of.

No wonder Hetty had been on edge and tremulous – she had been excited, thrilled to the skies, no doubt, by the man in her life coming back to her.

Now, he felt angry. Gone were all his dreams, his plans. He had been a fool. At his age he should have known better. Well, he wouldn't hang around to see the reunion between them, the wedding even – he would leave the coast clear for Hetty. Then he softened. She deserved some happiness after all this time, and the children deserved a father. He wished them well, but couldn't stay around and watch it all happening before his eyes. He would get out now. There was obviously going to be a war, and people would not be buying antiques and books then.

193

He must return to the shop and put things in order. He would write to her, he couldn't telephone, then go up to Uncle Malachy in Oxford. He might even join up, if they'd have him.

He couldn't imagine life without her.

That afternoon, Hetty found a letter addressed to her in Oliver's writing on the mat in the hall. She opened it curiously.

My dear Hetty,

Forgive the haste, but I am on my way to Oxford to visit my uncle, who has been ill. I expect I shall be away some time, so may I ask you to carry on in your own efficient way? It is on the cards that war will be declared tomorrow, in which case there will be no time for good book sales and first editions – so do feel free to close that part down and carry on as you will. You have my full permission to do just as you think fit about the antiques side of the shop.

Incidentally, I was pleased to meet David Ogilby. May I take this opportunity to wish you both every happiness for the future?

I will be in touch,
Oliver.

Hetty stood still, staring in front of her. Oliver gone – it wasn't possible! How could she carry on without him? He had always been there when she needed him and more than anything she had wanted to tell him about Freddie and David, and ask him what she should do for the best. For Oliver would know, he was so wise, and she loved him so much . . . She brushed away an angry tear, and read the letter again, "Wished them both every happiness?" Oh, he hadn't thought that she and David . . .

She folded the letter hurriedly and put it in her pocket as she heard Vida come in with Freddie from the garden. What would the children say when they knew Oliver had gone? They adored him.

What a weekend. She would remember this forever, the second of September, and who knew what tomorrow would bring?

194

Chapter Twenty-Four

On that fateful Sunday morning of September the third, a whole nation listened to Neville Chamberlain announce with the utmost gravity that England was at war with Germany. People who remembered the First World War saw none of the exuberance, the sheer wave of patriotism that overtook the country then. Now, after the rumours and doubts, the talk and prevarication, the mood was one of resignation. The institution of conscription and a national register of occupations had been put in force a few days before the declaration, but the first to be called up were the regulars and the territorials.

Hetty sat silent and pale, the events of the last twenty-four hours uppermost in her mind. The children watched her every reaction. The air raid siren sounded, and Hetty did the first thing which came into her head, shepherding the children into the cupboard under the stairs. There they stayed, unaware of what was going on in the rest of the street until "All Clear" sounded and they joined their neighbours who stood in little groups outside their homes.

"False Alarm," they said, until the sky was rent with the sound of low-flying planes zooming almost overhead. The onlookers ducked automatically. As the planes disappeared it became clear that they were British, from Biggin Hill one know-all said.

Hetty talked to the neighbours for a spell, discussing plans for the children's evacuation. Some of them had left London the previous Friday and were already in their new foster homes by the time war was declared.

It was something Hetty could not come to terms with, having the children sent away from her to unknown foster homes in the country, but many parents deemed it the wisest thing to do. Hetty had seen lines of them outside Blackheath station, with their sad little bundles of luggage, in some cases mere carrier bags, gas masks slung over their shoulders in cardboard boxes, each child with a label clearly denoting its name and the address of its destination.

I would rather take them away somewhere, she thought, as long as we can to together. After all, what is there to keep me here now?

She felt the absence of Oliver acutely, a sense of loss pervading every task she tackled. It didn't seem possible that he would not be around to give her a hand, and she realised how much she had come to depend on him.

Vida's pretty face had looked sulky ever since she learned that Oliver had gone away. She stared at her mother accusingly.

"It's all Mr Ogilby's fault," she said. "If he hadn't arrived when he did . . ."

"That's enough, Vida," Hetty said sternly. "His visit had nothing to do with Oliver's going."

But Vida's expression conveyed that she thought it did. Had it? Hetty wondered. Had Oliver really believed that she and David would marry in the future? She wished she could see him and explain.

The news of the war was received with no surprise by David Ogilby, who had heard it along with several other guests in the lounge of the Connaught Hotel. It took the announcement of a war to deflate him momentarily, for since the news of his son, he had been walking on air.

But now he was troubled, worried for the boy and the rest of his family. What would they do? They could hardly stay in London with the threat of bomb attacks, it didn't bear thinking of, but before he could do anything he must see his solicitor again since he was in London. He would return to Barnsdale on Monday evening, for Dorothy would be coming home sometime this week. It was with a mixture of pride and concern for her that he faced the homecoming.

After seeing his solicitor and laying his cards on the table as to all the possibilities, David felt in a much better frame of mind. He made the journey back to Yorkshire in a train with darkened carriages. Now and again when they stopped at a station, he lifted the blind to see the platforms in darkness with no signs to tell passengers where they were.

Nothing could depress him after hearing about Freddie, for if any boy was his father's son, young Freddie was his. Although he was not looking forward to the confrontation with Dorothy, nothing mattered as much as the fact that he had a son. Surely Hetty would come to see it his way, even if a lot of water had to pass under the bridge before then?

He saw Alderbourne with new eyes when he returned home. He felt a surge of pride as he saw it sitting there in the late autumn sunshine, surrounded by its land. Just wait until young Freddie saw all this! He felt like a new man, with something to live for now, and mounted his horse and rode over the fields, exhilarated as he had rarely been before. After two or three days of this euphoria he had no compunction at all about facing Dorothy.

They sat in the drawing room after dinner, uppermost in Dorothy's mind the declaration of war with Germany.

"David, what will it mean to us? Will you have to go?"

He smiled back at her, and took her hand. He really was so pleased to see her again.

"Of course, my dear," he said. "I don't have to, not yet awhile, but I must. The colonel would turn in his grave otherwise."

And they both smiled ruefully at this reference to his father.

"Oh, I can't bear it," she said. "I wish now I hadn't left you to go home."

"Well, I'm not going off tomorrow," he teased her. "In any case – " and he sobered up " – I have something to tell you. Something quite important."

Her blue eyes looked at him seriously and trustingly. He hated what he was doing to her.

He came straight to the point. "I have found Hetty."

"Hetty?"

"Hetty Jessops."

"Oh, darling, I'm sorry – of course, Hetty. Where? How?"

And she felt what was almost a physical pain go through her. She had never, in her wildest dreams, imagined this could happen.

"In London." And he began to tell her, slowly and carefully, of the events that led up to his meeting with Hetty.

She listened, eyes grave, not interrupting.

"It's quite a story," he said, "but that's not all."

And it was then that her heart seemed to turn over, for she almost suspected what was to come. She had always had an intuition about it.

David had thought carefully about the way to tell her, had rehearsed the words he would use, but now they came out clumsily in spite of his efforts.

"Hetty gave birth to a son – and he's mine."

"Oh, David!" She buried her face in her hands while he put his arms around her, holding her close. Had she not, all that time ago, wondered for a fleeting instant if anything might have happened as a result of that brief liason between them?

"Dorothy – Dorothy dear."

"Just leave me alone for a while. Don't say anything. Just leave me alone – please, David."

All the joy and exhilaration left him. He had never felt more miserable in his life than at the thought of what he was doing to her now, how she must feel. He realised, for the first time, how much he really loved her.

He left her, going to stand over by the window where he stood staring out but seeing nothing. He had hurt the two people he loved most in the world.

After what seemed like an age, he heard a slight sound and knew that she had come to terms with herself, that her grief was under control. He glanced over towards her, and saw that she was tucking her hankie in her sleeve and looking at him, an expression in her eyes he was unable to fathom. He rushed over to her and put out his arms. She smiled at him, whereupon he put them around her and held her close.

"I do love you, Dorothy," he said. "I really do."

"I know you do," she said, and gave him a wan smile. "But I cannot pretend that it hasn't been an awful shock – and are you quite certain that the boy is yours?"

He knew he had no right to object to the question.

"No doubt whatever."

"And what about Hetty?" she asked him. "It must have been a bolt out of the blue to her."

"It was," he said grimly, "and I can tell you she took it rather badly at first."

"How did it happen?"

And David told her from the accidental encounter right through to their parting. By then she was horrified.

"David – how could you? Oh, poor Hetty! It must have sounded like a threat – to want to take him away from her."

He felt emotionally drained.

"I suppose it did, but she will understand when she thinks it over."

"And what about her? Has she never remarried?"

"No, but she is in partnership with this chap – an antiquarian bookseller. They run the antique shop between them, and I suspect . . ."

"You think there may be something there, a romance of some kind?"

"I don't know. I could tell by the way he looked at her that he was fond of her. Nice chap, I liked him."

The thoughts were going round and round in Dorothy's head. From what David was saying, he and Hetty no longer saw each other as they once had, for which she was profoundly grateful. There remained the question of the boy, something which might be resolved later on. It had been a fine homecoming to receive news of this sort, but then David could hardly have kept it to himself overnight, and deep down she was pleased for him. His dream had come true. Perhaps she could learn to share it with him? After all, Hetty might have his son, but she had David, and that was what mattered most to her.

In London life settled down into a kind of routine with the air raid sirens occasionally splitting the air with their raucous sound. People got used to going up and down to the shelters at their command but by the end of October began to ignore the warnings. A phony war, people said, and began to carry on normally, while theatres and cinemas re-opened as people grew more confident.

Hetty waited for news of Oliver. She had heard nothing from him since his departure for Oxford, and had no address to contact him. She closed down the book department and regretfully put a notice in the window to the effect that the book shop would be closed for the duration of the war. In those first few weeks, she had few customers. If business were to continue like this, she knew she would have to do something else to supplement her income. Without sales, the shop was not viable. After a time she had many requests to visit homes to buy furniture from people either going into the services or moving away. There came a time when she had to refuse any further purchases, particularly as petrol rationing was introduced in October and every journey was precious.

Life developed a sort of pattern, people carrying on as they had before, but with a heavy cloud over them. The British Expeditionary Force was in France, and men and boys were being called up in great numbers. Behind the scenes great preparations were being made, things hotting up for the real war.

By the end of October trade was so bad that Hetty knew she would have to close the shop, at least for the time being. She decided to open only on Saturday mornings, and put a notice in the window to that effect. Presumably, she thought, Oliver wouldn't mind what she did. It was certain he would understand. And then a letter arrived from him, post marked Oxford.

She tore it open eagerly, her heart beating with excitement – then slowing down with disappointment as she read the brief note.

Dear Hetty,
I am sorry to have left you so suddenly, but I was in a hurry to get away. My uncle has a very good housekeeper, so I am leaving him in good hands. By the way, I have settled the rent for the next two years on the shop – although let's hope the war won't last that long!

I am going away, Hetty, abroad perhaps, on work of a nature I am not able to divulge, but I am pleased that at my age my scholastic studies have not been wasted, and someone feels I may be of use! You will be able to get in touch with me through my solicitor in the unlikely event that you need to, at the address on the enclosed card.

You must let me know if you need any help, although knowing you, I am sure you are coping, and I expect your young man is around to give you moral support.

You must make your own plans, Hetty, of course, but I hope you will consider getting out of London in case of raids. Take care. Love to the children,
Oliver.

She turned the card over. It gave the address of a firm of solicitors in Oxford.

She felt a bitter sense of disappointment. It could have been a letter to anyone. She read it again – he was going away, perhaps far away – she might never see him again. "Your young man" – by which presumably he meant David, the implication being that he was still around, had come back so that they could be together . . . She had a sudden thought which put a gleam into her eye.

Was she being over-fanciful to imagine that perhaps Oliver had been a mite jealous when David arrived on the scene? Dare she interpret his sudden disappearance as a wish to leave her free to manage her own affairs – to get back together with this man who had arrived out of her past? Oh, if it were true, if he loved her as she loved him . . . But now he had gone, perhaps abroad. She could have wept, she felt so desolate.

She read the letter again. Well, you could interpret it like that – or not. Wishful thinking, she told herself, and put the letter away. She would read it again later.

After a few days she wrote to Oliver, telling him of her plans and asking him, if it were at all possible, to come and see her, perhaps before he left, or if and when he obtained leave of absence. She particularly wished to see him, she stressed, as she had something to tell him. Then she posted the letter care of his solicitors, and sat back awaiting his reply.

In mid-December, she finally decided to find herself a job, out of necessity rather than choice. Hearing of a vacancy in a local doctor's surgery where the receptionist had enlisted in the WAAF, she went for an interview and was hired. The pay wasn't too good, but the job was congenial and the hours suited her. The patients liked Hetty's pleasant manner, and her understanding of people's problems always stood her in good stead.

Still with no letter from Oliver, she decided to store the antiques and his books until the end of the war. When the storage van arrived and the men began packing she could not help wondering if this was the end of an era. She watched the van move away across the heath, wishing with all her heart that Oliver would write and tell her everything was all right.

When a hoped for letter did arrive, it was from Mrs Harding way down in Cornwall, suggesting that in the event of air raids, Hetty and the children might like to go down there, where they would be very welcome. If not Hetty, then perhaps the children? She couldn't bear to think of them in danger in London.

Hetty was pleased with the letter – a friend out of the blue, she told herself, and the suggestion deserved thinking about. She really wouldn't want to leave Blackheath and the empty shop, but it certainly might be a good idea for the children. She wrote to Sylvia Harding, thanking her for her kind offer, saying she would give it some thought.

Life wasn't easy in those first few months, adjusting to wartime conditions. The blackout was the most difficult thing, travelling to and from home in darkened streets where there was no lighting and the only means of seeing one's way about was with a darkened torch. The winter seemed long and dreary, although people told themselves it could be worse; they must think of the men out there in France and pray for their safety. Comforts for the troops was the first order of the day, and as in every war, women got together in order to supply them. The shops began to be in short supply, and things which had been easy to obtain now became more scarce. The sound of the air raid siren was heard less and less until people began to wonder what the shelters and sandbags were for. The possibility of air attacks became more remote and the more daring began to travel again and visit relatives, the prospect of being caught in an air raid seeming more unlikely.

A Woman's Voluntary Service depot was set up in the village, and Hetty helped out there when she could, and the Citizen's Advice Bureau could always do with help. Hetty found herself busier than she had ever been. There was a great camaraderie between everyone; people spoke to each other where they would never have done so before. Loneliness was a thing of the past, and the war, hated thought it was, cut across all class distinction. Titled women worked alongside the most lowly born, and thought nothing of it.

It takes a war, Hetty thought. I wonder how long it will last?

In January she received a letter with a Yorkshire postmark in handwriting she didn't recognise. Opening it, she turned to the end and saw it was signed "Dorothy Ogilby".

She began to read the beautiful clear writing, her sense of trepidation fading as she read.

Dear Hetty,

I know you will not mind my writing to you – David has told me so much about you that I feel I know you already.

I have a request to make of you, but first I must tell you that David has joined his father's old regiment. I am afraid there was nothing I could do to prevent him, so I am here holding the fort until his return. He is in training camp "somewhere in England" before presumably being sent to France.

David has told me about Freddie, your son, and I don't have to tell you how much joy he takes in the knowledge that there is an Ogilby to follow on after him. Be that as it may, you and I know, as women, that there is much more to life than this – heartbreak and suffering, joy, and much more besides. I have taken four evacuees from Doncaster into our home, two girls and two boys, all under ten years of age – I can only hope that they are enjoying it as much as I am!

In view of this, Hetty, I wonder whether you would allow me to have Freddie for a spell? I know there is no urgency at the moment, but I would so love to have him for a time to get to know him – for David's sake. He will not be short of other children's company. Will you write to me and let me know how you feel about this?

Best wishes to you and your family,

Dorothy Ogilby

When Hetty put the letter down her eyes were full of tears.

Chapter Twenty-Five

"Why not agree?" Vida said when Hetty told her of the letter she had received from Dorothy Ogilby. "I think it is very nice of her, and it would be good for Freddie too."

"I don't know if I can make you understand just what it's like up there in Alderbourne," Hetty said. "It's a way of life you can't imagine. They have staff, maids, gardeners . . ."

"If it's good enough for evacuees," Vida said, "it's good enough for Freddie." And Hetty had to laugh. Vida was growing into such a down to earth little person – she never minced her words and said exactly what she thought.

"The war will change a lot of things, our teacher said. From what you've told me about life at the Ogilbys', I can't imagine that sort of thing will exist when we've come to the end of this war. There shouldn't be all this difference between people just because they were born into certain families. Everyone is the same deep down – it's just that some are luckier than others to be born into privileged families."

A little socialist in the making, Hetty thought. Sometimes she would have given anything for Oliver to walk through the door so that she could confide in him.

Perhaps she should allow the boy to go? He was seven now, old enough for such a visit, yet at an impressionable age – and apart from that she faced the unpleasant duty of telling Freddie his real parentage, that he and Vida had different fathers, which was not going to be easy.

"In any case," Vida said, as though to close the subject once and for all, "you should be jolly proud of Freddie – he's a well brought up little boy. You could take him anywhere." And Hetty felt quite chuffed.

That settled it then. No longer in doubt about it, she tackled the problem of telling him about the proposed visit.

He was sitting on the floor playing with his Meccano when she put down her sewing and folded the garment she was making.

"Do you remember when Mr Ogilby came to see us, Freddie?" she said. "Uncle David? It was some time ago – before Christmas."

He looked up. "Yes, I do. He was nice."

They had so few male visitors he was bound to remember him, Hetty thought, and seeing those blue eyes looking up at her, she took the plunge.

"He came down to London to see you especially," she confided.

"Why?"

"Mr Ogilby is your real daddy, Freddie," she said, and saw him look up with shocked surprise, his mouth open. After a moment he looked at her suspiciously. "I thought my daddy was dead?"

Hetty swallowed. "It was Vida's father who died." she said. "You have a different father – sometimes it happens. It's something you will understand when you are older."

"Why didn't he come to see us before?" Freddie said artlessly.

"Well, he lives a long way off, and when we came to London he married another lady. She is very nice, and has no children of her own, so she wondered whether you would like to go and stay with her for a short while?"

"She won't be my new mummy, will she?" he asked a little tremulously.

She gave him a hug. "Of course not! It's only for a little while. They have a lovely house, and there are other children staying there – evacuees who are billeted there, so you will have someone to play with. It will be like a holiday."

He began to look quite excited, then he frowned. "Are you coming? And Vida?"

"No, I think it's more fun to go on your own," she said. "It will be a special visit."

"But how will I get there on my own?" Now he did looked worried.

"We'll have to work something out," Hetty said, wondering the same thing.

She wasted no more time in doubts, and wrote to Dorothy the next day, saying that after giving it some thought, she was quite prepared for Freddie to stay for a while during the Easter holidays. As the time wore on she became more used to the idea, and began to prepare for the visit.

A letter arrived from Dorothy suggesting two weeks in April during the Easter holidays. She wondered if Hetty would agree to the Estate Manager of Alderbourne coming down to London to meet him, and taking him back at the end of his stay? Mr Lethbridge was a trustworthy man with children of his own, and if it was convenient, perhaps Hetty could arrange to meet him at King's Cross at a fixed time? She added that David was due for a brief leave before going to France, and she hoped it might be during Freddie's stay, for it would be wonderful if they could spend some time together.

If Hetty had any misgivings on this score, she kept them to herself. What was to be, would be, she decided – she wouldn't go back on her word now.

When the day came, she and Freddie and Vida caught the train to London. Hetty decided that after Freddie had gone, they would go shopping to buy Vida something nice, and she would take her to tea at Gunter's, then to a musical show at the Stoll Theatre.

She was so proud of Freddie as he walked off, his hand held firmly by Mr Lethbridge, the man holding his luggage while Freddie carried his raincoat and a small attaché case containing his dearest treasures. Hetty bit her lip, and Vida, glancing at her as she waved until the train was out of sight, took her arm. "Come on, Mummy, let's go and have some tea – I'm starving."

It seemed to Hetty that from then onwards the war began in earnest. The newspapers and radio gave grim reports; the Germans had invaded Denmark and Norway, and everyone became aware that at last things were under way. There would be no holding Hitler now. Hetty could hardly wait for Freddie's return, but the two postcards he sent her pleased her in the interim.

206

When the day of his return came, she and Vida were at King's Cross a good hour before they needed to be. They sat in the tea room, and watched travellers arrive and depart for a good while before Freddie's train was due. When it did arrive and the passengers spilled out of the train, Hetty craned her neck and could see Mr Lethbridge head and shoulders above the others. And there was Freddie! Did she imagine it, or did he look different? There was no doubting his pleasure at seeing her, for he let go Mr Lethbridge's hand and ran straight towards her. "Mummy!" She hugged him, giving an apologetic look at Mr Lethbridge who smiled at the little group.

"He's a fine lad," he said. "We've had a wonderful time, haven't we, lad?"

It seemed to Hetty and Vida that Freddie never stopped talking about the visit.

Most important of all, he had seen his father. He had been home for two days, was a soldier and was going to fight in the war. Freddie could not have been more proud of him. "I went for a ride on the pony. My daddy held me so that I was safe." And Hetty glanced at Vida, who was listening to every word. It was very hard on her, she decided, and she had been a little brick about it.

"He read a story to me at night, and said I could go up there whenever I liked. I could take Vida, if she wanted to come. And I saw swans on a lake, and ducks, and my bedroom was so big and there was a rocking horse in it that my daddy said he had when he was a boy. Then we went to the stables and I saw the horses, and Auntie Dorothy has a mare – that's a she horse – and she and daddy went for a ride and we stayed . . ."

"We?" Hetty asked. She could picture the scene so exactly.

"Yes, the other children: William and Bobbie and Ginny – her real name is Virginia – and Sarah. I wish we could have them down here to stay – except Sarah, Sarah's bossy and pushes everyone."

"Oh," Hetty laughed.

He was breathless from excitement. "Then we went to the kennels so see the dogs – and one of them had puppies, and I said I would like one, and Auntie Dorothy said I could have one, but I would have to ask you first."

"Did you thank Auntie Dorothy for having you?" Hetty asked.

"Yes, I did." Freddie looked quite shocked. "I wouldn't forget that – you told me to, anyway. I wish you could have been there. Can I go again?"

"I expect so," Hetty said, relieved that it was over and done with, except that this would not be the last time, she was sure of that.

"So your daddy had gone off the war," she said as casually as she could.

"Yes, he's in the Royal Artillery." Freddie said proudly. "That's the regiment my grandfather was in."

"I hope he doesn't become unbearable," Vida said in an aside to Hetty, who laughed.

"Thank goodness it went off so well," she said. "It could have been quite difficult."

Hetty wrote to Dorothy and thanked her for having the boy, then settled down to life in wartime London.

The news from abroad was grave, for in May Germany invaded France. Hetty's first thought was for Oliver. Where was he? His letter had been vague but she was sure he had gone abroad. If he had been in England surely he would have answered her letter? Then she wondered about David, probably somewhere in France.

It was mid-May, hot and sultry weather, and the German 2nd Panzer Division had in one great surge gone forty miles in fourteen hours, cutting Allied Forces in two. Nearly a million men, French, Belgian and the British Expeditionary Force, were now trapped in Flanders with their backs to the sea.

The 32nd Field Regiment of the Royal Artillery knew nothing of this. Placed as they were, facing the Belgian River Dyle, their job had been to prevent the Germans from crossing the river. Many of the enemy had been killed, there was talk of twenty-seven thousand Germans being taken prisoner, and the news was received with triumph.

It was with shock that they received the news that General Gort had ordered a new line, the River Escaut, sixty miles to the rear. Gort was a fighting man, and not likely to give up lightly. Such was the confusion that the 32nd Regiment knew nothing of this, and all hell was let loose when the news filtered through. Marching under a blazing sun, they came across broken down vehicles, traffic jams, burned out cars, and desperate refugees pushing prams containing their belongings.

"Get going as fast as you can!" came the orders along the line. "The Jerries are coming."

The roads were alive with people fleeing for their lives when Stuka dive bombers came out of a brilliant sky, diving low over the people and vehicles at roof height. Trying to avoid being hit at any cost, the marchers pressed on through the night. As another warm day dawned, the threat of renewed bombing came with it. David's men looked up as they heard an observation plane overhead.

"Take cover!" he shouted, and the men dived into ditches or anywhere else in an attempt to escape the attack. A dozen enemy bombers appeared, and swooping low strafed the weary crowds below them. One of David's men lay wounded just ahead. David went to him, turning his head to face him. He knew the boy, who could not be more than eighteen and now had a badly injured foot. There was a look about him of young Freddie, with his pale fresh skin and fair hair. David lifted him to his feet, and putting the boy's arm around his own shoulder, helped him along. Back came the bombers for the second time, striking again, their screaming terrifying roar immediately overhead.

David was calculating just how far it must be to the coast. The Germans had allowed them to penetrate a long way into Belgium without hindrance. Now they were trapped, and the way out was a different story. They had seen nothing of the RAF, and still the hideous attack went on. With toy whistles attached to both planes and bombs (they called them the trumpets of Jericho), the Germans nose dived at car height, pulling up only to dive again and again, strafing as they went.

The first time he was struck, David sagged to the ground, taking the boy with him, knowing he had been hit in the back. The second time it was a bomb, which killed them both outright.

Only afterwards did one of his men recall that, in his last minutes Lieutenant Ogilby had aided an injured soldier, and he took pleasure in writing to the officer's wife to inform her of the fact. He though she would be pleased to know.

When Dorothy received the news, she felt as if she had expected it all along. From the time that David had left she had feared the worst, yet when it came, nothing helped to minimise the shock – only her strong religious convictions managed to sustain her through those early days.

She waited two weeks before letting Hetty know in a brief letter which gave her no details other than the news that David had been killed in action.

Alone, Hetty wept tears of grief for a young man who had had so much to live for and had died too soon. Hetty was anti-war, and felt the hopelessness of it all, but David Ogilby was of another mould, and would gladly have given his life for his country, she knew.

Poor Dorothy.

She folded the letter and put it away, drying her eyes. She wouldn't tell Freddie yet – it would be too cruel. She would choose a time and a place sometime in the future. For the moment she must act as though nothing had happened.

As the threat of air raids grew, and Britain prepared to face the onslaught, Hetty thought more seriously about getting the children away from London. She herself was steeped in local war work, and had no wish to go. She had almost made up her mind to ask Mrs Harding to have them in Cornwall, or to find them foster homes down there, when another letter came from Dorothy Ogilby.

Dear Hetty

I will make this letter brief, since I hope I will be seeing you. I am coming down to London in early June. Would it possible to come and see you then – the 2nd or 3rd perhaps? I have something of importance to discuss with you.

Sincerely,
Dorothy

Having agreed on a date, Hetty waited, feeling a little nervous of what was in store.

She had written back and invited Dorothy to lunch,

210

knowing that the children would be at school, and had arranged for Lillian MacDonald to pick them up afterwards in order to leave her free to entertain Dorothy.

She glanced at her watch. Almost time to meet the train. Putting on a jacket, she picked up her gloves and handbag and her car keys. What sort of a woman would she see she wondered?

She parked the car and walked into the station foyer where they assured her the train from Charing Cross was on time. She heard it come in below her, heard it grind to a halt, and waited.

There were only three passengers getting off the train, and one of them was Dorothy. She knew Hetty in an instant and came towards her, hand outstretched in greeting. "You must be Hetty?"

She saw a tall, slim woman, extremely pretty in a delicate kind of way, with ashen-coloured hair done in a simple page boy. She wore no hat but an English-style raincoat, for it was a damp day, and carried a beautiful leather handbag. Her eyes were very blue, and full of lively curiosity. "Hetty, my dear."

Dorothy saw a small woman, almost exactly as she had imagined her, so well had David described her. Hetty had lovely brown eyes, warm and friendly, soft dark hair and a fine complexion – as all Englishwomen had. No wonder, she thought, David had fallen in love with her.

"Dorothy?"

Hetty took her hand and received a firm handshake. "How nice to see you."

She led her towards the car, chatting as she did so to put Dorothy at her ease, but there was no need. Dorothy was a very composed person.

She looked curiously about her as they drove the short journey to Hetty's home, noticing with approval the Victorian house with its early tulips in stone urns.

"You are much more forward down here," she said in her soft American accent. "Our tulips are nowhere near ready."

Hetty unlocked the door and led her guest in, taking her into the drawing room where although the day was mild, she had a cosy fire.

211

"How nice," Dorothy said. "And what a lovely room."

Hetty offered her a glass of sherry, which she refused, and over lunch they talked of everything except the reason for Dorothy's visit. Afterwards, in the drawing room, they sat over coffee. Hetty was the first to speak.

"It is difficult to tell you – "

"No need, my dear," Dorothy said. "We both know how shocked and horrified we were at the news, but we have our memories, both of us." She gave a small smile. "What I have come about is David's will."

Hetty looked at her in astonishment. She had thought she might have come to say something about Freddie – but David's will?

"I'll come straight to the point – David has left Alderbourne Grange in trust for Freddie until he comes of age."

Hetty's face paled.

"Oh! But . . . ."

"What about me? you were going to say. Well, I have a life interest, which means that for as long as I live it can be my home. I am very happy with that. It was something we discussed before David went."

Hetty covered her face. "You mean, you talked about the possibility – you made you plans – I had no idea."

"It is what David wanted – it is what I wanted," Dorothy said kindly. "It had to be. Freddie is an Ogilby, he has a right to Alderbourne." Hetty looked so shocked, Dorothy felt compunction for not having prepared her for the news. "With the bequest come provisos – that he goes to David's old school and spends a part of the year at Alderbourne."

Hetty nodded swiftly. "Yes, I understand all that. It's just that I never expected – "

"I have a copy of the will here, although there is much there that does not concern you, but you may like to read it?"

She got out an envelope from her capacious handbag and produced the will. Marked with crosses was the relevant part which concerning Freddie's legacy.

Hetty read it in silence, then looked up.

"Freddie is young yet," Dorothy said, "but until he is of an age to take over, the estate manager will run things – and up to now, we have had excellent staff. What will happen, with the war, I don't know – we can only hope." She looked at Hetty closely. "What do you feel about this?"

Hetty was silent for a time, then she spoke.

"I suppose I am shocked more than anything – it just never occurred to me that David would do anything so – so drastic as this. I also feel proud, for Freddie's sake. The very idea that my son . . . You do understand, don't you?"

"Of course I do!" Dorothy smiled at her re-assuringly. "You know, I have always had everything easy – well, apart from losing my fiancé. But then I found David. And I had loving parents, and I suppose what you would call a comfortable background, so I have never really had to work hard as you have done, fight against the odds, that sort of thing."

But you can't have a child, Hetty thought, and I would deem that one of life's greatest sorrows.

"I do admire you, Hetty. You've got – spunk." Dorothy smiled. "That's a good old American word for pluck. Well, now we are sisters-in-arms – what do you think?"

How could Hetty put into words just what she was feeling! Freddie, her small son, to be the heir to someone like David Ogilby. Who would have thought such a thing would come to pass?

"Aside from that," Dorothy was saying, "I wondered if you would allow him to come up to Alderbourne for the summer holidays? I suspect there will be air raids by then – everything points to it after Dunkirk, doesn't it? And you may be pleased to get him out of London. Your daughter, too. Both are welcome."

"Thank you," Hetty said. "I expect Vida would rather stay with me – although if things really do hot up, I am thinking of going down to Cornwall and would take her with me."

"Does that mean you will allow Freddie to come?" There was no doubt about Dorothy's eagerness to have him.

"Yes, of course," Hetty said. "It would be sheer obstinacy on my part to refuse."

She had to think of the boy and not her own feelings. Behind Dorothy's words was the unspoken thought, that the sooner Freddie got used to life at Alderbourne Grange and all that it stood for, the better for him it would be.

Hetty said nothing to Freddie or Vida about her visitor, deciding to wait for a while before she spoke. It would certainly be a solution to the evacuation problem, for plans were being got underway again to send the children to places of safety.

The next day, she got out her box of treasures, finding Freddie's first pair of shoes, the children's birth certificates, their christening cards, even her engagement ring with the seed pearls. It all seemed so far away now. The picture of them all at Alderbourne, with herself and David and the dog – what was his name? She sat back on her heels and wandered back into the past. It did no harm to do this sometimes, it was not often she indulged in harmless reminiscing. From her box of private papers she saw the letter from Dorothy informing her of David's death, and unbidden tears rolled down her cheeks.

She began to put everything away neatly, drying her eyes. There was a knock on the front door, and hastily she stood up, made sure there were no vestiges of tears on her face in the hall mirror, and opened the door.

"Hetty?"

She gasped for the smiling visitor was Oliver, and the shock was so great that she burst into tears of relief. He was safe – her dear Oliver. Then pulling herself together she remembered that no words of love had passed between them – he had simply come to see her as a friend and business partner.

It was hard, though, for she wanted to throw her arms about him and tell him how glad she was to see him.

Instead, she smiled through her tears. "Oliver! It's wonderful to see you – where on earth have you been?"

He smiled at that. "It's a long story," he said, as she ushered him into the dining room. Then he saw the box with the papers spread out over the table. "What's this?"

She hastily crammed the things back into the box, explaining as she did so, "Oh, nothing, really – I was just going through my papers. Please sit down, Oliver. Oh, it is good to see you."

"Well," he said drily," it's nice that you missed me so much that you wept upon seeing me, but I have a shrewd suspicion that you were crying before I arrived. Am I right?"

She flushed. "Well, to be honest, I had shed a tear. Still, you don't wish to hear sad news as soon as you arrive."

"What sad news?" he asked sharply. "It's not the children?"

"David," she said. "He was killed in France in May."

Poor little thing, he thought. She really has the most confounded luck. Had she married the chap? Perhaps that was why she was going through the papers. Her wedding certificate . . .

"His wife came to see me yesterday," Hetty began.

"His wife?" Oliver almost shouted the words.

"Yes, of course. We had some business to discuss – I'll explain later." She made a vow to tell him the whole story before the day was much older.

"I've come at an awkward time," he said stiffly. "It must have been a terrible shock for you."

"Yes, it was, particularly since I had only seen him again recently – it was like finding an old friend all over again. We grew up together."

Oliver felt a ray of hope.

"Anyway," Hetty said briskly, "enough about me. Did you ever get my letter? I sent it care of your solicitors."

"Yes, but not until a month ago. The wheels of war grind exceeding small. You said you had something to tell me?"

"Yes, I had. But first let me make some tea – I'm sure you could do with a cup."

The English answer to everything, Oliver thought. How was she to know how he felt?

He followed her into the kitchen. "I am really sorry to hear about your friend," he said. "It must have been a frightful shock. He couldn't have been out there long."

"No, a matter of weeks."

"Poor chap. Some people have really bad luck. I wish I could do something for you – to help."

Hetty turned surprised eyes to his. "Oh, Oliver, that's nice of you, but really it was much worse for his wife, You see – "

"Yes?" He grabbed at any explanation.

"Well, it's hard to put into words," she said. "I have so much explaining to do. I owe you that, at least."

"Did you love him very much?" he asked, taking the tray from her.

"When we were children, and when I was very young – it was a boy and girl affair. He lived in the big house and my family lived in a cottage. My father was the groom."

She poured out the tea.

"Oliver, sit down and tell me about yourself. Can't you tell me where you have been? Was it important work? Secret work?"

"Important? I like to think so," he said. "I've been abroad to a place I know very well, or did in my youth – that's why they sent me."

"And will you have to go again?" she asked, dreading his answer.

"No, I think not. But, Hetty, please tell me – "

And she had a sudden feeling that she was right – he had left hurriedly because of David's arrival. There was a twinkle in her eye when she spoke.

"You left awfully quickly," she said. "I couldn't believe you had gone."

"No, well – I felt *de trop*," he said.

"You couldn't have been more wrong." she said gently. "I missed you more than I can say."

His serious grey eyes were looking at her as though he couldn't believe what he heard.

"It wasn't David I wanted," she said softly, "it was you."

"Hetty!" he said, and jumped up to take her into his arms.

"Is that true? You mean – "

"Yes I do," she said. "And you, Oliver, are you pleased to see me after all this time?"

He kissed her slow and long until she broke away from him to look up at him, her eyes like stars.

"Oh, Oliver."

They stood hugging each other for some time before she said gently. "There's a lot to tell you, though. The story of my life – and the children's."

They sat side by side on the sofa, he with his arm around her.

"Freddie is David's son," she began, "and he has left his estate in trust for him – that was what Dorothy came to tell me. She wants him to go up there in the summer holidays. "Oh, Oliver, there have been so many times when I needed your advice."

216

"Well, I'm home now," he said, kissing her. "Hetty, we've wasted an awful lot of time – how about getting married?"

"And you don't want to hear the rest of the story?" she teased.

"Some other time," he said.

Also available from Woman's Weekly Fiction

Betty Paul

CONDITIONS OF LOVE

Overwhelmed by personal tragedy and the breakdown of her career as a singing star, Caroline retreats to a remote seaside hideaway. The last thing she needs is to meet a bedraggled and desolate young man, ten years her junior and even more in need of a helping hand than she.

Despite her own problems, Caroline cannot turn her back on her uninvited guest but Trevor has his pride. He will only accept help if he works for her in exchange. Delicate and discreet, the relationship between the stage star and the down and out starts off as strictly business and ends up so much more...

Further titles available from Woman's Weekly Fiction

While every effort is made to keep prices low, it is sometimes necessary to increase prices at short notice. Mandarin Paperbacks reserves the right to show new retail prices on covers which may differ from those previously advertised in the text or elsewhere.

The prices shown below were correct at the time of going to press.

All these books are available at your bookshop or newsagent, or can be ordered direct from the address below. Just tick the titles you want and fill in the form below.

Cash Sales Department, PO Box 5, Rushden, Northants NN10 6YX.
Fax: 01933 414047 : Phone: 01933 414000.

Please send cheque, payable to 'Reed Book Services Ltd', or postal order for purchase price quoted and allow the following for postage and packing:

£1.00 for the first book: £1.50 for **two books or more per order.**

NAME (Block letters) ....

ADDRESS ....

.... Postcode.................................

☐ I enclose my remittance for £........................

☐ I wish to pay by Access/Visa Card Number ⬜⬜⬜⬜⬜⬜⬜⬜⬜⬜⬜⬜⬜⬜⬜⬜

Expiry Date ⬜⬜⬜⬜

☐ If you do not wish your name to be used by other carefully selected organisations for promotional purposes please tick this box.

Signature ....
Please quote our reference: 3 503 500 C

Orders are normally dispatched within five working days, but please allow up to twenty days for delivery.

Registered office: Michelin House, 81 Fulham Road, London SW3 6RB

Registered in England. No. 1974080